Yes,
You're the best!!!
I wouldn't have been able
to format this book in InDesign
without your help!!!

Thanks for your support!

Love,

1

DEVIANT COLONY

Salacious Pilgrim Tales

AN INAPPROPRIATE COLLECTION OF TALES BY

MICHAEL ANTHONY MCLAFFERTY

This book is a work of fiction. The characters, incidents, and dialogue are drawn from the author's imagination and not to be construed as real. Any resembalance to actual events or persons, living or dead, is entirely coincidental.

First Edition

Cover Design by Craig Gates

ISBN: 978-0-692-54599-7

This book is dedicated to two of the most influential people in my life.

To my mother, Maryanne McLafferty, for allowing me to watch *Melrose Place* when I was in elementary school. I wouldn't be the smartass that I am today without your love and wisdom.

And to Cedric Hines, for teaching me that the only sense of humor worth having in life is an inappropriate one.

INTRODUCTION

Pilgrims.

We, in America, tend to think we know all there is to know about them. In school we're all taught their story and unsavory plight; fleeing Europe for religious freedom and looking to settle in an exciting new world where they could escape persecution and practice their faith. We celebrate them for their trailblazing efforts every year during our beloved Thanksgiving holiday as we gather with extended family members, many of whom we barely like, and stuff our faces with enough tryptophan-laced turkey to take down Dwayne "The Rock" Johnson. And we do all this to show our appreciation to them for dining with those pesky Native Americans way back when. But how much do we really know about those adventurous little rascals?

Yes, we know they battled foreign diseases, shortages of food, and had various conflicts with the natives, but what was *really* going on behind closed doors? Were they dealing with some of the same personal issues that we deal with as a society today? Was infidelity a creeping thought in some of their minds? Was sibling rivalry causing rifts between family members? And most importantly, were neighboring bitches just being ole' haters back in the colonial days as well?

In this collection of short stories, we carefully examine the inner-workings of a small colony of these settlers and the Native Americans who neighbored them. What some Americans fail to realize about this period of our history is that the pilgrims didn't originally land in Virginia, the location where the majority of them would eventually colonize. In all actuality, the first piece of American soil they encountered was what is known today as Cape Cod, Massachusetts. There was much debate amongst the passengers of the Mayflower as to whether or not they would stay in Massachusetts or travel further south toward Virginia, which was the destination they originally had in mind.

Some felt like they should stay on course and tough it out just a little while longer until they got to Virginia. While others, quite frankly, wanted the *fuck* off that ship. The Mayflower was great and all, but it wasn't exactly a Carnival cruise to Cozumel. The pilgrims were serious about striving for religious freedom, but two months on a boat that wasn't equipped to house that many passengers, and with food and supplies beginning to fade, it was enough to make even the most stringent believers want to chew off the faces of their fellow voyagers like a bath salt zombie.

So a select few passengers decided to depart from the pack and set-up their home along the shores of Cape Cod. They figured times would be difficult and they would certainly face many hardships as a small colony, but considering the fact that severe bouts of dysentery were beginning to make the Mayflower a bit too *Slumdog Millionaire* for their taste, they decided to take the chance. This is their story. These are the pilgrims you don't learn about in school. These are the pilgrims you don't see every year when *The Charlie Brown Thanksgiving* airs on TV.

These are the gangsta pilgrims.

PART ONE

LUCY SKEEZABETH AND THE BIGGLESWORTHS

CHAPTER ONE

"Darling, have you seen my pearl necklace?" said Jane Bigglesworth as she ruffled through her expansive set of baubles and trinkets inside her jewelry box. "Do you know the one I'm talking about? The strand the Dutchess of Cambridge gave to the family on our wedding day. I simply cannot host a dinner party without those pearls, my love."

Arthur looked up from his desk where he was quietly journaling about his day to find his fresh and supple wife standing topless in the doorway of their bedroom.

"My dearest Jane, now that right there is the perfect outfit," exclaimed Arthur as he proceeded to pounce off his desk chair and lift her up into the air and toss her onto their perfectly decorated bed. "Why I don't think I've ever seen such a perfect specimen on this entire earth. I must say I think I married the finest pair of tits on this side of the Atlantic."

"Oh Arthur Bigglesworth, keep your paws off my coochie until later,"[1] said Jane with a seductive giggle as she proceeded to push him off

---

1   W.A.S.P. Translation: Don't touch my vagina until after dinner has been served.

of her and rearranged her luxurious blonde curls back into her bonnet. "And you're damn right about my breasts being the best set on this side of the Atlantic. I mean, who would be my competition? Those natives and their orangutan titties? The good lord didn't mean for a woman's breasts to hang so low with no support like that. It's simply unseemly! By the time they're in their 30's they'll be using them to Swiffer the forest grounds. Anyway, I don't have time to entertain your perverse thoughts, I must glaze that chicken in the kitchen before Lucy gets here for dinner so please keep it in your britches."

"Such a prude, Mrs. Bigglesworth," said Arthur as he gave her a gentle smack on the ass as she rose from the bed.

"Oh, I'm a *prude*? Is that so?" she said as she glanced back toward her husband with a stunned look in her eyes. "Am I the same prude who just gave you some 'Becky' out by the river yesterday?[2] There's a lot that could be said of me, my dear husband, but we both know that *prude* is certainly not one of them. Now see if you can locate those pearls, my dear."

Arthur laughed as he watched his wife button the top of her blouse and head toward the kitchen. The Bigglesworth's were a newlywed couple from London, England. They both came from very well to-do families with major connections throughout the country. Arthur's father had hit it rich in the exporting business when he was very young, which subsequently enabled him to grow up without a care in the world as his father lavished the family with the finest things in life. Like most "new money" families, they basically spent their fortune much like MC Hammer back in the '90's, buying over-the-top bullshit and superfluous items to heighten their influence in the country.

Meanwhile, Jane's family was very "old money." They had their hands in English politics for generations and had managed to amass a fortune and had garnered significant influence throughout the years. She attended the finest schools and was constantly surrounded by some of the

---

2   W.A.S.P. Translation: "Becky" is urban slang for oral sex. Thus, Jane is implying that she slobbed on Arthur's knob by the riverbed.

most powerful citizens in all of Britain.

Coincidentally, Arthur and Jane ended up attending the same university and briefly laid eyes upon each other at an annual fraternity party. Their interaction was momentary, and while no words were spoken as they exchanged glances from across the crowded room, from that moment on they became very much aware of each other's presence.

As luck would have it, a few months later Arthur's father joined forces with Jane's uncle to form a business partnership that would surely be a profitable union for everyone involved. As soon as the ink dried on the agreement they orchestrated a massive dinner celebration for both families. While he thought it would surely be another stuffy and boring dinner party with the typical prehistoric guests that he was used to dining with when it came to family functions, Arthur became overjoyed when he made his way into the vast dining room and locked eyes on his soon-to-be wife, Jane. From across the dinner table they spotted each other and they could both feel the love immediately flow over them like a cascade of rushing water.

Jane looked even lovelier than Arthur had remembered (most likely because he wasn't tipsy on Patron like he was at the frat party) and Jane could see just how handsome and virile Arthur truly was. Everyone at the party knew from that first meeting that these two young aristocrats were headed for a union of their own (which would also be a major coup for both families).

They began to see each other on a daily basis. The bond they quickly formed was unlike any relationship either one of them had ever experienced. For the first time in their lives they felt real and true love. But as their courtship progressed they quickly learned that money and power weren't the only factors that brought Arthur and Jane together.

They harbored a dark secret that very few knew about; a secret that, if uncovered, would not only be disastrous to them as a couple, but also tarnish the names of their families, forever.

Arthur and Jane were swingers.

Yes, swingers.

What are swingers, you ask? Well, for those of you who aren't familiar with that term, they are individuals who, even though they are married, still enjoy sexing other people down.

It's all very Parisian, right?

These rich and influential youngsters enjoyed engaging in sexual escapades with other people.

But, I do feel it's also very important to note that they only "swung" as a couple; I mean they were sexual deviants and all, but they still had some values and traditions. If they were going to be "knocking-the-boots"[3] with strangers then dammit they were going to do it together as man and wife. They had taken vows after all.

But as one might imagine, this type of lifestyle wasn't exactly looked upon as favorable back in 1600's England. Arthur and Jane knew that if they wanted to live the lifestyle that they wanted they would have to leave their homeland for a different place to plant roots. They had thought about trying out France, but Jane preferred her conquests to be freshly shaven. She disliked the fact that all the French sexual partners she'd encountered seemed to look like they were smuggling Micheal Bolton's mane (circa 1993) between their legs. Jane felt it was much like when you get an Easter basket and you have to dig through all that plastic grass just to find all the little candies at the bottom; who wants to invest that much time and effort into uncovering the goodies?

With France out of the question, they began to hear murmurs and whispers about a ship that would soon be taking off for the New World.

What an exciting prospect they thought. How fantastic would it be to help colonize the New World and usher in a new sexual era where their lifestyle would not only be accepted, but rather celebrated.

---

3   W.A.S.P. Translation: An urban term implying sexual insertion; for a more in-depth analysis, YouTube search for H-Town "Knockin' The Boots." Classic '90's R&B jam.

They would forever be looked upon as trailblazers and revolutionaries to their cause. They could live their lives out in the open and no longer hide behind the shadows of the harsh puritanical laws of the day.

At least this is what they thought at first.

A minor tidbit that Arthur seemed to miss out on was the fact that the majority of this ship to the New World would be filled with zealots fleeing Europe for religious freedom. You can imagine their surprise when they boarded the Mayflower to find a boat full of Puritans. Arthur and Jane exchanged glances and for a brief second thought about jumping overboard and swimming back to shore. Living in England as swingers was hard enough, but being stuck on a boat with this kettle club of inhabitants was just not working for either one of them.

But then they saw her.

Beaming from across the ship, they spotted Lucy Skeezabeth.

She was a nubile beauty with the kind of body and smoldering sensuality that would make Megan Fox look like Betty White. Arthur and Jane couldn't see her cleavage, but they could tell that she was stacked like a Caucasian Selma Hayek under all those layers.

But the brazen sexuality that she was effortlessly exuding wasn't even her finest attribute. It was actually her hair. You see Lucy had the most radiant red hair in all of England. The hue of her hair was hypnotic and mesmerizing to anyone that laid eyes upon it. The long strands seemed to encircle her face like a ring of vibrant amber flames. It was impossible to look upon her and not be completely enraptured in her appearance.

Her beauty briefly paralyzed the Bigglesworth's on that very first visual exchange on the boat. Lucy seemed to be staring right into their souls as she glanced in their direction, almost as if to say she knew exactly what they wanted and it was theirs for the taking. And in that momentary interaction, the Bigglesworths began to fall in love with the young beauty.

They simply had to have her.

One way or another they were going to get all *Wild Things* on her ass.[4]

Over the course of the next few weeks at sea the Bigglesworths began to form a friendly bond with Lucy as they attempted to learn as much as they could about her. She was traveling to the New World with her older sister, Natalie, and her husband, Edward, where she planned on putting her knowledge of sewing to good use and becoming a seamstress in the colony. She was a carefree girl who, unlike most people on the Mayflower, wasn't going to the New World for religious freedom; rather, she was making the trek just for the sheer adventure of going somewhere new. In her short nineteen years of life, Lucy had managed to travel much of Europe and seemed to rebel against conventional life and authority.

These traits bode well for the Bigglesworths.

Upon first glance they figured it was going to be tough to get into some Puritanical panties like Lucy's, but finding out she was a free-spirit with a wild side to her made them tingle with excitement. They knew once they docked this damn boat they would be free to explore their relationship with Lucy on a more *personal* level. The Mayflower was a decent sized ship for the most part, but all those Puritans around them were kind of a giant cock-block to be completely honest.

So after months of sheer torture and sexual torment, tonight would finally be the night they had been waiting for.

It had now been a few months since the small group of settlers decided to leave the Mayflower and colonize along Cape Cod instead of going down to Virginia with the rest of their shipmates. Setting up the colony had been exhausting for everyone involved, and with the harsh winter weather beginning to creep upon them they knew they still

---

4   *Wild Things* refers to the 1998 erotic crime thriller in which Neve Campbell, Denise Richards, and Matt Dillion get all buck wild in a steamy threesome. It would also be the first of many times that Denise Richards boobs would be brought out in order to prevent anyone from noticing just how bad her acting was.

had many obstacles ahead of them in this new land. But those everyday stressors were to be put on the backburner this evening because the Bigglesworths were finally going to make it rain on the young maiden of their dreams.[5]

Arthur made his way into the kitchen and snuck-up behind his wife and placed the pearl necklace around her delicate throat. "I swear sometimes you're as blind as a bat, my dear. They were laying right on our nightstand where you left them."

"Thank you, sweetheart. I don't know what I'd do without your eyes sometimes."

Arthur let out a laugh as he made his way from the kitchen into the living room.

"Arthur, be a dear and put another log on the fire," Jane said from the kitchen as she put the finishing touches on the dinner. "I feel a draft in the cabin. I want it to be nice and toasty when Lucy arrives."

"Anything you wish, my dear," replied Arthur as he leisurely tossed another piece of wood into the blaze. "Do we have anymore of that Pinot Grigio that my father gave us at the wedding? That might be a good way to get everyone loosened up."

"Oh, I'm sorry my love but I drank the last bit of the bottle the other day while you were busy working," she said. "That insufferable Mary Higgins had come over and was bitching about her lousy turnip garden for over an hour and I had to pour myself two glasses in order to numb my pain or else she was bound to get a shotgun cap in her ass."[6]

"Yes, that whole Higgins clan is a giant mess aren't they?" said Arthur with a grin as he took a seat in his favorite chair in front of the fire

5   W.A.S.P. Translation: The term 'make it rain' is an urban expression referring to when someone brings a wad of cash into a strip club and proceed to throw it in the air at strippers so that it looks like it is indeed raining money while they dance. Hence, Arthur and Jane were ready to get the party started.
6   W.A.S.P. Translation: When Jane says she was going to put a 'shotgun cap in her ass,' it means that she was so annoyed with Mary Higgins that she was about to shoot her. With a musket. In her ass. Literally.

and outstretched his legs. "Her husband Baxter isn't much better. During our last counsel meeting the only thing he wanted to discuss was how much he hated the natives. It's like okay, we know you don't like them but why are you so obsessed with them? Let the bitches breath, you know?"[7]

"I completely agree," said Jane. "They should spend more time parenting those little misfits they call children and worry less about those ever-pleasant natives. I've yet to have any sort of real issue with them. Why one of the female natives even helped me prepare the chicken for this evening's dinner."

"Really?" he asked. "How so?"

"Well, you know how much I despise cutting off their heads when they're still alive," she responded. "All that squawking and shrieking is just plain dreadful. Why it quite reminds me of that time we saw Shakira live in concert back home. Anyhow, I spotted one of the female natives watching me from the woods and I enticed her to come over and lop the head off the chicken for me."

"And she did it just like that?" asked Arthur.

"Oh yes, you should have seen how at ease she was while doing it too," answered Jane as she set the forks and knives on the table. "I let her keep the chicken feathers as payment for her work. You know they like to keep those feathers for some reason. What they use them for I simply have no idea. They clearly don't use them for tops or blouses since their tits are always exposed."

Jane could hear her husband chuckle at her analysis of the natives.

While the Bigglesworths were a very open-minded couple, it should still be noted that they were both bred from English aristocrats and raised with silver spoons shoved up their haughty asses; so, needless to say, the Native American culture they encountered was certainly deemed "beneath them," but they simply tolerated it much better than most of their other fellow settlers.

---

7   W.A.S.P. Translation: Leave them alone and let them handle their business.

"What time did you say Lucy was coming over, dear?" asked Arthur.

"She should be here any minute now. I told her to come at nightfall. I figured the later the better, that way less people could see her making her way to our home. You know these neighbors we have like to be all up in our business."

"That is certainly true, my love," he responded. "All the insistent gossip always frustrates me. It's like jump off our dick and leave us alone, you know?"[8]

"I completely agree, my truest," she answered.

Just then they heard a knock at their door. The sound sent a shiver of exhilaration through their bodies. The moment of truth had finally arrived. After months of fantasizing, the indecent engagement they had longed for was finally about to come to fruition. They would be alone with Lucy at last.

Arthur sprang from his chair and raced toward the door to greet their guest. Before he could open the door he gave an excited, yet anxious, look to his wife. She ran towards the door to help greet their guest, as well. There she stood, right by his side. He gazed into her hazel eyes and took in all her glorious beauty. At that moment he realized just how truly lucky he was. Not only was his wife gorgeous, and an excellent homemaker I might add, but she was also willing to let him play in another woman's playground for fun.

Arthur Bigglesworth was living the American dream before there was even an American dream to speak of.

"Arthur," whispered Jane. "Can you open the fucking door already?"

"Oh yes, sorry dear," he said in a brief state of shock as he came back down to reality.

---

8   W.A.S.P. Translation: An urban term meaning to get off our back and mind your business. Hence, he's telling his neighbors to back the hell off.

Arthur quickly opened the door to greet their guest. "Lucy, how good it is to see you. Please do come in."

Lucy made her way into the cabin and out of the brisk chilly air from the outdoors.

"Hello Arthur and Jane, how great it is to see your smiling faces," Lucy happily said. "Oh my, it sure is getting colder with each passing day. I shutter to think what this winter will be like."

Arthur and Jane both just stared at Lucy in amazement. They had seen her a hundred times before, but something was different this evening. Neither one could figure it out. Maybe it was the fact that she was finally all alone in their home. Or maybe it was because the radiant candlelight throughout the house was making her appearance glow even more intensely than normal. Whatever it was, both Arthur and Jane were ready to get this cabin rocking.

"Oh yes, I completely agree," said Jane, as she shook herself out of the hypnosis that Lucy had over her. "I quite hope it doesn't get much colder. The cold air is horrendous on my skin. It's impossible to get a good facial out here in this wilderness. I'm looking so haggard lately."

"I find that hard to believe Jane," said Lucy. "Such beautiful and luminous skin like yours would be impossible to look flawed."

"You're too kind," said Jane with a grin. "Please let me take your coat and make yourself at home. The chicken just finished roasting and the potatoes are looking stellar."

"That's fantastic. This bitch is hungrier than Precious on Weight Watchers right about now!"[9] Lucy exclaimed. "I brought a bottle of Merlot with me as well. I'm quite a horrible cook so I figured this could be my contribution to our little soiree."

"Thank you so very much," said Arthur as he took the bottle and

---

9   W.A.S.P. Translation: Lucy is referring to the 2009 Oscar-nominated film Precious, which is a dramatic tale of a plus-sized girl in 1980's Harlem. Lucy's implying that she's hungrier than Precious would be if she were on the weight-lose program. In other words, a bitch is really hungry.

showed her to the kitchen table. "How are your sister and her husband doing by the way?"

"Oh they are doing well for the most part," answered Lucy as she took a seat at the table. "Though lately Natalie's been acting quite funny towards me. I'm not really sure what's got her panties in a bunch this time, but she's always been a bit of a twat when it comes to me so I'm not *totally* surprised."

"I have a hard time believing that anyone could be unpleasant with you Lucy, you're such a darling," said Jane as she sauntered back toward the kitchen to grab the platter of chicken.

"Oh, why thank you Jane, but yes, bitches always seem to be tripping when it comes to me and my dealings,"[10] said Lucy.

"I'm quite aware of how petty women can be," replied Jane as she made her way back to the dining room table. "I remember when I was away at boarding school in Wales, I had quite a few haters myself back then. Was it my fault that I developed early in life and you could bounce a quarter off my robust cakes?[11] I should think not!"

"She's right you know," Arthur interjected. "I'm not sure if we've told you Lucy, but I first met my lovely wife at a Pi Alpha Theta house party in college as she was doing her best Amber Rose impression; that is to say she was dancing on a ping-pong table as men pitched shillings at her. Why you've never seen such a wholesome girl bounce her ass to a dope beat quite like my beloved here.[12] In the words of that fellow T-Pain, I was madly and deeply in love with a stripper."[13]

"Oh you flatter me, Mr. Bigglesworth," said Jane with a wink at

---

10   W.A.S.P. Translation: Lucy is stating that other women tend to be haters toward her. This is most likely because she's very pretty and the other women in the colony tended to favor Lassie the dog.

11   W.A.S.P. Translation: The term 'cakes' is urban slang referring to someone's buttocks. In other words, Jane's ass was quite nice.

12   What Arthur is trying to convey with his statement is that while his wife is the picture of wholesomeness, she can also drop it like it's hot when the right song comes on.

13   Arthur is referring to the 2007 hit song "I'm in Love with a Stripper" by singer/rapper T-Pain in which he croons about being in love with the lady giving him a lap dance for cash.

her husband as she took her seat at the table.

"My-oh-my, I would have loved to be privy to such a performance," said Lucy as she seductively glanced towards Jane.

That rather small and relatively minute comment seemed to make time stop for the Bigglesworths.

You could almost cut the sexual tension in the air as they both stared at Lucy from across the table. To hear Lucy be flirtatious with them made the couple tingle with excitement. They knew this conquest would be a cakewalk.

"Well, the night is still young my dear," said Jane as she placed some chicken on Lucy's plate. "Who knows what might occur once the Merlot starts flowing."

"That is true, Mrs. Bigglesworth," said Lucy. "That is *very* true."

The dinner party continued to go off without a hitch. The chicken that Jane had prepared was succulent and her mashed potatoes were like buttery clouds on a plate. They conversed for hours about everything from their social backgrounds to the current state of politics back home in England. Everyone was having a fantastic time and before they knew it they had finished the entire bottle of Merlot and they could feel it slowly going to their heads.

"I can't say it enough Jane, but that meal was utterly fabulous," said Lucy as she gently placed her napkin on the table.

"Thank you so much," said Jane. "I'm so happy that you enjoyed it. Oh, I got so enraptured in our conversation that I completely forgot that I prepared a lovely raspberry tart for dessert."

"Let's cut the crap and forget about that dessert, I'd rather have your raspberry tart, Mrs. Bigglesworth," responded Lucy in a very self-assured tone.

The response caught both Arthur and Jane off-guard.

They hadn't anticipated that Lucy would be so forthright.

"Excuse me, my dear?" said Arthur, trying to make sure he had heard exactly what he thought. He had to verify that his mind hadn't magically concocted such a response from their guest.

"Come on you two," said Lucy. "You guys have been trying to butter my biscuit since we boarded that bloody ship months ago. Let's not play coy any longer. Are we going to get this party popping or what?"[14]

Arthur and Jane glanced toward one another. They didn't need to speak a word, but they both knew exactly what the other one was thinking.

Jackpot.

"Of course we are," said Jane with a semi-drunken giggle. "But I must ask, were we really that transparent? How were you so sure?"

"Jane, I've traveled all throughout Europe. I've spent semesters in Paris, summers in Amersterdamn, and winters in Berlin. You think I don't know how to read lust when I see it? I knew from that first day at sea that you two wanted to board *my* mayflower," Lucy answered gleefully and proud.

Arthur let out a chuckle upon hearing her response. He genuinely didn't think it would be *this* easy to persuade Lucy into a menage-a-trois, but here she was taking control of the situation and practically demanding it.

Lucy slowly reached for the tie on her bonnet and loosened it so that it fell to the floor, allowing her fiery locks to cascade down past her shoulders. Her blazing red hair seemed to illuminate the entire cabin; it seemed to unleash a new life into the Bigglesworth home.

She quietly rose from her seat and made her way around the table where she gently grabbed the hands of her hosts as she helped them out of their chairs. Arthur and Jane seemed to be genuinely shocked. They had shared multiple conquests over their short marriage, but they had never encountered a creature quite like Lucy before. She was so brazen and bold with her approach that they honestly didn't know what to expect next. It felt much like going on a first date with Charlie Sheen; you really had no idea what kind of shit was going to go down once that door closed and

---

14   Lucy was ready to get the party in her pants underway.

you're left all alone with no eyewitnesses. And truth be told, Arthur and Jane kind of liked that feeling.

Lucy led them into their bedroom and gently closed the door behind them. A tart was about to be eaten in the Bigglesworth household, but it surely wasn't the one sitting on the kitchen counter.

Four hours later the marathon had finally come to a conclusion. With the exception of a few farts from Arthur, the event had gone down marvelous (Jane made an excellent chicken, but her seasoning tended to leave Arthur with a severe case of gas. Needless to say he let one or two rip during some very inopportune moments of their tryst.)

Lucy lay between the Bigglesworths and let out an elongated sigh.

"So did you two enjoy yourselves?" she asked.

They both let out a laugh, simultaneously.

"Enjoy ourselves?" responded Arthur. "Last time we had that much fun was when Lindsay Lohan joined us during her last visit to London. You know there's no bigger freak in the sack than the ones with daddy issues."

"That's very true sweetheart, but all that crying during intercourse is quite a turn-off for me" responded Jane. "But Lucy, where did you learn some of those moves? I don't think I've ever heard Mr. Bigglesworth scream like such a little bitch during love-making before."[15]

"Jane, my dear, I traveled through Europe with Prince during his *Purple Rain* tour a quite a few years back. He gets all the credit for that," answered Lucy as she gently caressed Jane's hair and placed her head on Arthur's chest. "That little man has a tongue like a KitchenAid blender."

All three of them let out a laugh.

A peaceful silence then fell over the small room. They all stared toward the ceiling as they basked in the afterglow of the nookie that had

---

15   Lucy brought Arthur to tears with her vaginal tricks and magic.

just taken place.

"Well, I better start making my way home," said Lucy as she gently raised her head off Arthur's chest and began to make her exit.

"Are you sure you must go?" asked Jane. "You're more than welcome to lay between us this evening. I almost feel sad to see you go my dear."

"Jane is right," said Arthur. "You've certainly earned the right to stay the evening. I'm sure I can speak for my beloved wife when I say we knew this would be a splendid night, but we had no idea how bad a bitch you truly would be."[16]

"I certainly concur," said Jane.

"Oh, you two surely know how to make a young lady blush," said Lucy as she stood at the base of the bed reveling in all her lush nakedness. At that precise moment she knew she already had them both wrapped around her finger.

Mission accomplished.

"You know I want for nothing more in this world than to spend the evening with my two lovers, but I truly must get home before the sun rises and the others in the village realize I've been out all evening. Could you imagine the ruckus that Mary Higgins would cause if she saw me strolling through the village coming from your home at this time of the morning? That bitch would spread the gossip of my walk of shame faster than Wendy Williams."[17]

They were disappointed that she wouldn't stay the evening, but they both knew that what she spoke of was the absolute truth. If any villagers saw Lucy making her way home at this hour they knew they would become suspicious of such unorthodox behavior.

---

16   W.A.S.P. Translation: When Arthur refers to Lucy as a 'bad bitch,' he's speaking in street slang to infer that she's truly an amazing woman; specifically pertaining to her sexual prowess.
17   Lucy is basically stating that Mary Higgins has a big mouth and is notorious for being in everyone's business (i.e. much like a colonial equivalent of Wendy Williams, the famous TV hostess.)

"We will get to see you again though, won't we my dear?" asked Arthur.

"Oh course you will," answered Lucy. "Wild stallions couldn't keep me away from my two beloveds. Why it would be like Kim Kardashian dating a Caucasian man; quite impossible and ridiculous to even suggest such a thing."[18]

As Lucy began to sort through the piles of their clothes that had been strewn across the bedroom floor during their frantic race to get naked, she noticed something marvelous staring back at her.

Lying there on the floor next to Arthur's trousers was Jane's luminous pearl necklace. They must have come unlatched and fell to floor when Lucy had tore Jane's blouse open with her teeth.

They were glorious, nothing short of stunning.

She wanted them.

Lucy stood there for a brief second and internally debated as to whether or not she should pocket the gorgeous piece of jewelry. The Bigglesworths had been wondrous hosts and, quite frankly, the sex had made her feel more alive than she had in months (aside from Arthur stinking up the room a couple times). She knew that she would be wrong for taking the pearls, but the internal debate was futile.

Lucy knew she was going to take the necklace.

She quickly snatched the pearls off the floor and placed them inside her skirt pocket. Aside from the moonlight streaming in through the single window in the room it was completely dark and neither one of the Bigglesworths seemed to notice her devious action.

As she placed her bonnet upon her head she could feel subtle pangs of guilt begin to hit her, but they were subsided by the nervous exhilaration that was coursing through her body. She knew what she was doing was wrong but that didn't stop her. It felt far too good to be this bad.

She gradually finished dressing and made her way over to the side

---

18   Google "Kim Kardashian boyfriend" and see for yourself.

of the bed to bid farewell to her hosts.

"I can't thank you two enough for such a lovely evening," said Lucy as she gently placed a soft kiss on each of her conquests. "I'm already looking forward to round two."

Both Arthur and Jane were speechless. The look of compliance was written all over their faces. They all knew that no further words were needed.

As they watched her exit their tiny cabin and softly close the door behind her they both felt a rush of cold loneliness wash over them. It was certainly a feeling that neither one of them were used to feeling after indulging in their secret sexual desires.

What was this feeling?

They lay side-by-side in the bed, not daring to speak or touch, but staring blankly at the dark ceiling as if waiting for something to occur.

Neither Arthur or Jane slept that evening; for each of them was too busy falling deeper and deeper into love with Lucy.

CHAPTER TWO

The bright rays of the sun streamed through the window and gently caressed Lucy's cheek. It was hard for anyone to imagine that Lucy could possibly look more beautiful than usual but there she was, looking like a slumbering angel upon a fluffy white cloud in her tiny room of the quant cabin she shared with her sister Natalie and her husband Edward Williams. She seemed to exude a peaceful serenity in her sleep. A certain gracefulness that you dare not tamper with or attempt to interrupt out of fear that you would never get the opportunity to witness it again.

Unfortunately for our dear Lucy though, that just made the temptation even more sweet for Natalie as she stormed into the room.

"Wake up you lazy girl!" yelled Natalie as she flung open the door. "I know the Queen of Sheeba would like to lounge around all day and get her beauty rest, but we have much work to do and even your delicate hands are going to be getting dirty with the rest of us."

Lucy opened her eyes to find her older sister standing above her and awaiting for her to rise.

"Jesus, Mary and Joseph, Natalie," said Lucy as she squinted her eyes to adjust them to the radiant light of the morning sun. "Don't you know how to gently knock? I was sleeping so peacefully."

"Gently knock?" responded Natalie. "Bitch, what do you think this is? The fucking Four Seasons Resort and Spa? I suggest you get your derriere out of that bed sooner than later. You're on laundry duty today and you've got your work cut out for you; Edward's been eating baked beans by the boatload lately and his farts make Gary Busey's breath smell like fresh-cut gardenias.[19] They're going to need a thorough scrubbing."

"Huhhhhhhhh," huffed Lucy as she turned away from her sister and peered out the window. "I find it quite ridiculous that I have to wash *your* husband's undergarments. Isn't that your job as his beloved wife?"

"Lucy, you know very well that we rotate our chores in this house so I'll hear none of that nonsense," Natalie snapped back at her sister. "And you should consider yourself lucky, I was the one who had to have sex with his fat ass last night. I spent an hour in the tub this morning scrubbing the smell of bacon off of me. There isn't enough Dove body wash in the world, I will tell you that much."

"My God Natalie, I've never heard a woman speak so horribly about her husband," said Lucy as she threw the white covers off herself and proceeded to rise from the bed. "Why did you bother marrying him if you're just going to talk shit about him all the time?"

"Oh, so you woke up a dunce this morning did you?" questioned Natalie. "You know the only reason I married Edward was to get us out of England. The heat from the police was getting too severe and the longer we waited the greater chance that you and I would end up swinging from the gallows like pinatas on Cinco De Mayo. Now hurry up and get dressed, queen diva. We haven't got all day."

Lucy stared at her sister as she departed from her room. She could feel her blood boil as her body attempted to calm itself from the brash awakening that it had just endured. While Lucy genuinely couldn't stand her older sister most of the time, she did realize that Natalie had

---

19   Have you ever seen what his mouth looks like? It looks like he's been eating his breakfast, lunch, and dinner off of a dirty diaper for the last decade.

saved both their asses by marrying Edward and getting them aboard the Mayflower.

You see the Skeezabeth sisters came from a very reputable and aristocratic family back in England. Anything they ever wanted, they received; plush vacations, designer garments, the finest foods in the land, anything their hearts desired their parents put right into their hands. They rubbed shoulders with some of the richest and well-connected people in the country. They lived the sort of lifestyle that most people could only dream of.

But that lavish lifestyle still couldn't suppress the secret urge that both sisters seemed to inherently share.

Since they were children, both of the Skeezabeth sisters seemed to have sticky fingers. It started with innocent items like an apple here and there, or maybe a cookie from the bakery close to their home. But as they grew older the stakes got higher and higher. Before they knew it they were swiping jewels from rich neighbors and pickpocketing strangers on the street just for the sheer exhilaration of it.

The best part of the whole scenario was that no one ever suspected them. When one's jewels go missing you tend *not* to point the finger at two rich girls who already have the world by the balls. They already have it all, why would they resort to stealing, right?

The Skeezabeth sisters were pure risk-takers and rebels (but it should be noted that Natalie didn't share her sister's sexual prowess. She knew that her sister got down with some freaky shit, but she wasn't really aware of how deep it went.)

But, as with most good things in life, it all had to come to an end sooner or later.

The Skeezabeth sisters had been invited to a rather swanky dinner party at the home of Mr. and Mrs. Reginald Richards and, of course, they knew they had to take the opportunity to delve through their hostess' jewelry chest while everyone was busy mingling downstairs.

Lucy immediately took a fancy to an immaculate diamond ring

that was big enough to make Elizabeth Taylor wet her knickers. And Natalie simply couldn't resist pocketing a massive ruby necklace that she knew would go perfectly with her black bathing suit on their next vacation to the South of France.

Weeks later the sisters figured they had made a clean getaway from the scene of their thievery since no questions seemed to arise. But, unfortunately for them, that all came crashing down as late one afternoon a detective came to the door to ask them a few questions about the missing jewelry. Apparently Mrs. Richards had become inconsolable upon finding out that her priceless pieces had been swiped and she was promising a hefty reward to the person who could find the culprit.

After the detective finished questioning the Skeezabeth sisters, they both knew he had a bad vibe about them and that sooner or later he would be back to arrest them. They had to think fast and act even faster.

That's when Natalie came up with the perfect plan.

For months she had been dodging proposal after proposal from Edward Williams. While he was very rich and had many connections throughout England, he also had the hair of Donald Trump and the body of John Goodman (a Ryan Gosling he was not). But during their last visit together Edward had told Natalie that he planned on departing for the New World aboard the Mayflower and that he wanted her to join him as his wife.

Of course, at the time, Natalie would have preferred getting a pap smear from Captain Hook instead of marrying Edward's rotund ass; but now, with their fates hanging in the balance, she knew that if she accepted his proposal and convinced him to take her sister along with them to the New World they would both be free and clear.

And that's exactly what she did.

Natalie gave in to Edward's proposal and got him to agree to a small, and hurried, ceremony; three days later, all three boarded the Mayflower and the fugitives sailed off into the sea under the blanket of protection that Natalie had crafted for them.

And now, here they were.

They were safe in the New World and thousands of miles away from their shady past.

Although, as time went on, Lucy wondered which was the worse fate between the two: being hung for larceny or being forced to wash Edward's tighty whiteys in a river behind the cabin.

As Lucy sat on the edge of her bed, she knew that she should feel more gratitude toward her sister for her sacrifice to save them, but she hated owing Natalie anything. While they were sisters, Lucy knew that Natalie always had an underlying hatred toward her. It had always been that way. Natalie had always been jealous of Lucy and the amount of attention she received because of her beauty.

Natalie berated her with hurtful words and always tried to bring her down. She secretly hoped the constant harassment would damper her luminous appearance, but of course it was to no avail. Lucy was honestly surprised that Natalie had even gone out of her way to make sure Edward secured her a spot on the Mayflower with them. She could have easily left her behind to face the consequences of their mischievous doings but she didn't.

Most would think this was because Natalie was protecting her sister and making sure she got out of danger as well, but Lucy knew what the real motive behind her actions was. Natalie wanted to plan Lucy's demise herself. She wasn't about to let her sister get off the hook that easily. Lucy knew that whatever fate Natalie had planned for her would certainly be worse than death by hanging.

For as far back as Lucy could remember she had always battled with Natalie about everything under the sun. That was, of course, everything except for their love of thievery. It was the one thing that bonded them. The rush and danger of it seemed to be the only genetic connection they shared between them.

But Lucy didn't have time to dwell on her unhealthy and bitter bond with Natalie. She slowly reached under her pillow and pulled out

Jane Bigglesworth's long pearl necklace that she had snuck off with the night before. She gently caressed each pearl as she rolled it between her fingers. It had been months since she had stolen anything and she had to admit it felt damn good to sneak off with the piece of jewelry. She had quenched the urge that had been gnawing at her for what felt like forever.

Lucy had become so enamored in staring at the beautiful piece of jewelry that she failed to realize that her sister had made her way back toward her doorway.

"Lucy, what is that?" asked Natalie.

Lucy was startled by the interruption and nearly jumped out of her flawless skin.

"Oh, it's nothing," Lucy hastily answered. "Just a piece I brought with me from back home. I couldn't bear to leave it behind."

"You lying jezebel!" yelled Natalie. "Where did you get that necklace from? I know for a fact you didn't bring that with you. In fact, I've never seen you with those luxurious pearls before."

"Natalie, you don't know what you're talking about," said Lucy as she shoved the pearls into the pocket of her nightgown. "I'm telling you I brought them from home. Now please get up out my face about it."

"What kind of idiot do you take me for Lucy?" said Natalie. "Do I look like I graduated from the University of Florida? Where did you steal that pearl necklace from, girl? You stole it from the Bigglesworth home, didn't you?"

"What?" said Lucy. "Why would you even imply such fuckery?"

"Because I know that's where you were all last evening," responded Natalie. "And let's not even get started on that because I know you snuck in through that window at an ungodly hour. I don't even want to know what perverse sexual antics you were getting into, but I'll be damned if you're going to take us down by stealing some freaky housewife's jewelry out here in this new land. I didn't marry this fat ass bastard for you to get caught snatching a set of janky pearls and blowing our cover!"

Lucy knew she had screwed up.

Here they were attempting to restart their lives in a new country, free from their criminal past, and she had given in to past temptations so easily. She stared at the ground in disappointment.

"I'm sorry," she said. "I'm not sure what came over me."

"Oh, I know what came over you, Winona Ryder, you saw something shiny and nice and decided to snatch it!" snapped Natalie. "I don't know what your going to do but somehow you better get those pearls back into that house before that freaky bitch realizes you made off with them. And try to keep your panties on this time, young lady. Our parents are probably spinning in their graves knowing what a sleazy trollop you've become."[20]

"Excuse me Natalie, but don't hate the playa, hate the game,"[21] responded Lucy. "Don't be upset with me because people actually enjoy sleeping with me."

"Bitch please," snipped Natalie. "You go through fuck-buddies faster than Taylor Swift and don't think I haven't noticed it."

"I'm a free-spirit and your sexual judgements will not change or alter my lifestyle."

"Free-spirit?" asked Natalie. "Is that what they call whores these days? Keep your legs closed to married men you little bootleg Kim Zolciak![22] I've had enough of this conversation. I've told you what must be done and I expect it to be accomplished sooner than later young lady. Now get dressed and get the laundry done."

Natalie stormed out of the room.

Lucy knew she didn't have much of a defense in this situation.

She had messed up. Big time.

But she wasn't overly worried because she knew getting back into

---

20   While Natalie often plays dumb about Lucy's salacious impulses, she's very aware that her beautiful sister can be a bit of a hooker at times.

21   Lucy has no shame for her whorish tendencies.

22   Natalie is referencing the now infamous line delivered by Mrs. NeNe Leakes on *The Real Housewives of Atlanta* during a heated exchange between herself and consistent frenemy, Kim Zolciak. As you can see, Natalie is an avid fan of the Bravo TV line-up.

the Bigglesworth home wouldn't be an issue. She had put it down on both of them the night before and knew they would be back for more.[23] She would simply plant the necklace back into their bedroom on her next visit and neither of them would be any the wiser.

Lucy pushed herself off the bed and began to dress herself. She knew that she had a busy day ahead of her; aside from the required washing of the laundry, she also had to finish sewing two blouses for the Higgins daughter and Dr. Stevens would be by later in the day to pick up his khakis which needed tailoring. All in a days work the most talented seamstress in the colony.

Lucy was truly the Donna Karan of this new world. Villagers came to her for everything fashion related. If they needed a dress stitched, they called upon her. If they needed pants hemmed up, they called upon her. If they needed a new garment constructed, they called upon her. It seemed unfair to most that such a beautiful creature could also be so incredibly talented as well. The things Lucy could do with a needle and thread would make Marc Jacobs look like he was designing frocks for Wal-Mart.

Needless to say these impeccable skills and talents only added fuel to Natalie's blazing hate for her sister.

Lucy spent much of her day by the river scrubbing the laundry and singing songs to herself to pass the time. She unleashed her fiery hair from her bonnet and let it blow in the wind as she scrubbed the family's unmentionables in the cool stream. It was truly a magnificent vision to see her locks twirl in the air with each gust of the breeze. Villagers would pass by and do a double-take upon seeing her; their first thought was that a luminous goddess had appeared right before their very eyes. It took them squinting and blinking hard to refresh their vision to realize it was only

---

23   Lucy knew she had sexed them like a true professional so she was very sure they would be back for a second helping.

one of their own. And, of course, this just made them secretly despise her even more (not surprising considering the majority of the others in the village were about as visually appealing as a bunch of zombie extras from *The Walking Dead*.) Her beauty made them love and hate her all at the same time.

Much of the rest of her day went by like any other; Lucy finished her required household chores and even managed to make Edward's Fruit-of-the-Looms look brand new again, which was no easy task. As the evening was settling in, Natalie and Edward departed the cabin to have dinner with the Fayes, a neighboring family. Lucy politely declined the invitation because she knew that Dr. Stevens would be coming by later in the evening to pick up his trousers, and quite frankly, the thought of having to play nice with her sister in the company of others was not appealing to her at all. She much preferred a quiet night at home in front of the warm fire with a giant glass of wine to loosen herself up from the work of the day.

Just as she got herself comfortable in the living room she heard a brash knock at the door.

"Fuck," Lucy whispered under her breath as she gently placed her glass of wine on the table. She could tell from the heavy knock that it was Dr. Stevens on the other side of the door. She dragged herself towards the front door to allow her guest entry.

"Hello there Lucy," said the doctor as he entered the cabin. "Good evening to you."

"Evening to you as well, doctor," answered Lucy. "How are you doing this weekend?"

"Huh," exhaled Dr. Stevens in an exhausted manner. "I've been busier than Demi Moore at a Boy Scout's meeting, my dear. This winter wind rolling through has left quite a few of our fellow voyagers with a case of the sniffles so I've been tending to them all day. I hope you're bundling up and keeping warm young lady?"

"Oh yes, I certainly have," she answered. "I'm far too busy these days to get ill so I've been taking the proper precautions. Would you like to have a seat by the fire and enjoy a glass of wine with me for a little while? I think you deserve a little relaxation after such a taxing day."

"That sounds fantastic," said the doctor as he made his way towards the couch.

"Would you like some white or red wine, sir?" asked Lucy.

"I prefer my wine like my bitches, that is white,"[24] responded the doctor as he shot Lucy a seductive glance.

She had never looked at the doctor in that way before, but something in that moment seemed to ignite from within him. Seeing him against the light of the fire she realized just how handsome he truly was. There was something very Clooney-esque about the dear doctor that she had never realized before. His chiseled face was not only extremely sexy, but it was also inviting at the same time; it was the kind of face that made you want to spill all your secrets to it. Sure he was old enough to be her father, but Lucy always enjoyed the company of an older man. The boys her age were just that, boys. She had no need for a boy. And besides, the doctor was in better shape than practically every other man in the village. In that moment she thought she might throw him a bone if the opportunity presented itself.[25]

Lucy sauntered over towards the couch and handed the doctor a hefty glass of wine.

"Thank you so very much Lucy," said Dr. Stevens as he grinned toward his hostess.

"You're very welcome. I'll be sure to include it in your tab," giggled Lucy.

"Oh, is that so?"

"What can I say doctor, I'm all about my paper,"[26] said Lucy as she made herself comfortable across from him on the couch.

---

24 W.A.S.P. Translation: Dr. Stevens is implying that he prefers the company of Caucasian bitches.
25 Lucy is saying that she might drop her draws and give the dear doctor a little action.
26 W.A.S.P. Translation: At the end of the day, the bands are what makes Lucy dance.

"That's good to hear young lady," he responded. "There's nothing more attractive than a boss bitch making her dough."[27]

"I know that's right, doctor! So many of the women in this village don't take advantage of their skills in order to turn a buck. But that will never be me; a dolla makes me holla quicker than Honey Boo Boo!"[28]

The doctor let out a boisterous and hearty laugh. "You truly are quite the character, young lady."

"I'll take that as a compliment coming from a man of your stature, doctor."

"As you should."

They locked eyes and at that very moment you could cut the sexual tension in the air with a knife. The glare of the fire seemed to set Lucy's hair alive with fluid effervescence. The doctor could only stare and marvel at her beauty. They had settled into the colony for months now, and yet Dr. Stevens actually knew very little about this fascinating creature. He had to know what made her tick.

"I hope this is not too forward of a question to ask a young lady, but how is that no gentleman has put a ring on that delicate hand of yours? I would think men would be clawing at each other in order to lay claim to such a beauty as yourself."

"Oh, my dear doctor, I hope to not sound conceited but I've been fielding off proposals for years now," she answered as she swirled her wine glass in her hand and stared off into the fire. "I don't really know if I'm the marrying type of girl if I must be honest. Maybe one day in the near future I'll settle down a little bit, but sometimes I wonder if I'm just too full of passion to ever be quenched. I often think I've been cursed with these feelings of mine."

"Maybe you just haven't found the right gentleman to tame that ferocious wild cat of yours?"

---

27   W.A.S.P. Translation: Dr. Stevens is implying that an independent woman gives him a boner.

28   The addictive catchphrase brought to infamy from American royalty, Honey Boo Boo.

Lucy swiveled her head toward the flirtatious doctor. The seductive look in his eyes was a glare she had become accustomed to over the years with her dealings with the male species.

"Wild cat? My dear doctor, if that is a metaphor referring to my coochie then let me assure you that wild cat doesn't do it justice; it's more like a *Thunder Cat* residing in my pantaloons."[29]

Dr. Stevens let out a loud cackle of a laugh and slapped his leg to further illustrate just how tickled he was with her.

"I know that's not the most 'lady-like' thing for me to say to a gentleman like yourself, but if there's one thing you'll quickly learn about me it's that I truly give about zero fucks what anyone in this village thinks of me."

"No," responded the doctor. "I actually find it refreshing to converse with such a self-assured and confident young lass like yourself."

"Well that's good to know, but what about you? What's your deal, dear doctor? I mean here you are, an older man, intensely handsome, educated, and rather sweet, and yet no wife? This is probably the wine talking for me, but if I didn't see the bulge in your pants getting progressively larger since you sat down next to me I might think you were into the fellas."

"Oh my," said the doctor as he quickly stared down toward his crotch to inspect and reorganize the referenced area.

"Please don't be embarrassed, I'd be offended if you weren't at least a little excited sitting here next to me in this romantic setting."

"That would be quite impossible, my dear," said Dr. Stevens as he took a swig of wine. "But back to your original question, I used to be married to the love of my life. Her name was Margaret and it was quite a marvelous marriage, but as with most good things it came to a crashing end a few years ago when I came home early from work one day and

---

29 Lucy is comparing her vagina to the *Thunder Cats*, a 1980's cartoon about wild, alien cats with vicious superpowers.

caught her getting salacious with our cook. He was taking her right there in the kitchen and let's just say he was stuffing more than a turkey that evening."

"Sweet Jesus, Mary, and Joseph! How did you survive such traitorous fuckery under your own roof?"

"Well, my dear, I tossed the bitch out in the streets with the rest of the trash where she belonged. You know you can't turn a hoe into a housewife. I should have followed the code of the streets with that one. As for my ever-attentive chef, well you know in England you're only as good as your reputation and after I got finished socially murdering him no one would dare employ such a scoundrel. Last I heard he was cooking Grand Slam breakfasts at Denny's. That will teach the young fellow to dip his ladle into another man's pot."

"Remind me never to cross you," said Lucy with a little giggle. "Please excuse me for bringing up such a sore subject, I suppose my curiosity got the best of me."

"No worries at all, my dear," replied the doctor. "And as much as I am enjoying this little rendezvous, I do think I should be getting on my way shortly. Much like today, my schedule tomorrow is sure to be packed thanks to all these ill bastards in our village."

"I completely understand, but I must insist that you do try on your pants before you depart. I want to make sure the alterations I made were a success. They are hanging on the door in the bathroom if you'd like to change in there."

"Surely, that's a fantastic idea."

The suave doctor gently placed his wine glass on the coffee table and rose from the couch. Lucy caught herself watching him out of the corner of her eye as he made his way into the bathroom. There was something about this man that intrigued her. Before this evening she thought he was just like the rest of the lame pilgrims she was surrounded by, but after being in his company in such an intimate setting she realized there was something sexy and mysterious about him, almost dark. As she gazed off into the fire she let a brief rush of girlish optimism take over herself and thought maybe this friendship with the doctor could be something more. Something real. It was a rare occurrence for her to click with others like the way they had. But all in due time she thought; there was no point in counting her chickens before they hatched.

Behind her she could hear the lock on the bathroom door click and footsteps getting closer to her.

"Well, I think this fit is quite perfect, Ms. Lucy," announced the doctor.

As Lucy stood up from the couch to turn and inspect her amazing tailoring she caught a glimpse of the dashing doctor standing there in all his nakedness.

"Why, Dr. Stevens, I think you've misplaced your clothes," said Lucy as she turned her head attempting to be modest and hide her excitement.

"I've misplaced nothing, my dear," replied the doctor as he made his way closer to the beauty. He took her head into his big, masculine hands and began to passionately kiss her. At this point Lucy threw all modesty out the window and began to claw at the doctor like Scooby Doo in heat. He forcefully turned her around and began to gently kiss on her neck as he pushed her lush red hair to the side and gave it a soft pull for effect. His hands made their way to the buttons of her bodice where he gradually undid them all one-by-one. He turned her around once more and stared into her eyes as his hands cupped her perky bosoms. Here he was, the most respected member of this colony, standing in this beautiful stranger's home, completely naked, and although he knew she was the village Blanche Deveroux he still had to have her.[30] There was something about this jezebel that he couldn't resist. He grasped her on the back of her thighs and lifted her into his arms as he made his way back toward the

---

30 Dr. Stevens knew that Lucy was like the infamous and slutty *Golden Girl*, but he still wanted to thank her for being a friend.

couch.

He threw her on the couch and climbed on top of her. Neither one could keep their mouthes off one another; it felt like that kind of rare, intense and volatile passion that one rarely gets to experience. It was very Angelina Jolie and Billy Bob.[31] Lucy closed her eyes and basked in the feeling of ecstasy that was taking over her body. She barely knew this man, but that's what turned her on the most about the whole scenario. She could feel the doctor reaching under her skirt grabbing ahold of her panties as he ripped them off and began to thrust himself into her.

Not more than four thrusts later, a total of about 10 seconds, the dear doctor let out a loud shriek and then proceeded to lay his head down between Lucy's supple breasts. She opened her eyes to survey the situation. *Was it really over? Did I fall asleep during the whole thing? But how?* Lucy thought to herself. *I mean I've heard of minute-men, but I've had banana's with a longer shelf-life than this asshole!*

Lucy let out a soft chuckle under her breath as she gently brushed the hair out of her face and pat the doctor on his head.

Dr. Stevens lifted his head and glared up at the beautiful girl with an inquisitive smile. "And what may I ask is so funny, my dear girl?"

"Oh nothing, nothing at all," she answered with an even deeper chuckle.

"No really, what's so funny? I'd love to know," he asked once more, a bit more serious this time.

At this point in the evening the wine had made its way to Lucy's head and she was feeling a bit "loose" so it's not very surprising what came out of her mouth next.

"I say this with no intended disrespect, but if that's how long a normal fuck with you typically lasts then I must say I'm not terribly surprised your dear old wife was letting Chef Boyardee pound her cakes to smithereens next to the breadbox on the kitchen counter."

"Excuse me?" responded the doctor, completely aghast as he

---

31   A.K.A. white trash loving.

lifted himself off of her. "What's that supposed to mean? Didn't you enjoy yourself? I thought that our tryst was fantastic. I cannot believe what my ears are hearing."

"Fantastic? In what world is a 10-second plow defined as fantastic? Michael Douglas could've given it to me better than that,"[32] she sarcastically said as she sat up and buttoned up her bodice. "But try not to feel so bad, it happens to all men at some point. Or so I've heard."

Dr. Stevens quickly stood up from the couch, feeling completely and utterly humiliated. "I cannot believe you. What an ungrateful child! Did you ever think maybe it was your fault?"

"My fault?" she said with a boisterous laugh as she watched the doctor storm off towards the bathroom to dress himself. "How on earth could this be construed as my fault? It's my fault for having a good coochie? No one told you to fuck me faster than Seabuscuit![33] I thought you were different, but you're just like every other man; putting your shortcomings onto a woman to rectify yourself of guilt. Well, I'll be damned if you'll treat me as such. I ain't the one, boo!"

The doctor stormed back into the living room, throwing his coat over his shoulders and making a beeline for the front door.

"Mark my words, Lucy Skeezabeth, you will regret the shame and humiliation you just inflicted upon my character. It may not be tomorrow. It may not be this month. But trust and believe me, you will feel my wrath."

"Feel your wrath? That's a tad bit dramatic isn't it, doctor? You sound like Shredder from the *Teenage Mutant Ninja Turtles* right now."

"Laugh it up now you young hussy, but it is I who will have the last laugh. You can bet your bottom dollar on that," he said as he reached

---

32 Lucy is implying that even the prehistoric actor, at the tender age of 132-years old, could have pleasured her better.
33 Lucy is referencing the award-winning 2003 film *Seabiscuit*, in which a thoroughbred race horse scores fame for his incredible speed. Unfortunately for Lucy, sex with the doctor was not nearly as enjoyable as the film.

for the door handle to leave this cabin of shame.

"Hey, Speedy Gonzales, aren't you forgetting something?" she said as she reached for her glass of wine on the table to take another swig. "You owe me 25 cents for the pants and another 25 cents for the glass of wine. I'll refrain from charging you for the sex; I'll just claim it as a tax deduction under 'Charitable Contributions' considering it was a pity lay. Most of the pity going towards myself for actually having to endure that misery."

"Here, take your 50 cents you dirty trick!" he responded as he reached into his pocket and threw two quarters in her direction before he stormed out of the house into the brisk night air.

Lucy got up off the couch and fixed her disheveled dress as she made her way towards the money. She picked it up off the floor and placed it in her skirt pocket. She returned to her spot on the sofa and set her sights back onto the hypnotic fire. She knew she would wake up tomorrow and feel a little guilty for being so hard on the poor doctor, but a drunk tongue only speaks the truth. Surely the doctor wouldn't hold a grudge against her for too long. It was just a few little jokes after all.

Either way, the worst of it was over now. No sense in harping over it for too long. Lucy was just happy that her little secret fling with the doctor would end, right here and now. But little did she know that peering through the kitchen window someone had witnessed the events of the evening and had much different plans for the newly acquired information.

CHAPTER THREE

As Natalie stood outside in the cool air and stared through the small kitchen window of her charming little cottage she knew she had just struck gold. Baring witness to the humiliating interaction between her sister and Dr. Stevens had brought a wicked smile to her face. What would she do with this precious little gem of information she had just stumbled upon? How could she use it to her advantage to annihilate her sister? She wasn't entirely sure yet, but she knew proper planning had to be done.

But what luck had fallen into Natalie's lap; she had simply left the Faye's dinner party momentarily to grab another bottle of wine from their private collection to bring back to the gathering. And while she was having a fabulous time at the party, nothing could quite compare with the knowledge she had just acquired.

Natalie slowly made her way towards the front door and sauntered into the warm cabin.

"Natalie, what are you doing home so early?" asked Lucy. "Where is Edward?"

Wouldn't you like to know, you little 25-cent trollop, Natalie thought to herself, but ultimately decided to keep her inner disdain at bay.

"Oh, Edward is still over at the Faye's home. The party is still going on but I ran home quickly to grab another bottle of Chardonnay. You know that Laurie Faye doesn't know when to stop drinking and she's managed to polish off an entire bottle completely by herself. Such an uncouth miscreant she is, but the bitch sure knows how to make a mean meatloaf; I'll certainly give her that."

Lucy let out a half-hearted giggle and turned her head to resume gazing at the fire.

"What have you been up to this evening?" asked Natalie as she made her way towards the cupboard to grab the wine.

"Nothing too eventful. I've just been relaxing for the majority of the night. Please make sure you send my apologies to the Faye's for not attending the dinner party this evening. I haven't been much in the mood for company today."

Oh really? You're not in the mood for company huh? Is that why you just let our dear doctor pound your hot pocket faster than Usain Bolt at the London Olympics,[34] thought Natalie.

"Don't worry, I'll be sure to pass along your message to them. I'm sure they'll take no offense. There's always next time," said Natalie as she smiled at her unsuspecting sister.

"What's that grin for?" asked Lucy.

"Grin? Why whatever do you mean? It must be the wine going to my head," said Natalie with a giggle.

"I see," said Lucy as she rose from the couch and walked towards the kitchen to place her wine glass in the basin. "Well I think I'll be off to bed now. I really am quite exhausted for some reason."

Yeah I'd be exhausted too if I just got banged like a clearance-bin Bangkok whore, thought Natalie.

"Oh okay, well get some rest. I suppose we'll see you in the

---

34   Usain Bolt broke the world record for the fastest 100m dash in history. Dr. Stevens broke the record for the fastest premature climax almost as quickly.

morning," said Natalie as she watched her sister make her way towards her bedroom. "Aren't you going to bathe before bed?"

"I bathed after you and Edward left for dinner. What do you care anyway?"

Because, you dirty skank, you just had sex with a stranger! You'd think you'd want to take a sponge to that filthy muff of yours to wash off the shame, thought Natalie.

"No reason; just making conversation I suppose. Anyway, let me head back to the party before it gets too late. Don't want them sending a search party after me," said Natalie as nonchalantly and friendly as possible.

"Yeah right, have fun."

Natalie watched Lucy make her way towards her room and close the door behind her. She waited until she heard Lucy close down the latch on her lock before she gave in to the fit of laughter that had been bubbling up inside her since she came into the cabin. Natalie had to cover her mouth with both hands and run out the door into the chilly nighttime air as to keep her delight a secret from Lucy. The last thing she wanted to do was to make Lucy suspicious.

As she slowly made her way back to the Faye's cabin she breathed in the fresh night air and let the feeling of glee rush over her. She had surely struck it rich this evening. *Oh, what a joyous night it has been thus far*, she thought. *Not only will I humiliate that skank of a sister with this new piece of delicious information I've bared witness to, but, maybe it's all the wine in my system this evening, but Edward actually seems, well, fuckable this glorious night. It surely must be the wine because normally the thought of him naked would make me feel like I'd just contracted the early symptoms of Swine Flu. Oh well, I'm in a mood of sheer bliss this evening so maybe I'll throw him a little blow job when we get home to reward him for not being completely repulsive for once.*

Fast forward 3 hours (and 4 more bottles of wine) later....

While the rest of the colony slept their night away, Natalie and Edward drunkenly stumbled through the blackness of the evening toward their home. They leaned into one another for balance as they giggled like tipsy schoolgirls at the most minuscule jokes.

"I must say my dear, I can't remember a time when you've ever been more pleasant," said Edward as he placed his arm around his wife and pulled her closer. "I'm going to have to keep you drunk on wine more often if this is who you are when you're loaded."

Natalie let out a wild giggle.

"Oh, you hush Mr. Williams! I've just had a good evening is all; I'm not a miserable bitch all the time, you know?"

"Of course not, my love. I knew when I put a ring on that delicate finger of yours that you had more personalities than Sybil, but I surely do enjoy this one. It seems as though you've removed the stick from your ass tonight," Edward said jokingly.

"What a lovely thing to say to your wife, you fat bastard," Natalie responded with a girlish slap to Edward's arm before bursting into a fit of laughter.

Edward came to a stop and grabbed Natalie's hand and proceeded to place a gentle kiss on the back of her palm. "It just brings me such joy to see you so very happy. I know it's been quite a stressful voyage since we left England to come to this new world, but I certainly do think we shall be happy here now that everything is finally getting settled."

"I agree," said Natalie as she stared into her intoxicated husband's eyes. "Now stop being such a sentimental little bitch and carry me home. This wine has me feeling a bit *feisty* this evening."

Edwards eyes widened and a sinister smile came over his pudgy face.

"Feisty? Is that so?" he said as he proceeded to pick up his wife off the ground and began sprinting toward their cabin. The two of them could barely contain their amusement as Edward's big ass ran through the settlement, carrying his petite wife over his shoulder at the sheer hope of getting laid. If one were to bare witness to this sight they would have immediately thought they had seen a chubby, caucasian Yogi Bear chasing after a pussy picnic basket.

When they finally reached their front door Edward was completely out of breath and had to put his wife down before he had a major cardiac episode right there on his front steps.

"Are you okay?" Natalie asked as she rubbed his back to comfort him.

"I'm more than okay," he responded as he caught his breath and grabbed her by the hand. "Let's go."

They raced into the cabin, attempting to keep their drunken delight to a minimum as not to wake Lucy from her beauty rest. As they crept into their bedroom they began to strip layers of clothing off one another.

Boy, I really must be drunk if I'm actually anticipating fucking this tubby idiot, thought Natalie as Edward ripped open her blouse and began to motorboat her ample cleavage. Natalie let out a devious giggle. *He's licking on my breasts like they're a 10-piece bucket of all-white meat chicken from KFC with a side of mashed potatoes and a biscuit. I've got to be careful he doesn't take a bite out of me.*

Edward picked up his wife and threw her on the bed. They were clawing at each other like rabid badgers in heat as he climbed on top of her and entered his woman. Needless to say, the scene was very hot and heavy....for about 25 seconds.

One minute Edward was taking Natalie to pound town, and actually doing quite a good job Natalie thought, and the next second all action ceased. Natalie looked down at her husband's head lying between her breasts.

"Edward," Natalie said as she tapped him on the cheek. "Edward, wake your fat ass up!"

There was no response.

"My gosh Edward, I would think you'd at least dismount me before you fell asleep. And to fall asleep on top of me, you know my brittle bones can't handle all this weight. Get off me and let me finish myself off; at least my fingers never disappoint me."

Natalie gathered all her strength and pushed her husband's body off her and onto the other side of their bed.

Go figure, the one night I'm actually into the idea of letting him into my cookie jar and the chunky hippo falls asleep mid-hump! she thought. *Whatever, not even this little ordeal is going to bring me down from this high that I'm feeling tonight.*

Natalie put her hands behind her head and stared off into the space of night. She was anxious for the new day to begin so that she could get her plan for Lucy's demise underway. She had spent so much of her life living in the shadow of her gorgeous sister, but now was Natalie's time for a little retribution.

Only a few hours later the sun began to rise on a brand new day. As the warm rays of sun began to creep through the crisp and chilly windowpanes, Natalie opened her eyes and took in the new day as a mischievous grin began to run across her face. She had only slept a handful of hours, but she awoke completely refreshed and ready to get her day started.

She turned her head to the other side of the bed to find Edward still fast asleep in the same position he had passed out in the night before.

"Edward," Natalie said with a gentle push on his shoulder. "Wake up. The sun is up and much is to be done today."

There was no response.

"Edward Williams, if I would've known you were going to turn into a lazy lump after a few months of marriage I would've just accepted my first proposal of marriage from my Mexican gardener, Alejandro. I'm sure he wouldn't have taken a siesta whilst still in my chocha,"[35] Natalie sarcastically snapped toward her husband.

Still, Edward didn't budge from his location.

This is what happens when you let fat people indulge too much, thought Natalie. *I'll let him sleep it off a little more while I go run my errands, but this Fat Albert-looking bastard better be awake when I get home.*

Natalie hopped herself out of their queen-sized bed and proceeded to rummage through her closet to find the perfect outfit for the day. *Oh, what to wear on such a glorious morning*, thought Natalie. *I'm so tired of these neutral tone dresses and these horrendous bonnets. I feel like I'm some butter-churning Mormon bride. What's a bitch gotta do to find some colorful frocks in this new world of ours? I'd kill for a Zara right about now.*

As Natalie buttoned-up her dress she caught a glimpse of herself in the mirror above her dresser. While she wasn't as gorgeous as her sister, there was a peculiar beauty about Natalie that seemed to be more intensified today. Her subtle sexuality seemed to be shining through more than ever this morning. She was getting a twisted boost of self-confidence knowing that she had finally secured a plan to seemingly destroy her sister. She watched herself as she slowly tucked her thick brunette hair into her bonnet and gradually made her way out of the bedroom, quietly closing the door behind her.

She didn't want to draw any attention to the fact that she was exiting the house this early, so she tip-toed her way through the hallway before making her way into the living quarters. Natalie knew Edward was out cold, but she wanted to make sure Lucy continued her slumber as well. Natalie wasn't in the mood for any incessant questioning from her this morning. She quickly made herself a small cup of coffee to brush off the minute hangover and headed out into the village.

While it was still early, the village already seemed to be ripe with people. Natalie made her way through the village and greeted her fellow

---

35   Natalie is putting her knowledge of the Spanish language to good use this morning by telling her husband that even the gardener wouldn't have taken a nap whilst humping her.

settlers with gracious (yet phony) waves and bits of forced small talk.

Oh, how I wish this bitch would've brushed her teeth before she started speaking to me, she thought as old Mrs. Robbish leaned in closer to tell her about the devious rabbit she had caught the previous day running rampant in her cabbage garden.

Does this dumbass not realize he has a giant bogger dangling from his nose, she said to herself as Tom Wilard cornered her a little further down the road to invite her and Edward to his cabin next weekend for a feast.

I wonder how much those Pamela Anderson tits cost her, she thought to herself as she smiled and greeted Mrs. Gwen Coolage, whose massive breasts seemed to be resting right below her chin.

Natalie certainly didn't have the fondest things to say about her fellow settlers, but that was just her character. Over the years she had learned to cloak herself in sarcasm as a means to stay guarded and she never liked to let anyone get too close to her (both physically and emotionally). It goes without saying that she wasn't winning any Miss Congeniality awards any time soon.

Just when she had thought she was finished with the insipid small talk she heard a woman beaconing for her from behind. She turned around to find fellow newlywed Jane Bigglesworth racing toward her trying to get her attention.

"Why hello there, Mrs. Bigglesworth," said Natalie. "How are you this lovely morning?"

"I'm doing well. It certainly is gorgeous weather outside today isn't it?"

"Yes, it truly is. According to Al Roker's weather forecast it's supposed to be fantastic all week. But then again I never fully trust those weathermen you know? The only advice I really trust from Al Roker is where I can get the best B.L.T. on the east coast."[36]

---

36   Natalie lived by a very simple philosophy when it came to good food: always trust the recommendations of fat people (even former fat ones) because they know where the good shit is at. Who are you going to ask for the best burger in Hollywood, Brad Pitt or Kevin James?

"I fully concur," Jane said with a giggle. "It's much like Rihanna giving singing tips, isn't it? How are we supposed to take your advice seriously when you sound like a bag of rabid cats being hit with a stick, right?"[37]

"You got that right," Natalie agreed as they made their way down the road together.

"I wanted to ask you about your sister Lucy, how is she doing?" asked Jane.

Natalie stared at Jane out of the corners of her eyes with skepticism. "She's fine. Why do you ask?"

"Oh, no reason in particular. It's just that my husband and I had her over for dinner a couple days ago and we just wanted to make sure she was doing well. That's all."

"I see. Well yes, my sister is doing fine."

"We would love to have her over for dinner again this evening if you wouldn't mind passing along the invitation. I was thinking about glazing a chicken for supper..."

Before Jane could even finish her sentence Natalie brought her to a halt and interrupted her neighbor. "Jane, let's keep it all the way 100, the only thing you want to glaze is my sister's cooch again."[38]

"Why, excuse me?" Jane said, shocked.

"Jane, do you think you and your husband are the first couple my whorish sister has turned out? You think I didn't realize how late she got home the other night? You expect me to believe you guys were over there playing Candyland or Shoots and Ladders until the wee hours of the morning? You must think I was born yesterday."

"Mrs. Natalie Williams, all we were doing was enjoying each others company and engaging in some fascinating conversations," Jane

---

37   Rihanna has some of the most amazing and catchy pop tunes of the last ten years, but I've heard women who are 10-centimeters dilated in the midst of childbirth who are on pitch better than she is most of the time.

38   W.A.S.P. Translation: By saying "keep it all the way 100," Natalie is requesting that Jane be 100% honest with her about the fact that she wants to butter Lucy's muffin one more time.

said, trying to deflect the accusation of a freaky-deaky menage-a-trois.

"You were enjoying the fascinating conversations?" Natalie said with a hearty laugh. "Really? That's the best excuse you could come up with? I once had a fascinating conversation with Margaret Thatcher over a lovely dinner, but I didn't eat her out after dessert."

Jane Bigglesworth's jaw seemed to drop to the ground as she clutched her basket closer to her chest. "I'm shocked and appalled."

"Listen up Jane. Take heed to this warning that I'm offering you. You and your husband seem like nice people, but I've seen this happen before. You weren't the first and I'm fairly certain you won't be the last. I could tell from that first day on the boat what you and your husband were after; you wanted the nookie, and by the looks of it I would say that you finally got it. But this scenario isn't going to end well for you and your beloved husband. After she works her magic on you and gets you both to fall head-over-heels in love with her she'll tire of you both and throw you to the side faster than Jamie Lee Curtis can gobble down an Activia. Just take my advice and move on."

Natalie twirled around and proceeded to walk off, leaving poor Jane all alone in the middle of road with a bruised ego. Natalie knew what she had said was harsh, but Jane needed to hear it; and much like ripping off a Band-Aid or seeing a Jennifer Lopez film, it was best to get it done quick and be finished with it. Natalie knew that Lucy would eventually hurt them and as far as she was concerned she had just done the Bigglesworth couple a major favor. And besides, Natalie didn't have time to play pimp to her sister's hooker-like endeavors; she had more pressing matters to tend to as she strolled closer and closer to Dr. Steven's cottage.

KNOCK, KNOCK

Natalie rattled on the massive wooden door of the beloved village doctor. A moment later the doctor came to the door and a look of pure fright seemed to wash over his face. *What is she doing here*, he thought. *Has that jezebel of a sister told her what happened last night?*

"Why, hello there Mrs. Williams. What brings you over so early this morning? Is everyone in your home feeling well?" he said, attempting to fish for information.

"Oh yes, everyone is quite perfect in our household," she said with a smile. "But may I come in? There's something I would like to discuss with you."

"For sure, please come in," he said as he opened the door wider for her to enter.

Natalie glided past the doctor into his cabin like she owned the place. She had seen enough Beyonce performances to know how to turn on her very own Sasha Fierce walk when needed. She made her way around his living quarters, casually inspecting and auditing all of the medicinal bottles strewn throughout his shelves and cabinets. There seemed to be no method to his madness when it came to the organization of all his tubes and vials, but this was the case with most insanely brilliant people Natalie thought.

"Was there anything in particular I could help you with Mrs. Williams? Is everyone back home feeling okay?" said Dr. Stevens, attempting to feel out exactly what this unexpected visit was in reference to.

"My dear doctor, you've already asked me that question haven't you?" she responded as she peered at him over her shoulder.

"Oh, why I believe I have. I'm sorry, I suppose I'm still a bit tired being that it's so early and all."

"It's quite alright. But I must say doctor you seem a bit uneasy to see me this morning; nervous, in fact. Is everything okay with you?"

She was right. You could read the tension and nervousness in the doctor's body language from a mile away. He looked about as comfortable as Mel Gibson at a Bar Mitzvah.

"With me? Of course, I'm fine. Like I said, I suppose I'm just a bit exhausted attempting to care for all of those in the village who have fallen ill with this weather. You would think some of these parents would know how to dress their children in such conditions, but instead they have them running these colonial streets like Dennis the Menace with nothing more than a simple t-shirt and slacks. And then they wonder why their children are projectile vomiting like Linda Blair in *The Exorcist* the next day."

Natalie could see the honorable doctor was rambling out of discomfort; she let out a small laugh to ease his tension. She made her way towards his desk and politely sat down in the guest chair at the front of it.

"Would you like to sit down, doctor? I have a proposition for you that you may enjoy hearing."

"A proposition? Is that so?" he questioned as he made his way towards his supple leather chair behind his desk. "Let's hear what this is all about."

"I shall get right to the point. As I understand it you were a guest at my home last night while my husband and I were away at dinner."

"Why yes, I came to your home to pick up my slacks that your sister Lucy was hemming for me. She did quite an amazing job. I must say…"

"Doctor, doctor, doctor," Natalie interrupted as she placed her hand in the air to halt him from another winded diatribe. "Believe me, I could give a fuck about how well your Docker's fit. That's not what I'm here for."

A look of embarrassed panic quickly ran across his face. She knew what had transpired at her residence the night before.

"What are you talking about, Mrs. Williams?" he said as he leaned back in his chair.

"Well Dr. Stevens, it just so happens I had to return to my home early last evening to fetch another bottle of wine for our hosts, and when passing my kitchen window I was quite surprised, as you can imagine, to find my sister spread-eagle on my couch as our distinguished doctor proceeded to jackhammer her as if she were an old road in need of renovation. As if that wasn't scandalous enough, the whole ordeal lasted a whole 30-seconds, if that much. I mean really doctor, I've got to say I've cooked Uncle Ben's Minute Rice that actually took longer to finish than you did last night."

Dr. Stevens went completely pale. If one could die of embarrassment than he would have crocked right then and there.

"But your horrific sexual performance isn't exactly why I'm here," she continued. "I saw your interaction with my sister after you two *finished* and I bore witness to her rash treatment of you. She has quite the wicked tongue, doesn't she?"

Dr. Stevens couldn't figure out where this conversation was headed. Was he supposed to agree with her? Was she setting him up as retribution for her sister? He thought he had best tread very carefully because if Natalie was as cruel as her sister he could be in a world of trouble.

"Well, the things she said weren't exactly the nicest. I shall say that much," he said.

"I'll say; I mean it's not your fault you came faster than the Road Runner being chased by Wile E. Coyote. I know you men tend to get excited very easily, but that doesn't excuse her wicked tongue now does it?"

"You're absolutely right," he responded, inquisitively.

"That's what brings me to your dwelling this morning, my dear doctor," she said as she proceeded to rise and saunter behind his chair gently outlining the frame of it with her finger. "I've seen my sister hurt too many people and I think it's time someone teaches her a lesson that these actions don't go without consequences."

Dr. Stevens was intrigued; this certainly wasn't the direction he was expecting this visit to go. "What exactly do you have in mind, Mrs. Williams?"

"I think you and I could be formidable team to show my sister that these kinds of things are unacceptable. With your knowledge of all these interesting potions and medicines, and my know how of her idiosyncrasies and weaknesses, I think we could show her a thing or two."

Dr. Stevens couldn't believe his ears. He had every intention on getting Lucy back for her disrespectful treatment of him last night, but the last thing he expected was her own sister standing in his home offering up her help to potentially destroy her. He still wasn't entirely sure he could trust Natalie; what was her reasoning for wanting to hurt her own flesh and blood? He rose from his chair and walked toward Natalie, "This sounds well and good Mrs. Williams, but why? I haven't seen this kind of secret sisterly disdain since I dined with Mary-Kate and Ashley Olsen over Memorial Day weekend. What is fueling your fire in this situation?"

Natalie stared directly into Dr. Stevens eyes; she wanted him to feel her passion on this topic. "Dr. Stevens, do you know what it's like to spend your life in the shadow of a sibling? Since my sister came along I've become a non-factor to everyone in our lives. Her beauty has made her the commodity and turned me into an afterthought; well, I'm tired of being the Khloe Kardashian of this family. At a certain point even the most devoted sister stops giving a fuck and wants a little shine for herself. It's my turn to be the Kim!"[39]

Dr. Stevens couldn't believe his ears. She was serious about this; very serious, actually. He could see the hate illuminating in her eyes as she profusely declared her disdain for her sister. He knew she would be a worthy partner in this act of retribution.

"Well, how do you propose we get her?" he said with a smirk.

Her own smile grew cold and wicked. She knew she had baited him.

"Tell me dear doctor, what do you have that can aide in the loss of hair?"

---

39   Khloe can shower Kim with as much Twitter and Instagram love as she wants, but there isn't a doubt in my mind that she wouldn't take a Louisville Slugger to her sister for a Vogue cover.

Twenty minutes later Natalie Williams exited Dr. Stevens cottage. Inside her basket, laying between some fresh eggs and a plethora of tomatoes, lay a vile with the contents that would change her life forever.

CHAPTER 4

The walk home from the doctor's cabin seemed longer than Natalie remembered, but she didn't mind. She didn't mind one bit.

Dr. Stevens had provided her with a vial of highly corrosive liquid that she was going to use to take away the source of her sister's power. That little vial in her basket was carrying the source of all her future happiness.

As she maneuvered her way through the village she began to relish and bathe in the deliciously devilish thoughts that filled her head. After a lifetime of secondhand treatment, Natalie Skeezabeth-Williams was finally going to get her due reward. She felt anew, as if she had awakened this morning to a fresh beginning in her life. She pranced and skipped down the road like one of those strange women in a tampon commercial who seem suspiciously jubilant even though they have a giant cotton ball shoved up their coochie.

She drank in all her surroundings. With every step she took her smile grew wider and wider. If you didn't know any better you would've thought this was a genuinely happy-spirited young lady. You probably never would've thought the reason for her smile was because she was a borderline psychotic.

Natalie turned the corner at the main road and her lovely demure cottage came into view in the distance. She suddenly felt a cool chill rise up her spine; the kind of chill that made the entire body shutter and quake from within. At first she couldn't explain the surprising feeling that overcame her, but she took it as a physical reaction to the joy that was bottling up inside her.

The sheer thought of seeing that horrific bitch-of-a-sister completely bald, without those pretty tresses of hers, is actually bringing me close to climax, she thought to herself. *I must remember to check my panties when I get home. I think all this plotting and scheming is making me a bit moist in my Victoria Secret pantaloons.*

When Natalie finally reached the house she triumphantly lunged herself through the doorway and immediately spotted Lucy standing in the kitchen, delicately washing off an apple.

"Well, someone's surely up-and-at-it quite early this morning," said Lucy with a sneer. "I'm shocked you didn't stampede through my room at the ass-crack of dawn like a manic rooster to wake me up too."

Natalie drank in the contempt that Lucy was spewing her way and spit it right back at her.

"Well, after I saw how rough and rugged you looked last night I figured I would let you get a few extra hours of sleep. By the looks of those sandbags under your eyes I suppose even you need some serious beauty sleep every now and again. Has anyone ever told you that you bear a striking resemblance to Bea Arthur when you're tired?"[40]

"You wish, bitch," Lucy said with a chuckle as she bit into her ripe apple and made her way towards the comfort of the living room couch.

"Lucy, did you already finish pruning the hedges outside?" Natalie questioned. "You know that's your chore for the day and there's no sense in you getting too comfortable if you haven't already completed what's

---

40   Natalie is implying that when Lucy is tired she resembles the late and great Bea Arthur (a.k.a. Dorothy from *The Golden Girls*), who, while she was insanely hilarious, surely wasn't winning any Miss America pageants in her day.

expected of you."

"Listen here Diane Sawyer, you should be less worried about my daily doings and more concerned with why your dearest husband still hasn't awakened from his slumber yet. I heard the rumblings coming from your room last night, but you must've twerked it on him real good if he's still asleep at this hour. Kudos to you, Miley Cyrus. Didn't realize you were turning into such a glorious slut puppy!"[41]

Natalie laid her basket on the kitchen table and spun her head toward her sister's direction.

"What do you mean? Are you saying Edward still hasn't awoken yet?"

"Did I stutter or are you just slow, Rain Man?" Lucy clapped back at her sister. "Yes, your husband is still in bed; so all that quizzing me about the damn hedges should be directed at him and why he hasn't chopped the firewood for the day. If it gets any colder in here at night my poor nipples are going to freeze right off."

Natalie looked perplexed. It was quite unlike Edward to sleep-in like this, especially on days when there was work to be done around the house. She made her way towards her bedroom and swung open the door.

There, lying in their bed, just as she had left him hours ago, lay Edward completely lifeless. Natalie closed the door behind her and ran over to the bed where she began shaking and prodding her motionless husband.

"Edward, wake up this instant," she demanded as she gave him a slap to the cheek. "I swear to everything holy in this world Edward if you don't wake up this instant you're never getting laid again!"

It was no use and Natalie knew it.

She was attempting to wake the dead; it was a useless endeavor.

---

41   Anyone with two eyes and pulse has had the privilege of watching Miley's steady progression from Disney sweetheart to Hollywood Boulevard streetwalker over the past couple years.

No matter how many smacks she gave to Edward's bloated face she knew that he wouldn't be chopping firewood anytime soon. In the heat of the moment last night poor Edward's heart must have simply given in. Natalie had warned him numerous times that all those Popeye's Fried Chicken value meals would catch up to him one day; she just wasn't expecting that moment to occur when his pants were down around his ankles.

Oh damn you, Edward Williams, she thought to herself as she lay beside her deceased husband. For a second she could feel tears begin to well up in her eyes; while she genuinely despised being married to the man, she did realize how much he loved her and how that love had ultimately saved her life back in England.

But the sentimental feeling was fleeting. She wiped the tears from her eyes and sat up on the bed as she pondered how the untimely death of her husband would play into her plans of the destruction for her sister. This wasn't what Natalie needed on her plate right now.

She rose from the bed and walked over toward the mirror above her dresser. She straightened out her skirt and tucked in the few loose strands of hair that had escaped from under her bonnet. Natalie knew there would be a bunch of gawkers and busy-bodies coming to the house once word began to spread that one of their own had passed, but there was no reason to look like a disheveled mess when they did. *There was no rule that a wife in mourning had to be a busted-looking bitch*, she thought to herself as she made her way towards the door.

As Natalie wandered into the main living quarters of the cabin she found Lucy still sitting on the couch polishing off what was left of her apple.

"Lucy, please do me a favor and go forth and fetch Dr. Stevens."

A look of dread rushed over Lucy's face; she was hoping to avoid the doctor's company for a while after their awkward altercation the previous night.

"Dr. Stevens? What do you need him for?" questioned Lucy as she rose from the couch and meandered toward the kitchen wastebasket. "Is Edward not feeling well?"

"Oh, he's dead is all," Natalie said very nonchalantly as she withdrew the eggs from her basket and placed them in the refrigerator.

Lucy dropped the core of her apple on the floor in shock. "Dead? Natalie, what do you mean he's dead? How the fuck did he die?"

"Hell if I know, that's why I need the doctor to come here. I'm assuming he had a heart attack during our lovemaking last night," she answered with a light yawn as if the conversation was dreadfully boring her. "I did find it a bit odd when he drifted off right in the middle of it, but I figured the wine had just made him sleepy."

"Natalie, how can you be so lax about this? I know you didn't love the man, but my lord woman, don't you think you should show some kind of emotion? I mean you slept in bed next to your dead husband last night."

"You're right, Lucy. And thank you for reminding me of that! After you fetch the doctor please stop off at old Mrs. Pacish's place and pick me up a new set of sheets. There's simply no way I can sleep on those sheets again knowing that Edward's fat ole self had expired on them. Oh, and please get the Egyptian cotton ones; those Jersey knit ones tend to make me sweat when I sleep in the nude, and you know I like to let my bits and pieces get some fresh air when I slumber."

Lucy was stunned.

She'd always known that her sister was a cold-hearted harpy, but witnessing just how selfish and wicked she could be shocked her to the core. How could she be related to such a callus bitch? For a brief second she realized what it must feel like to be related to Theresa Guidici from *The Real Housewives of New Jersey*.[42]

"I simply cannot believe you, Natalie! How do you know he's really dead? Maybe he's just in a deep sleep," Lucy retorted.

---

42   Anyone who follows the series is very well aware that there's a strong possibility that she's Lucifer's bride.

"Lucy, you naive fool, the man is dead," she said with a huff of annoyance as she faced her sister for the first time since breaking the news. "I could shove a grenade up his ass and that still wouldn't wake him. People die little sister, it's the way of life. Edward certainly was a great man and he saved our tuckus' by taking us with him on this voyage, but what do you expect from me? You know there was no love there on my part so I'm not going to sit here and pretend otherwise. Now please, if you want to make yourself useful go and get the doctor so we can get Edward's body out of this house; you can't leave a dead body for too long or else we'll never get rid of the scent. No amount of Febreeze will be able to kill that odor."

"You're truly a hopeless bitch, Natalie," Lucy said as she stormed out of the house and slammed the door behind her.

She knew her sister wasn't completely off-base.

Natalie knew she was a bitch and she was fine with that. But one thing she wasn't was stupid; she knew that she was going to have to push back her plans to ruin Lucy, at least for a few days. With Edward's death about to be front-page news throughout the colony she didn't want to overdo it and burn her sister's hair off when everyone's eyes were sure to be on the household already.

Natalie reached into her basket and withdrew the vial that Dr. Stevens had given her. She held it up to the light shining through the kitchen window and peered at the thick oily liquid; her eyes were transfixed on it as she shook it up and watched it slowly creep up the sides of the glass casing. As much as she wanted to make her way into the bathroom and pour the contents of the small vial into Lucy's shampoo bottle she knew that patience was going to be key in this plan.

Natalie had become so hypnotized by the acidic cocktail in her hands that she seemed to lose track of time; she must have been enraptured in it for quite awhile because before she knew it there was a knock on her front door. The brash knock brought Natalie back down to reality. She looked out the window to find numerous neighbors converging on her doorstep, presumably to shower her with condolences on her lose. She knew word would travel fast, but she didn't think this fast.

In a rush to get to the door she opened up one of the kitchen cabinets and gently placed the vial of acid inside; she figured this would be a good hiding place for the moment. The last thing she needed right now was one of the neighbors seeing the container and raising any questions about its contents.

Natalie quickly looked at herself in the small mirror next to the door; she knew she needed to look like she was in pain and emotional anguish so she scrunched up her face like Kristen Stewart and thought to herself, *There you go, now you look like a miserable bitch in mourning.*[43]

She opened the door and was bombarded by a barrage of hugs and kisses as each neighbor made their way into her home.

"Lucy told us what happened! He was such a good man."

"He will surely be missed among the colony."

"I know it's tough right now, but remember that Edward is in a better place, dear."

"We all know how much he loved you. He was such a fantastic husband, wasn't he?"

Natalie could barely tell who was saying what.

After awhile it was all a giant blur.

At a certain point she just turned her brain off and zoned out so she didn't have to listen to their redundant well-wishing's. She knew they were all just trying to be friendly and comfort her during her time of "loss," but frankly she could honestly give a shit. It had already been such a long morning and all she wanted to do was climb in her bed and take a nap, but she surely wasn't going to do that with her husband's corpse still in there. This wasn't *Weekend At Bernies: Vacation in the New World* after all.

---

43   You would assume with a wildly successful acting career with all those *Twilight* films and millions of dollars at her disposal the young actress would be able to smile once in awhile rather than looking like someone just got done pissing in her Cornflakes day-in and day-out.

The one positive thing about the entire situation was that each and every villager brought a hearty helping of food with them to help console Natalie. Her kitchen was filled with warm breads, tender chicken dishes, bountiful salads, cheesy casseroles, and various cakes to help ease the pain of her husband's demise. *Maybe this wasn't such a bad thing after all,* she thought to herself. *At least I won't have to lift a finger in the kitchen for the next week or so. #Winning!*

Just as she felt her annoyance about to overflow, she looked up to find Dr. Stevens entering the cottage behind Lucy.

"Oh doctor," Natalie wailed as she lifted herself from the couch and ran into the doctor's arms. "You must go look at my dear husband and tell me what happened. He was fine before we fell asleep last night and now I come home from my morning errands to find him dead in our bed. I'm sorely heartbroken, doctor. You must tell me how my poor husband passed on to the heavens."

Lucy looked on at the wondrous display of acting that she was witnessing. Somehow, as if to really swing the point on home, Natalie even managed to squeeze out a few tears as she embraced the doctor. To everyone else in the room it looked like a distraught wife severely saddened by the loss of her husband, but Lucy knew this was some serious Hollywood acting she was seeing. *This ho could give Meryl Streep a run for her money*, thought Lucy as she rolled her eyes in disbelief.

"All right, all right Mrs. Williams," said the doctor as he gently tried to soothe the newly crowned widow. "Let me go take a look at the body and see what I can uncover. Until then, I think it's best that we let Mrs. Williams have a little privacy so that she may grieve with her sister without the entire colony looking upon them."

One by one, each villager filed out of the house as they waved their goodbyes and gave some last minute condolences. After everyone had gone, Natalie showed Dr. Stevens toward her bedroom where she left him alone to look over Edward's deceased body. She closed the door behind herself and made her way back into the kitchen to join Lucy until he was finished.

"Well, well, well, that surely was the performance of a century, my dear sister," said Lucy as she dug into one of the warm loafs of bread. "I haven't seen acting that good since the last time I watched Whoopi Goldberg pretending to like Elizabeth Hasselbeck on *The View*."[44]

"Why, whatever do you mean, beloved sister? I'm just a poor little widow who's beside herself at the loss of her husband, whom she loved very much." Natalie said with a sneer and a light chuckle.

"Lordy, you truly are psychotic," said Lucy as she began walking towards the front door.

"And where do you think you're going, young lady? Don't you think it's in poor taste to leave your grieving sister all by herself while you go out chasing dick around town?"

"Not that it's truly any of your business, dear sister, but I'm going over to the Bigglesworth house to put back these pearls from the other night."

"And how exactly do you plan on accomplishing that?" questioned Natalie. "Are you just going to walk in their house and say, 'Oh, remember the other night after you both plowed me like a cornfield, well I accidentally took your pearls when you weren't looking.'"

"Don't you worry yourself in how I plan on doing it," Lucy rebutted. "Just know that it'll get done and it won't happen again."

"It better not Lucy Skeezabeth, because we need to be on-guard even more now that Edward is gone," Natalie said in an elevated whisper as not to draw any attention from Dr. Stevens in the other room.

"I'm aware of that Natalie, now leave me to my business and you worry about your own. You have enough to worry about at the moment, wouldn't you agree?" Lucy questioned as she sarcastically blew her a kiss and walked out the front door.

---

44   Whoopi tried with all her might, but anyone with at least one working eye could see that she wanted to go straight "Mortal Kombat" on Elizabeth's ass on a daily basis.

That stupid tart better not screw this up, Natalie thought to herself. *The last thing we need right now are these dense ferrets in this village getting wind of thievery on our part. They'll surely burn our asses at the stake for such an offense! But no sense in worrying about that, I know Lucy can connive her way into that house and find a way to place those pearls back into their rightful home.*

A few minutes later Dr. Stevens emerged from the bedroom and made his way towards the living room where Natalie was sitting quietly.

"Well Mrs. Williams, it looks as though it really was a heart attack that took your husband from us," he said as he sat down next to her and placed his medical case on the floor. "As I'm sure you're aware, your husband's diet and lifestyle most likely led to this outcome. I severely apologize for your loss."

"It is what I expected, doctor. It honestly doesn't shock me to find that this was the cause of his demise. My husband's idea of healthy eating was slathering his fried chicken in ketchup because the tomatoes in it would be his daily serving of vegetables. He also had a penchant for anything sausage and bacon related as well; maybe it's a blessing in disguise that he's passed because within a few more months on this new land he would've most likely eaten every hog within a 12-mile radius and ultimately cause the rest of us to starve."

Just like earlier in the day, Dr. Stevens couldn't get a proper read on Natalie Skeezabeth-Williams' personality. Was she joking to ease the pain of losing her husband or was she really that malicious?

Natalie could detect a look of minor distaste spreading across Dr. Stevens face. "Oh, please excuse me for my inappropriate humor, doctor. It's simply how I cope with stressful situations. My poor husband, he truly was a great man." Natalie managed to squeeze a few more tears out of her eyes as she buried her head in her hands.

"There, there, Mrs. Williams," he said as he gently rubbed her on the back.

Dr. Stevens attempted to be as supportive as possible, but he knew there was a lingering topic that had to be addressed between the two of them.

They were both painfully aware that there was a massive pink elephant standing in the cottage that had to be spoken on.

"I hate to bring up this matter during such an emotionally difficult time for you, but regarding that topic that we discussed earlier in the day, maybe it isn't the best time to be plotting revenge against your sister," said Dr. Stevens reluctantly. "Have you given any thought to that, my lady?"

Natalie lifted her head from her hands and stared him straight into the eyes with the coldest glare that he had ever seen.

"My dearest doctor, no matter will stand in my way from enacting the plan that we discussed earlier today," she responded cool and calmly as a sinister little grin formed on her face. "But all in due time, all in due time. Don't you worry your handsome self about it."

Dr. Stevens could feel a chill race up his spine as he looked Natalie in the eyes. In that brief moment he came to question who, or what, he had aligned himself with in this scenario.

CHAPTER FIVE

Lucy strolled down the trail towards the Bigglesworths cabin very slowly. The brisk breeze in the air felt nice on her skin as she lost herself in thought. She still couldn't believe that Edward was gone; while they didn't exactly have the closest connection in the world, Lucy still recognized the fact that she would most likely be dead had he not agreed to marry Natalie and take her with them on this voyage. Lucy couldn't help but feel like poor Edward got the raw end in this deal.

Did he realize how much he was being played? thought Lucy as she stared off into space. *He had to know that Natalie never loved him. Why did his poor soul choose to stay with such a wretched woman like she?*

Lucy shook her head to bring herself back down to reality.

As much as she felt for him, much like her sister, Lucy didn't have much time to mourn poor Edward at the moment. She had the more pressing matter of these stolen pearls to tend to.

Lucy still hadn't come up with a definite plan as to how she was going to get the pearls back into their bedroom, but one thing she did know was that she did some of her best work when she was forced to improvise. She placed her right hand in her dress pocket and fished around until she felt the smooth pearls in her petite fingers. They felt so marvelous as she wrapped them around her slender digits and imagined how fantastic they would look as they dangled down from her long, slim neck and rested between her ample bosoms. *They would surely be the perfect accessory to any outfit,* she thought to herself.

Just then she stopped dead in her tracks.

Snap out of it, she thought to herself as she quickly removed her hand from her pocket of shame. *That kind of thinking is what got you into this mess in the first place. I have to break myself of this dreadful habit before I end up serving 10-to-20 on cellblock D.*

Lucy closed her eyes tightly and took in a deep breath of the brisk air. As she exhaled she imagined herself releasing her deviant desires into the surrounding wilderness and freeing herself of their demanding clutches; while she knew this wouldn't "heal" her of her demons, she was proud of herself for actively attempting to expel them from her being. She opened her eyes and commenced walking once again. She could see the Bigglesworth cabin finally coming into view in the distance, but before she could reach the dwelling she heard someone bellowing her name from inside the forest along the trail.

"Lucy Skeezabeth! Why Lucy Skeezabeth, is that you?" yelled the deep voice.

Lucy squinted her eyes in attempt to make out the figure in the distance; after a moment or two she finally realized it was Arthur Bigglesworth waving at her. It took her a moment longer to realize he was holding an axe in his right hand as he was undoubtedly chopping firewood for the impending chilly evening.

"Come over here Lucy, give me a hand bringing this wood to the cabin if you would," Arthur beaconed to his lovely guest.

Lucy galloped through the woods, dodging tree branches and leaping over stray logs to get to her friend.

"Hello there, Arthur," said Lucy as she reached him. "I was just on my way to your cabin to see how you and Jane have been doing. I've missed my *friends* quite a lot, I must say."

Arthur could detect Lucy's subtle flirting, but he had to try his best to keep himself composed.

"Oh, we're doing quite fine my dear," he assured her. "Except for the little conversation that your older sister had with my wife earlier this morning. I must say it has left her quite upset."

"Conversation?" asked Lucy as she stared intensely into Arthur's eyes. "Whatever do you mean? What did Natalie say to Jane?"

"I'll simply say they certainly weren't the most pleasant things a sister could say about her own sibling," answered Arthur.

Lucy let out a soft chuckle as she shook her head in disbelief.

"Please lend me your ear Arthur, do not believe anything that comes out of my sister's mouth. Especially about anything that involves moi. You're more likely to find a trustworthy Republican candidate for the presidency than to get any shred of truth from that scandalous sister of mine."

Arthur looked genuinely perplexed.

"But I don't understand. She told Jane…"

"Arthur, I don't even want to know what she told Jane because it's only going to make me despise that cheap wench even more. She's a bonafide hater, my dear. And what do we know haters to do, Arthur?"

"Haters are going to hate," Arthur responded as he pressed his ax on ground and leaned against it.

"Exactly," Lucy said as she snapped her fingers in the air. "You got that right! So believe me, anything that she said is pure falsity. And I would hate to see her poison the great connection I have with you and Jane. I feel so close to you two; why, I did things with my tongue to you and your wife that would've made Tommy Lee blush.[45] Do you think that's commonplace for a classy bird like myself?"

---

45   Considering Tommy Lee has the sexual prowess of an Olympian on Ecstasy, it's easy to infer that the things that transpired between Lucy and the Bigglesworths were certainly too hot for TV.

Arthur stared into Lucy's eyes. While he hadn't known Lucy very long, he could tell that she was telling the truth. He knew that he could trust her wholeheartedly. Then again, Lucy had him and Jane so pussy-whipped that she probably could have told them that her real name was Gary Coleman and that she was a black midget and they both would've believed her implicitly.

"Alright, alright," Arthur answered. "No need to explain any further. I believe you and I'm sure Jane will as well. I suppose we just didn't realize there was such friction between you and your sister."

"My dear Arthur, friction doesn't even begin to describe how my sister and I feel about each other. We make Mariah Carey and Nicki Minaj look like fucking B.F.F.'s from one of those *The Babysitter's Club* books."[46]

"Well, at least it all makes sense now that you've fully explained yourself. Now let's get some of this firewood back to the cabin. I'm sure Jane will be happy to see you and hear this fantastic news as well. You had to see her come home this morning, my dear Lucy; she was crying profusely and sweating right through her blouse from the sheer despair she was feeling. Why, I don't think I've seen a woman react that way to something since Paula Deen was presenting at the BET Awards."[47]

Lucy let out a hearty laugh as she reached down to grab a few logs to carry to the house. "Poor Jane, I don't like to hear of her being disheartened. I'll have to give her some extra special attention to make up for the unwarranted stress she's had to endure today."

Lucy gave Arthur a wink just to drive the point home.

"I'm sure she would absolutely love that. And I can say I surely wouldn't mind seeing that as well."

"Oh Arthur Bigglesworth, such a fresh boy you are," said Lucy. "Now let's be on our way; this forest is far too chilly to be chillin' out

---

46   It's not exactly classified information that Mariah Carey would rather drink Wal-Mart quality champagne or wear synthetic fabrics than be within a 50-mile radius of Nicki Minaj.

47   Could you imagine Paula presenting at the Black Entertainment Television Awards? She would be sweating Crisco oil from every pore on her body.

here for too long. A bitch ain't trying to catch pneumonia these days, you know?"

"I concur, shall we bounce?" asked Arthur.

"Yes, let us. Lead the way."

As Arthur led them out of the woods Lucy couldn't help but think that Natalie's underhanded attacks were beginning to get too close for comfort. She knew her sister had it out for her, but this was getting out of hand. The last thing she wanted to do was get innocent people hurt in this situation and that's exactly what was beginning to happen.

I have to deal with Natalie's venomous attitude sooner than later, thought Lucy. *But right now let me focus all my attention on the Bigglesworths. I can't afford to slip up now.*

As they reached the cabin, Arthur set the logs of wood he was carrying down by the front door and then turned back towards Lucy to relieve her of the armful that she was struggling with.

"Thank you for carrying those, my dear. I fully appreciate the favor," professed Arthur to his beautiful guest.

"Not a problem, sir. Don't mention it. But I will say I do find it humorous that every time I come to the Bigglesworth household I end up with a handful of wood," Lucy retorted sarcastically. "I mean that literally and figuratively."

"Well, you can never have enough wood in your life these days, you know," said Arthur with a laugh as he placed the remaining logs by the front door and reached for the doorknob. "Please come on in."

Lucy followed Arthur into the cabin. As she made her way inside she peered around to see if she could catch a glimpse of Jane. She didn't see her in the kitchen or lounging by the warm fire in the living quarters, but she knew Jane was nearby because the scent of her Chanel perfume lingered in the air.

With all the stress of the last couple days she had forgotten just how amazing that scent truly was.

"Jane, my love, I'm back from chopping firewood and I have brought you a sweet and supple surprise from the forest," hollered Arthur as he hung his and Lucy's coats up on the hook by the front door.

They could hear soft rumblings coming from inside the bedroom and the gentle clik-clak of heels on the fresh wood floor. Jane emerged in the bedroom doorway wearing a soft pink silk dressing robe and her soft curls cascading down past her shoulders. She was truly a vision to be seen.

"Why Lucy Skeezabeth, I'm quite shocked to see you today," said Jane as she made her way towards her for a soft embrace. "In fact, I didn't think I'd see you standing in my home ever again after the conversation that was had earlier today with your sister."

"Yes, I've just been informed of this spiteful conversation that took place during the wee hours of the day," said Lucy as she took her friend into her arms and gave her a tight squeeze. "I've already spoken to Arthur about it, but I just wanted to reassure you that whatever diatribe that was spewed from my sister's vengeful, whorish mouth was completely inaccurate and couldn't be further from the truth."

"Oh, is that so?" questioned Jane as she let her go of her embrace on her houseguest and slowly began to back away. "I must say I'm thoroughly confused, my dear Lucy. Why would a sister speak of her own sibling in such a manner? Something about this situation smells fishier than Christina Aguilera's panty drawer."

Lucy could feel Jane's apprehension mounting in the air. She knew that Jane was going to be a tougher nut to crack than Arthur was.

"You must understand Jane, there is no love lose between my sister and I. We have never been friendly with one another and this latest attack on my character that she's managed to involve you and Arthur in is nothing new. This is how that shady ho rolls.[48] But I insist that everything that came out of her mouth is false."

Jane eyed her houseguest up and down and took in what she was

---

48   W.A.S.P. Translation: Urban dialect to suggest that "this is how that mischievous harlot likes to act."

saying.

"My dear Jane," interjected Arthur, "I must say after the conversation that's been had between Lucy and I in the woods I have no further doubts about our dear lover. It seems as though this is a case of pure sibling jealousy; and let's be real here, who wouldn't be jealous of a bad bitch like our sweet Lucy? Clearly Natalie is reaching into her bag of tricks to try to contaminate what the three of us have formed."

Jane's eyes bounced back and forth between the two individuals in front of her.

She could tell that her husband fully accepted Lucy's excuse for what had occurred earlier in the day, but she was also well aware that he wasn't there to witness just how passionate Natalie was when she was warning her of the fate that awaited them if they continued down this sorted path with her sister. She could tell that there was certainly shreds of truth to what Natalie had spoke about, but to what degree she wasn't sure of just yet. Jane knew she was going to have to keep her eyes on this situation very closely to avoid any further conflict.

"Alright," she finally said as she turned and sauntered toward the kitchen. "I suppose we'll just chalk this altercation up as a minor misunderstanding."

"Oh fantastic, I can't tell you how happy that makes me, my dearest Jane," said Lucy as she smiled from ear-to-ear and clapped her hands together to illustrate her joy.

"But let's get one thing quite clear before we proceed any further," said Jane as she placed three wine glasses on the kitchen counter and gave Lucy a deadly stare. "You may be the most gorgeous girl in the village, and you may be able to work your tongue like the propellers of a Black Hawk helicopter, but if any bitch, whether it be your sister or any other scalawag, ever approaches me in these streets pertaining to you and/or how you're going to play my husband and I then I suggest you run for the hills now because I'll pull a straight-up Tanya Harding on your ass and bash in those pretty little kneecaps of yours. I'm fresh out of fucks to give these days and a bitch doesn't have time to play any games, comprende muchacha?"[49]

Lucy swallowed hard.

Up until this point Jane had always struck Lucy as being very demure and quite the "Disney princess" type of girl; apparently Jane, as she was quickly realizing, was equal parts Cinderella and Al Pacino in *Scarface*.

"I vow to you both this is something you won't have to deal with ever again. You have my word," Lucy sternly pleaded to them both.

"Well, fantastic then," Jane said with a gleeful smile plastered across her face as she made her way towards the refrigerator. "Now tell me, my sweet Lucy, which would you prefer, some Merlot or a little Pinot Grigio? I have a brand new bottle of Ramona Singer's Pinot Grigio on ice that I picked up earlier today at the market. You know I love that crazy, big-eyed New York housewife!"

"That sounds delightful, dear!" exclaimed Arthur as he led Lucy by her petite hand towards the living room couch. "I'll certainly have a glass of that. How about you, Lucy?"

"Oh the Pinot sounds absolutely exquisite, thank you," she answered as she made herself comfortable and took in the warmth exuding from the fireplace.

"Great," said Jane. "Arthur, my love, do me a favor and cut some of that fresh cheese I purchased this morning. That will be a glorious little snack to have with the wine."

"As you wish, my darling."

Lucy was happy to have a quiet moment to herself while her hosts were busy in the kitchen. She closed her eyes and breathed in a sigh of relief; she wasn't anticipating this visit to become as stressful and torturous as a dinner date with Kanye West, but once again her sister

---

49   W.A.S.P. Translation: The simplest way to translate Jane's warning speech to Lucy is this: don't fuck with me. Period.

had managed to make her life all the more complicated with her devious meddling. But she couldn't worry about that right now; she had survived the first part of this mission, but now she needed to tend to the real reason why she came here. She casually placed her hand inside her dress pocket to make sure the pearls were still residing comfortably in their hiding place. She had to think of a way to get inside that bedroom to put them back in their rightful home.

"Here you go, my lovely," said Jane as she glided into the living room and handed the glass of white wine to her houseguest. "I certainly hope it's chilled enough for your liking?"

"Oh yes, it's great, thank you so much," said Lucy as she slowly sipped from her glass. "But I must say, I originally came here today for an entirely different reason than what we've discussed thus far."

"Is that so?" questioned Arthur as he placed the cheese plate down on the coffee table and sat down next to his wife.

"Yes. And I hate to bring bad news, but sadly it seems as though my beloved brother-in-law, Edward Williams, has passed away in his sleep last evening."

"Oh my," said Jane as she gasped and grabbed ahold of Arthur's hand. "I'm so sorry to hear that, Lucy. What happened to the poor fellow?"

"Apparently he had a heart attack whilst sexing his frigid witch of a wife," Lucy said very casually as she took another swig of her wine. "I can't say I'm very surprised if I must be completely honest. She was always so stingy with the coochie; he probably had a heart attack at the pure shock that she was letting him get into those dusty panties of hers."

"Well, that would explain that horrific demeanor of hers this morning. Had I known her man had just 'bought the farm' during a roll in the hay maybe I wouldn't have reacted so harshly to what she had to say in reference to you, my dear," said Jane.

"No, I can assure you that's what she's like on a daily basis; dead husband or not, she's got about as much tact as Nancy Grace,"[50] Lucy exclaimed with a roll of her eyes to illustrate her point even further. "But I surely do feel bad for poor Edward; at the end of the day he genuinely was a good man, but he did eat pretty terribly which I'm sure aided in his demise."

"I fully concur," interjected Arthur. "Why, I had just seen him a few days ago at a town hall meeting, and come to think of it, I believe he was eating an Arby's Roast Beef and Cheddar during the proceedings. It's truly a shame though, the village will certainly miss him."

"Yes, they certainly will," said Jane. "But in all seriousness Lucy, how is your sister handling the news? She truly must be devastated, no?"

"She's handling it as well as can be expected," Lucy answered as believably as possible. She would've liked nothing more than to blow up Natalie's spot and tell them exactly how she reacted to her *beloved* husband's death, but she knew that would end up causing more of a problem for her if she divulged that at this very moment. But just then, at that very moment, Lucy was struck with a brilliant idea. "But that's partly the reason why I stopped by today. You see we've become inundated with so much food and treats from the other villagers that it would surely be impossible for my sister and I to consume it all before it spoils. So I was hoping you two would like to join us for a small intimate dinner tomorrow evening?"

Arthur and Jane exchanged a quick, apprehensive glance between one another.

"My dear Lucy, are you sure that's a good idea considering everything that's occurred with your sister lately?" Arthur questioned.

"Oh yes, it'll be fine! Don't even worry about," said Lucy very nonchalantly.

"But is she really going to appreciate a dinner party at her household the day after her husband's untimely demise?" asked Jane.

---

50   If you've ever watched Nancy Grace's news program then you know it's easier to swallow a cup full of glass shards than the way she delivers her opinions. Smooth, it is not.

"Well she certainly loves herself a good dinner party. I think she'd greatly enjoy it to be honest."

"But what about…" Jane attempted to ask.

"What's with all the questions?" Lucy snapped at her, becoming very visibly annoyed. "I simply invited you two to attend dinner at our home, I certainly didn't think that warranted a Barbara Walters barrage of inquiries. If I didn't think my *lovely* sister was up for the company I certainly wouldn't be inviting people into our home during this time. Now either you can make it or you can't, what's it gonna be?"

Jane's grip on Arthur's hand got a little tighter.

"Oh, I'm so sorry Lucy, I surely didn't mean to upset you," said Jane. "Of course we would love to come over tomorrow for dinner. We just didn't want to impose at all. Please do forgive our incessant questions."

"No, I'm sorry," said Lucy as she placed her wine glass on coffee table and took in a deep breath. "I had no right to explode on you like that. Who do I think I am speaking to you in such a manner? Alec Baldwin?[51] Please forgive my outburst, I'm simply feeling very stressed is all. It's been quite an emotionally taxing day, I hope you understand."

Arthur got up and walked over to be by Lucy's side. He began gently rubbing her back to comfort and calm her.

"Our poor Lucy, please try not to stress yourself like this," he said. "We hate to see you in such a manner. You need to try to relax a little bit."

"Thank you, Arthur," she said as she patted him on the knee. "You're absolutely right. I feel like you two are the only people in the colony who really understand me sometimes."

Jane got up from her spot on the couch and sat down on the coffee table directly in front of Lucy. "Well, the three of us have a very *special* connection. We're here for you if you need anything, dear."

Lucy felt a tad bit uncomfortable with Arthur and Jane being so

---

51   Waiters, photographers, flight attendants, his own children; is no one safe from a tongue lashing from ole' Alec?

close to her at the moment. She still had Jane's pearls sitting in her pocket and until that problem was resolved she had to be very aware just how close they got to her.

"Here you go Lucy, finish your wine. I'm sure that will certainly relax you a bit," said Arthur as he picked up the glass from the coffee table and handed it to her.

"Thank you," she said.

"You know what might also help?" Jane asked.

"What's that?" Lucy said.

Jane leaned in and planted a kiss on Lucy's soft lips. Initially, it caught her off guard, but Lucy went along with it; all drama aside, the sexual attraction between the three of them had certainly not dwindled in any capacity. Arthur looked on with explicit excitement. What began as a soft and tender kiss between the two ladies gradually intensified until Jane and Lucy were going at it like two college freshman at a frat party trying to impress the starting line-up of the football team.

The two girls came to a stop and turned their focus onto Arthur. He reached for the strings on Lucy's bonnet and yanked it off to release her fiery tresses from their imprisonment. They began to passionately kiss as Jane sat on the table and watched as her husband ran his hands through Lucy's hair, giving it little tugs here and there to show her who was in control.

Jane took them both by the hands and proceeded to lure them towards the bedroom. "Shall we take this into the boudoir, my dears? I just had the couch cleaned the other day and I'd hate to get it messy again if Arthur gets too *excited*."

This is perfect, Lucy thought to herself. *I need to get into that bedroom to get rid of these damn pearls*. She followed her hostess into the bedroom. Jane led her towards the bed and then proceeded to take off her robe to reveal a lacy lingerie set that left little to the imagination. Jane knew she was hot and she had no problem reveling in it. Both ladies turned towards the door just as Arthur was coming in carrying the plate of cheese along with him.

"Arthur, my sweet, why are you bringing that cheese in here?" Jane asked.

"I figured it might be a good snack in case we get famished," he responded absentmindedly.

"You thought *cheese* might be a good idea to snack on during a three-way?" she questioned as she cocked her head to the side in annoyance. "Why stop at cheese, Arthur? Why don't you go get a nice piping hot bowl of cabbage soup or maybe some enchiladas? It'll be *really* sexy when you start shitting the bed 10 minutes into our little tryst you dipshit. Go put the damn cheese down, man!"

Lucy couldn't help but giggle to herself. She knew it might come across a bit rude to laugh in the middle of their disagreement, but the wine had started to go to her head and she couldn't resist. It didn't take a genius to see who wore the pants in this marriage, but she found it strangely erotic to see Jane in such a powerful position in their union. *She certainly isn't like the rest of these timid pilgrim broads in this colony*, thought Lucy as she stared at her female lover.

"I swear Lucy, sometimes that man is dumber than a box of straws," Jane whispered to Lucy as she primped her hair. "He's just lucky he's got a schlong like an NBA Forward; that tends to make up for his lack of sense sometimes."

"It sure does," said Lucy. "I remember when I first saw you two on the ship all those many months ago, I thought Arthur was smuggling a can of Pringles in his trousers."

"Tell me about it. The first time we intercoursed I had to spend the whole next week with an ice pack in my pantaloons. I remember thinking to myself, 'Good heavens, he killed my poor little beaver!'"

Lucy let out a little giggle as Arthur walked back into the room.

"And what may I ask is so funny? Why are you two giggling like schoolgirls?" he asked.

"Oh, no reason my dear, just a little girl talk," said Jane. "Now bring that sexy ass over here, Mr. Bigglesworth."

Arthur proceeded to make his way towards his women. He began unbuttoning his dirty white shirt and revealed an upper body not unlike that of Hugh Jackman. His chest and abs were still glistening with sweat from chopping the firewood and he exuded a manly musk that took over the room. He took Lucy's soft face into his rugged hands and began passionately kissing her as Jane looked on from the side. Jane couldn't control herself for very long; she wanted in on the fun too. She came up behind Arthur and started to gently caress and kiss along his shoulders. But, as hot as the scene was, Jane couldn't hold back the feeling of disgust that immediately rushed over her.

"Oh hell nah," she barked aloud. "Hold the phone you two! Press pause on this shit!"

Arthur and Lucy turned around and peered at Jane in total confusion.

"What's wrong now, my love?" Arthur asked.

"What's wrong now? Arthur, you're sweatier than an orange picker in August! Do you honestly think you're about to get into our bed like that? These are 1,000-thread count Ralph Lauren sateen sheets and you're not about to ruin them, I'm sorry. Arthur, please go bathe yourself before this endeavor commences any further."

"But Jane, we're in the middle..." Arthur began to plead.

"Arthur, my dear husband, I don't care if you're three strokes away from climax. I don't keep a glorious home so you can mess it up within minutes of you returning from your work. I'll be damned if you treat our home like this is Honey Boo Boo's double-wide trailer. Now I'll not hear another word of this matter; go draw yourself a bath and don't forget the Calgon."

"Jane, this is quite embarrassing, wouldn't you agree?" he asked.

Lucy could see that Arthur was shamed; between reprimanding him for the cheese and now ripping into him for the state of his hygiene he looked completely emasculated. She knew she was going to have to interject to salvage this situation.

"Now my loves, I think I may have an idea that would please all parties involved. Why don't we all head for the bath together? That could be fun, right?" she said.

Arthur and Jane stopped arguing and stared at their lover with a look of interest.

"I suppose that could be a fun experience," Arthur said.

"Yes, very interesting," said Jane. "I don't think I've ever gotten frisky in water before actually."

"Really?" asked Lucy. "I surely have, but I can't seem to remember when the last occurrence was. Oh wait, that's a lie, I most certainly do remember; Matthew McConaughey invited me to exercise along the beach and one thing led to another and before I knew it that southern hippie had me doing naked toe-touches along the shoreline. But that's a story for another time, shall we make our way towards the bathroom?"

"Yes, let us go," said Jane as she grabbed both their hands and started to drag them towards the door.

"Why don't you two go get the bath started and I'll be right in there, I would like to fix my hair up rather quickly," said Lucy as she attempted to get some alone time inside their bedroom to rectify herself of the pearl situation.

"Your hair looks quite lovely already my dear, I can't imagine you getting it much better than it is at the moment," said Arthur.

"That's quite sweet, and such a horny man thing to say, but you know how women are with their hair. I'll be right in there. Make sure to get a lot of bubbles going for me," she said with a wink as Arthur and Jane made their way out of the room.

Lucy walked over to the mirror and began fiddling with her hair for a few seconds until she heard the running of the water in the bathroom. She quickly snuck over to the bedroom door and peered out to make sure the coast was completely clear; when she realized she had the room all to herself she dashed towards the dresser where Jane kept her jewelry box proudly perched atop.

Lucy flipped open the box to find a vast plethora of fabulous rings, bracelets, and necklaces all strewn throughout it. The sheer sight of such valuables nearly took her breath away; she had to muster all of her internal strength to keep from going on a thievery spree and taking every last fantastical piece inside of the box. She fished about her pocket until she felt the silky smooth pearls in her fingers and then quickly placed them back inside the jewelry box underneath a bunch of bangles as to not make it look too obvious that they had just been returned. She gently closed the lid on the box and breathed a giant sigh of relief.

Mission accomplished, she thought to herself as she stared at herself in the mirror. *One less thing to have to worry about; now let me get into that bathroom before they start wondering what's taking me so long.*

As Lucy made her way into the bathroom she was greeted with a glorious sight; Jane was straddling Arthur in their massive copper tub as a sea of bubbles were overflowing from the sides. They both turned their heads toward Lucy as she came into view.

"Come right in my dear, the water is the perfect temperature," Jane said seductively.

"Don't mind if I do," said Lucy as she lifted her dress above her head and closed the door behind her.

Three hours later Lucy exited the Bigglesworth cabin looking and feeling like a new woman in comparison to the one who entered it hours before.

It's amazing how a good ole' fashioned orgasm can truly refresh a woman and leave her feeling stress free, she thought to herself as she strolled along the dirt road towards the center of the village. *There's no wonder why that bitch Angelina Jolie doesn't have a single frown line on that face of hers.*

Things couldn't have worked out better for Lucy thus far today. She had managed to relieve herself of the stolen pearls, she had cleared the air with the Bigglesworths after Natalie had cast a shadow of doubt over her character, and she had even got them to agree to come to a dinner at the house the following evening, which she knew would surely get under her sister's skin to see that the trio was still intact.

While things were certainly on the upswing for her there was one thing that was becoming more and more apparent in her interactions with the Bigglesworths; she was beginning to see tiny cracks appearing in their union. The tiny altercations that she bore witness to earlier in the day were a surefire sign that there was certainly friction brewing amongst the newlywed couple. Maybe the "honeymoon" phase was beginning to die out? Or maybe they were simply just stressed out from acclimating to their new surroundings? Whatever it was, it was a situation that Lucy wanted to keep an eye on. One thing she knew for sure was that she didn't want to overstay her welcome if things were beginning to go bad already; that was one of the benefits of being the "guest" in this very untraditional relationship they were carrying on together. At any given moment Lucy was free to let it go and go about her way without any strings holding her down.

As much as I enjoy getting freaky with those two, and while it is hot to see Jane act like a boss bitch at times, I refuse to stick around if it's going to turn into The War of Roses *every time we attempt to get it on. But that shall be a matter for another day*, she thought to herself. *I simply cannot wait to see Natalie's face when they walk in for dinner tomorrow evening. It's going to be a glorious sight to see her look like the giant dickhead she is! Maybe this will bring her constant torment to an end.*

An end was certainly approaching, but to what degree no one could have foreseen.

CHAPTER SIX

Arthur and Jane quietly lay in their bed; they had barely spoken a word to each other since Lucy had exited their cabin. Similar to their last encounter, this one had left them both with that same bittersweet feeling as before. While they loved the feeling their sexually explorative relationship had afforded them, they were both reacting to Lucy's companionship in a way that neither of them had felt before. Each interaction had left them both with a feeling of longing, a feeling of wanting more and more of her. It was a feeling that was beginning to become very obvious within their marriage.

"Lucy really is such a lovely girl, I'm quite happy that we were able to make amends in regards to that horrid situation involving her sister," said Jane as she turned on her side and faced her husband.

"I fully agree, my dear," Arthur said. "It would have been such a shame to see our union spoiled by the wicked tongue of a jealous outsider."

"You're quite right, my husband. I feel as though the bond we've forged is too strong for that. But, as your wife, would you be offended if I offered up a minor critique in regards to our exploration with Lucy?"

"Critique?" asked Arthur as he turned his head towards his wife.

"Why whatever do you mean by that?"

"Well, I'm not trying to be obnoxious or nit-picky about your performance, but there are just certain things I think you could do that would enhance the experience for all three of us. It's simply that…"

"For the love of everything holy Jane, just spit it out!" barked Arthur, clearly annoyed that his wife would even dare mention that his sexual performance could be better.

"Well, first of all, I'm not even going to mention the *cheese* situation again, even though we both know that was a colossal fail of epic proportions, but what the hell was up with those noises you were making whilst you were mounting the poor girl from behind? I felt like I was baring witness to a National Geographic special on the mating rituals of the Grizzly Bear."

"Are you kidding me right now, Jane?" asked Arthur. "It's called being *passionate* and thoroughly enjoying the moment. Besides, Lucy was really into it so that's all that matters."

"Well I beg to differ, my love," snapped Jane. "If you could have seen her face you would have been able to tell she looked about as interested as Clay Aiken would be at a titty bar.[52] That's the only reason I bring it up."

"You know what I think? I think you're jealous."

Jane let out a loud laugh just to illustrate how ridiculous she found that notion.

"Jealous, my love? What exactly would I be jealous of? The fact that you sound like Wilbur from 'Charlotte's Web' when you're boning the poor girl?"

"No, you're jealous that I don't get that passionate when you and I make love. You're jealous that I don't have the same reaction to you. It's not my fault you aren't as good as she is."

Jane sat up and smacked Arthur across the face with all her

---

52   Considering that you could probably see Clay Aiken flaming all the way from the surface of the moon, it goes without saying that Jane is implying that Lucy wasn't really into it.

might.

"Have you lost your mind, motherfucker?" she shrieked. "Did you just say that to your beloved *wife*?"

Immediately after he said it Arthur realized he had crossed the line and gone too far. He knew he had just dug himself into a hole that was going to be virtually impossible to escape.

"I apologize Jane, that was over the line. I was only trying…"

"You're damn right that was over the line! I was simply providing you with a minor critique and you had the audacity to try to drag my sexual prowess through the mud like I'm not good at it! Well, let me tell you *something* Arthur Bigglesworth, I fuck like a thoroughbred *champion*! And those are Mick Jagger's words, not mine! Go ahead, call him; he'll tell you the exact same thing, verbatim!"[53]

She lay back down on the bed and turned away from her husband to give him the cold shoulder.

"Jane, I know that. I wasn't trying to insult you. You know that, my love. Sex with the two of you is simply different that's all."

"Different? That's an interesting way to put it when we both know that what you wanted to say is that she's *better* than me! And that's fine, you know why? Because she's actually better than you are too! At least when she goes down on me she knows how to find my g-spot; you couldn't find it if Rand McNally were there navigating you towards it!"[54]

Arthur lay there, stunned in silence.

"Sometimes I can't believe how viscous of a witch you can truly be," he finally uttered under his breath as he lay his head back down and closed his eyes.

"You haven't seen anything yet, my beloved husband."

The following day Arthur and Jane barely spoke a single word to one another as they went about their daily chores and activities. Neither

---

53   I presume having Mick Jagger's seal of approval on your sexual resume is like the equivalent of having Bill Gates as one of your contacts on your professional one.

54   It's a sad state of affairs when one's wife accuses you of needing a road map in order to find her "special" spot.

one wanted to admit it, but their individual feelings for Lucy were beginning to unravel their own connection at a detrimental pace. Not since Carmen Electra's ill-fated marriage to Dennis Rodman have you seen a union run its course so quickly.[55]

They had tricked themselves into believing that their nontraditional way of approaching marriage would prevent them from the traps and hindrances of it, but they couldn't foresee the barrage of unusual problems that they had inadvertently set into motion with their choices.

Making matters even worse, they now had to attend a dinner engagement at their dear lover's home this evening. Both of them were secretly overjoyed to see Lucy, but having to plaster on fake smiles and pretend like everything was perfect in paradise made them exhausted at the sheer thought of it all.

While they were getting dressed Arthur finally broke the silence. "Do you think we should cancel our appearance at dinner this evening?"

"Cancel? Why would we cancel?" Jane asked.

"I mean don't you feel as though we might be a little awkward with us not really speaking at the moment?"

"You may cancel for yourself if you'd like, but I fully plan on attending. I've been looking forward to seeing Lucy *all* day."

Arthur could feel the venomous tone in his wife's response. "As have I, my love. As have I."

Jane spun her head around towards Arthur and shot him the kind of fiery glance that could've melted ice.

"Was it something I said?" he sarcastically quipped back at her.

"Just shut up and get dressed you bloody idiot. We're going to be late if you don't speed up your primping and prodding. If I would've known my future husband would take longer than me to get ready every time we step out of the damn house I would've accepted Ellen DeGeneres'

---

55   The marriage between Carmen and Dennis would only last 9 days before an annulment would be filed. Kind of makes that whole Kim Kardashian and Kris Humphries marriage seem like it lasted a couple decades, doesn't it?

marriage proposal when I had the chance; at least lesbians can get ready in 5-minutes flat."

Nothing more was spoken between the two of them as they put the finishing touches on their outfits and headed towards the front door. Arthur and Jane walked along the dirt road through the colony and made fake pleasantries with their fellow villagers as they drew closer and closer to Lucy's cabin. To the untrained eye they looked like a happy newlywed couple taking an evening stroll; little did their neighbors know that a torrid three-way love affair was beginning to tear them apart at the seams.

When they finally reached the front door of the Skeezabeth household, Arthur broke the icy silence that they had been bathing in since they left the house. "I know this might be hard for you, my sweet wife, but do try to remove the thorny stick from your ass before we enter this house. I'm sure I don't need to remind you that Natalie Skeezabeth is still mourning the death of her husband and I'm sure the last thing she wants to deal with is a raving bitch. So try not to act like yourself this evening."

"I'll do my best, my beloved husband," she answered with a sweet smile spread across her face. "But I'll give no guarantees considering the sheer sound of your voice right now makes me want to bludgeon you with a rusty axe."

"Awe, there's the romantic wife whom I've missed so much," Arthur answered as he began to knock on the front door of the Skeezabeth cottage.

A few seconds later Lucy answered the door and greeted her guests with warm embraces. "Oh, how fantastic it is to see you two. I must admit, I've been looking forward to our dinner all day," Lucy said with a schoolgirl giggle.

"As have we, my dear," said Arthur as he held onto his hug with Lucy longer than your standard greeting. "If you only knew."

"Yes, he's been talking about it all day; it's actually been a bit creepy I must say," Jane interjected with just enough shade to embarrass Arthur.

"Oh, that's flattering," Lucy said sweetly as she led them both into the house and proceeded to take their coats. As she reached for Jane's coat her eyes were met with a sight that she wasn't expecting: the notorious stolen pearls delicately decorated her neckline.

"What gorgeous pearls those are Jane," said Lucy, attempting to make it seem like it was her first introduction to the shiny string of pricy jewelry.

"Why thank you, Lucy. I think you've seen them before though; I wore them the other night when you came over for dinner."

"Is that so?" Lucy nonchalantly questioned. "I probably didn't notice because my focus was on those Kate Upton-sized knockers of yours."

"Oh, you surely know how to flatter a young dame," Jane giggled.

As the Bigglesworths peered around the cottage, the first thing that caught their attention was the amazing spread set up on the dining room table. It was stocked with succulent meats, warm and hearty breads, fresh vegetables, and flavorful gravies.

"As you guys can see, we've been stocked to the brim with some fantastic foods thanks to the villagers since the untimely passing of my brother-in-law. I'm almost embarrassed to say how little of this epic feast I've actually prepared; the salad was all my doing and I'm quite proud of it I must say."

"It does look pretty damn delicious; had I known this village would be so generous to grieving spouses I would've killed this wretched harpy that I'm married to months ago," said Arthur with a sarcastic laugh as he put his arm around his wife and drew her near.

"I should be so lucky," Jane responded as she wriggled out of her husband's hold and pinched him on the cheek. "But we did bring some cupcakes for dessert. I wanted to make sure we contributed something pleasant to this amazing feast and show our support to your family during this grievous time. And don't worry, they're low-fat cupcakes so they won't ruin that pretty little figure of yours. I have to bake everything low-fat these days since my rugged husband is about two chocolate chip cookies away from needing a pair of industrial-strength Spanx to fit into his pants."

Arthur could sense an uncomfortable air beginning to settle around them as Lucy looked on with curious eyes. He let out a loud laugh as a means to loosen up the mood. "Oh, my dear wife, she's such a comedienne isn't she? Sometimes I feel like I've married my own little Tina Fey."

Though his efforts were commendable, Lucy knew all was not right in the Bigglesworth marriage. Since she had left their home yesterday she knew it was time to begin slowly removing herself from this relationship. But for the sake of the evening she figured she would play along and go with the flow.

"Why don't you two take a seat on the couch and relax for a moment," Lucy said. "I'll bring you both a glass of wine to indulge in while I put the finishing touches on our feast."

"That sounds marvelous, my dear," said Arthur as he took his wife's hand and led her into the living quarters. "Say Lucy, where is your sister anyhow? Is she still preparing herself for dinner?"

"She actually laid herself down for a nap a few hours ago before I began preparing dinner and would you believe that lazy whore is still asleep?" said Lucy as she took the wine glasses out of the cabinet.

"Oh, the poor thing," said Jane. "I'm sure she must be exhausted from dealing with the grief of losing her spouse."

"Don't let her fool you, Jane," said Lucy as she walked into the living room carrying two hearty glasses of wine for her guests. "My sister, or Satan's mistress as our nanny used to refer to her, has about as much human emotion as a wooden chair."

"Well surely she must be sad at the loss of her husband?" questioned Arthur.

Lucy knew she had to stop painting her sister in such a harsh light. She knew that her sister would make herself look bad enough without any help from her and she didn't want to look like the bitter one in the situation.

"No, I'm sure she is," she answered. "Please excuse my harsh demeanor when it comes to my sister. I think she and I are so used to being cold to one another that it gets tough when we actually have to support one another."

"Well, it's certainly understandable," said Arthur. "We can't choose our family in this life so you have to make it work the best you can; even in those moments when all you want to do is push them off a cliff."

"That's absolutely true," said Lucy. "But let's not plague ourselves with such dramatic conversation this evening. Let's attempt to enjoy ourselves the best we can. Now will you please excuse me for a moment, I'm going to finish preparing the salad and then wake my sister from her slumber so we can eat."

Lucy walked back into the kitchen and gently began to toss the salad around in a giant bowl. It looked quite delicious. The salad leaves were a vibrant green, the cherry tomatoes were plump and juicy, the pieces of cucumber were fresh, and the shredded carrots looked crunchy and crisp. It looked like Lucy had ordered it straight from The Olive Garden. The only thing she had to do now was add the dressing and finish mixing it all around.

Lucy knew that her sister had just visited the market yesterday morning and she was hoping she had picked up a new container of salad dressing. She began to search through the kitchen cabinets to see exactly what they had available to adorn it with. As she opened up the cabinet housing all their spices she noticed an unfamiliar vial with an oily looking substance in it. *Hmmmm, I wonder what this is,* thought Lucy. She grabbed ahold of the vial and shook it vigorously.

Looks like some vinaigrette dressing to me, she thought as she opened the bottle up and poured its contents into the giant salad bowl and mixed it around. She then placed the bowl in the middle of the dining table and made her way towards Natalie's bedroom door.

Lucy began to gently knock on the door but didn't receive any response.

"Natalie, my sweet sister, are you awake?" she called out as she knocked a little bit louder.

But still no answer.

"Natalie, I'm coming in the room so put your dildos away," Lucy called out in jest.

As Lucy entered she found her sister fast asleep in the bed with a string of drool hanging from her mouth. She had pulled the curtains closed and the room was pitch black. She walked over to the window and yanked the curtains open so the last remaining rays of sunlight from the day bled into the room.

"Wake up you lazy bitch, we have company for dinner," Lucy said as she stood over her sister.

Natalie had finally come out of her sound slumber and was none too happy with her sister.

"Jesus Christ, Lucy! Let me sleep! I have no intention of being awake right now. Leave me be!"

"It's quite annoying to be awoken in such a manner, isn't it? Now you know how I feel when you barge into my room like a drill sergeant. But we have company my dear sister. Didn't I tell you the Bigglesworths were coming over for supper this evening?"

"What?" Natalie asked as she opened her eyes and gave her sister a deadly glare. "You never told me the Bigglesworths were coming for dinner. What kind of game are you playing little sister?"

"Game? Why whatever do you mean by that?" Lucy asked innocently. "I simply invited some friends over to help you cope with the untimely loss of your dear husband. I thought having guests might take your mind off it. I must have forgotten to remind you of it though. Oh please do forgive me dear sister, but you might want to hurry up and get ready because dinner is ready to be served and the guests are patiently waiting for you to join."

Natalie was furious; she could read the facetious tone in her sister's voice from a mile away. She stood up from the bed and grabbed ahold of Lucy's arm. "You're up to something. I don't know exactly what it is, but I know when you're up to no good."

"Oh sweet Natalie, I don't know what you speak of," said Lucy as she wrangled her arm free and faced her sister. "I only had the best intentions by inviting them over. They are *quite* fond of you and wanted to make sure you were okay after the *horrible* ordeal you've faced, and I've spent the last couple hours preparing the feast for you. So please stop thinking so negatively and get yourself dressed for dinner; and do make sure you run a brush through that hair of yours because it's looking a bit nappy at the moment, boo."

Lucy exited the room with a smirk smeared across her face. She knew if she had warned Natalie that the Bigglesworths were coming for dinner she would have thought of some devious plan to embarrass her, but by springing it on her she was able to catch her sister completely unprepared.

As she sauntered into the living room she noticed that Arthur and Jane were sitting at opposite sides of the couch not even attempting to communicate with one another. You could almost cut the tension between them with a knife.

"My sister should be out to join us in a matter of minutes," said Lucy as Arthur and Jane swiveled their heads in her direction. "She is almost done getting ready for dinner. I had to light a fire under her ass and tell her to hurry up; she takes longer than RuPaul to apply her make-up and tend to her hair."

"Oh, it's no rush at all," said Arthur. "We were just sitting here relaxing by the fire."

"Yes, there's absolutely no rush at all," said Jane as she rose from her spot on the couch and made her way towards Lucy. "Was there anything I could help you with for preparation? I would be more than willing to lend a helping hand."

"That's so sweet of you to ask Jane, but everything is ready. We're just waiting on my *beloved* sister to grace us with her splendor."

Just then they heard the click-clack of heels walking heavy on the wooden floor; Natalie emerged in the doorway dressed in all black from bonnet to shoes. While it was evident that she was currently in mourning she still seemed to exude an air of confidence and strength in her demeanor.

"Hello there Arthur and Jane," Natalie said softly as she came towards Jane for a soft embrace. "I cannot thank you enough for coming over this evening to dine with us. It's such a pleasure to be around friends during a time like this."

Jane was taken aback. The last time she had seen Natalie in the village she was reading her up-and-down like her name was NeNe Leakes; and while she wasn't expecting the same type of treatment this time around, she was a bit perplexed at how pleasant she was. *Maybe Lucy had spoken to her and corrected the situation?* she thought. *Or maybe the loss of her husband had given her a change of heart?* Whatever the reasoning behind it was, Jane wasn't going to metaphorically "poke the bear."

"Of course, dear Natalie," said Jane. "We cannot express how sorry we are for your loss; Edward was such a lovely man and we know how crazy he was about you. You two were like the village Rihanna and Chris Brown, sans the domestic violence, of course."[56]

"Yes, he was a good man and a great husband. He will surely be greatly missed by the entire village."

"Natalie, I hate to be intrusive," said Arthur as he got up from the

---

56   The Romeo and Juliet of our generation. A true love story of the ages.

couch. "But have you already began preparations for the funeral? Did you need any help with that?"

"Oh, how sweet you are for offering," said Natalie. "But I've already finished all the planning."

"Already? My, that was surely fast," said Jane.

"Yes, I've come to the conclusion that Edward will be cremated after his wake next week. It's just a smarter decision that way."

"How so?" questioned Lucy from the kitchen as she began pouring her sister a glass of wine.

"For a multitude of reasons, my dear sister. First and foremost, do you know how many redwood trees we would have to cut down to make a casket large enough to house Edward's exorbitant sized ass for his eternal rest? It would be like trying to shove an elephant into a shoebox. We would surely have to clear out about 4 acres worth of wood to make that happen and I didn't think that was fair to do to mother nature. And secondly, I want to always have a part of Edward here with us in this house. I would just feel more at peace that way."

"Oh, how *lovely* a sentiment," said Lucy as she handed her sister the glass of wine.

Natalie knew her sister was being sarcastic, but she held her tongue and slowly took a sip from her glass.

"Why don't we all take a seat at the dining room table before all this delicious food cools off," said Lucy.

"Sounds like a fantastic idea," said Jane. "Your sister has done an exquisite job at preparing this feast for you, Natalie."

"Has she now? I didn't realize it was still considered 'preparing' if all she did was heat up food that others have already cooked," laughed Natalie as she walked towards the table. "My sister is skilled at many things in life, as I'm sure you two are both aware, but sadly cooking isn't one of them."

Lucy shot her sister an ice-cold glare. "You'll be quite happy to know that I made the salad completely on my own."

"The salad?" Natalie laughed even louder. "Well it's always reassuring to know that you're skilled in mixing some tomatoes in with some lettuce. Someone, quick, call Padma Lakshmi and sign this bitch up for *Top Chef* before it's too late!"

The room went completely silent as they all tried not to make eye contact.

"Oh for Christ sake, it was only a joke people! Come on guys, get a sense of humor; I'm the one that's supposed to be in mourning. Thank you for your efforts my dear sister, everything really does look fantastic. I greatly appreciate it," said Natalie as she tried to breath life back into the room.

"You're quite welcome, now how about you close that trap that you call a mouth and have a seat," Lucy said.

As everyone in the party took their seats at the table Lucy began to start dishing out servings onto their plates. "Please everyone, don't be shy. We have such a plethora of food that will surely go bad if we don't eat it all so feel free to pillage it as much as you'd like. Go full Carnie Wilson on these dishes, I beg of you." insisted Lucy.

"Well my appetite isn't exactly up to par at the moment since I've just awoken from my slumber, but please feel free to pass that infamous salad of yours this way. As much as you've bigged it up it had better be the best fucking salad I've ever tasted."

"Here take the whole bowl," Lucy said as she handed the entire bowl to her sister. "It's probably best that you stick with salad anyway; now that you're back on the singles market you might want to drop a few pounds if you want any potential suitors to be interested in you. I didn't want to mention it since you're in such a fragile state, but it's been looking like you've started smuggling a Michelin tire around the midsection of yours lately."

Arthur and Jane both began to giggle under their breath. While it was a bit uncomfortable to actually witness the two sisters snipe away at each other, they had to admit watching the battle of their quick wits was pretty damn funny at the same time. Especially considering it wasn't them fighting with one another for the first time all day.

"And what may I ask is so damn funny?" Natalie asked as she turned her glare towards her guests. "Maybe I missed the punchline of the joke where the younger sister disrespects her elder sibling during her time of duress."

"Oh no, it was nothing, please excuse us," insisted Arthur. "It was just a nervous reaction on our part. We've just never seen you two have a sibling tiff before; it's simply interesting to see you two in this light."

"Oh Natalie, stop making our guests feel uncomfortable," Lucy interjected lightheartedly. "You know very well I was simply joking with you. This is just how we communicate with one another. And besides, don't be so self-conscious; I'm sure there are plenty of men in the village who prefer a woman with some meat on her bones. Why look at Old Man Jenkins, when we were out at sea I caught him in the communal bathroom beating off to a topless photo of Kathy Bates. He could be your next meal ticket, my dear sister."[57]

Jane tried as hard as she could, but she couldn't hold back her laughter any longer. She dropped her fork on her plate and buried her face in her hands to attempt to buffer her outburst.

"Please excuse my wife, she'll laugh at anything," said Arthur as he began to rub his wife's back in order to rein her back in.

"Yes, please do forgive me for my outburst," said Jane as she regained her composure. "I only laughed so heartedly because I thought I was the only one who caught Old Man Jenkins getting frisky to that photo late at night; that horrid vision has sadly been burned into my brain as well."

"Mmmmmmm, whatever," said Natalie as she began to dish out a massive heap of salad onto her plate.

---

57   Say what you will about Kathy Bates, but that's an attractive older woman right there. I especially loved her with full beard on *American Horror Story*. That's my kind of lady.

"Dear sister, please try to save some of that for us," said Lucy as she began to nibble on a piece of warm chicken.

"Leave me be with my salad," said Natalie. "You all have a vast selection of things to dig into; let me indulge in my salad and hush."

"I must say this chicken is so succulent and juicy. Who was the angelic patron who prepared it?" Arthur asked, attempting to steer the conversation into less turbulent waters.

"It really is delicious, isn't it? I believe it was that lovely Mrs. Ravensworth. She really *did* that shit!" exclaimed Lucy.[58]

"I'll say," said Jane as she placed another forkful into her mouth. "I can't remember the last time I tasted a piece of meat so mouth-watering."

"That doesn't say very much for you, now does it Arthur?" Natalie questioned with a sarcastic wink as she took her first bite of salad. Her face scrunched up a little as she slowly began to chew and let the intriguing taste of the "salad dressing" envelope her taste buds. It was a bit harsh, but strangely tangy and sweet at the same time. She swallowed it down and went for another forkful.

"So how are you two newlyweds fairing on this new land? We haven't really gotten an opportunity to catch up with one another since we landed," said Natalie.

Arthur and Jane exchanged a quick glance as if to say, *Do you want to answer that one or should I?*

"Everything is going quite well," Arthur said as he took control of the conversation. "Of course we have our challenges trying to get accustomed to such a new and rugged land, as well as trying to make nice with the natives, but I think we've been doing fairly well so far."

"I see. And are you *both* still fucking my sister?" Natalie asked, wide-eyed and curious as everyone at the table raised their heads and stared in amazement. Nobody, Lucy included, thought that Natalie would have the audacity to be that forthright with the topic. The room became

---

58   W.A.S.P. Translation: By stating that Mrs. Ravensworth "did that shit," Lucy is emphatically stating that her chicken is tasty as hell.

dead silent.

"Oh come on people! Don't get all sanctimonious now! Everyone at this table knows what you three freaks have been getting into lately. I was simply wondering if you two were still smashing her Little Debbie cakes?"[59]

"Natalie, stick a sock in it and just eat your damn salad!" Lucy demanded.

"Was it something I said?" Natalie asked sarcastically as she took another bite of her salad and turned her head to meet the gaze of everyone at the table.

"Sweet Natalie, what happens in the confines of our home is our business and we shall leave it at that," Arthur said as he came to the defense of his unorthodox relationship with Jane and Lucy. "And I find it a tad bit uncivilized to bring up the sex lives of your guests who have come to your aide during your time of grieving."

Natalie went to respond to Arthur's explanation but suddenly began to find herself in a small coughing fit. When she finally caught her breath she said, "Oh yes, please excuse me for being quite *uncivilized*, my dear Arthur Bigglesworth. I suppose it was a tad disrespectful to bring up the fact that both you and your wife are currently getting your rocks off with my sister."

"That's quite enough!" Jane yelled as she slammed her fork down on the table and rose from her chair. "I don't know what your problem is bitch, but I've officially had enough of your mouth! I let you slide the first time you ran your mouth about our *friendship* with Lucy, but don't get it twisted because I will knock a bitch out if you keep testing me! Don't worry about what happens in my bedroom, is that understood?"

Everyone at the table sat in shock at Jane's explosion. Natalie had finally pushed the wrong person too far. Lucy finally broke the silence by

---

59   W.A.S.P. Translation: Natalie is using the popular, and delicious, Little Debbie snack cakes as a means to reference her sister's own personal goodies. The same goodies that Arthur and Jane had become enamored with.

clapping her hands and dramatically singing, "I second that emotion…"[60]

"Well excuse me, I didn't realize we had invited the cast of *Love &
Hip-Hop Atlanta* into my home this evening,"[61] said Natalie as she bowed
her head and took another bite of her salad. She had certainly misjudged
the type of girl that Jane was; Natalie had never seen her get buck like
that before, but apparently the demure Mrs. Bigglesworth had more bite
than she had assumed.

"I apologize for that outburst, but I prefer to keep my business
out of these streets and I don't like people speaking on situations they
don't know anything about," Jane said as she calmly sat back down and
went for a sip of wine.

"Let us move on," said Arthur as he patted his wife on the leg to
show his support.

But before anyone could even bring up a new subject of discussion,
Natalie broke into another intense coughing fit. But this time she could
feel a burning sensation begin to quickly work its way throughout her
chest. The pain had come on so fast and strong; it was beginning to become
almost unbearable.

Lucy stared at her sister inquisitively. "Are you okay, Natalie? This
is what you get for sleeping with the window open during these cold
evenings. You're bound to catch pneumonia one of these days."

The coughing began to get worse.

Natalie could barely catch her breath at this point.

Her chest felt like it was on fire.

She threw her fork down on the plate and stood up from her
chair. She made a quick run towards the sink to pour a glass of water. As
she made it to the cupboard to reach for a glass she discovered the culprit

---

60   Did I mention that Lucy was a big fan of Smokey Robinson & The Miracles?
61   W.A.S.P. Translation: Natalie is referencing the behavior of the ladies of the popular VH1
show in which wives/girlfriends/mistresses of famous hip-hop stars get paid to verbally, and
sometimes physically, attack one another at any and every opportunity available to them. In
other words, Natalie is inferring that Jane is acting like a hoodrat.

of her condition: the empty vial of corrosive acid.

It lay on the kitchen counter, completely empty.

Natalie could feel her heart sink. She grabbed ahold of the vial and turned toward the dining table.

"What did you do with this?" she managed to ask as she held up the container to the rest of the room.

"The dressing? What do you mean? I put it on the salad, of course," Lucy answered, slightly concerned at this point. She got out of her chair to attempt to console her frantic sister.

Natalie pushed her away. She grabbed ahold of her chest as she tried to catch her breath. She threw the container against the floor and it smashed into pieces.

Not a second later, Natalie fell to the ground as everyone got up and ran over to her side. She writhed in pain.

"What the hell is going on? What's wrong with her?" screamed Jane.

"Someone should run and get the doctor. She must be having a heart attack," said Arthur as he tried to keep Natalie calm.

But before anyone could do anything, Natalie became completely still.

Her body completely relaxed.

Her glassy eyes scanned the room and met the gaze of her sister, who stood over her in sheer confusion and anxiety.

"You fucking bitch, you win," Natalie whimpered as her last breath exited her body and she died right there on the kitchen floor.

The room was silent.

The three remaining patrons of the dinner party stood in complete disarray and awe.

No one dared to move, or even speak, for minutes. Time seemed to stand still as reality began to sink back into the room.

Finally, Arthur spoke up. "Lucy, what in God's name was in that vial?"

Lucy simply stood there staring down at her dead sister. She was completely vacant.

"Lucy, what was that shit?" he asked again as he grabbed ahold of her arms to shake her back to reality.

"I…I….I don't know. I thought it was salad dressing. I mean it looked just like dressing. I presumed that's what it was. I don't know," she finally mumbled.

"I think it's pretty safe to assume at this point that wasn't what it was," Jane said as she walked over and put her arm around Lucy. "But more importantly, what was she planning on doing with it?"

Lucy didn't know how to verbally answer that question, but in her heart she knew exactly what her sister was planning on doing with it. She had blindly and accidentally saved her own life. Her sister's jealousy and hatred ultimately led to her own demise. The poison that had meant to relieve her of her worldly burdens ended up being the tool that ultimately destroyed her.

"What are we going to do now?" questioned Arthur as looked at both women. "We must go get the doctor and inform him as to what has happened here."

"No!" Lucy barked. "They'll hang me for sure! They'll think I purposely poisoned my sister, especially now that Natalie was the sole inheritor of Edward's estate. There's no way we can tell anyone what occurred here this evening! Please promise me that you two won't say anything!"

Jane and Arthur looked at each other with tortured confusion. Neither one of them wanted to see Lucy hang over an accident, but they had to come up with something.

"Lucy, of course we don't want to see you get into trouble…" Jane began to say, but was interrupted by Arthur.

"Wait, I have an idea. We can't lie about the poison because the doctor will surely be able to tell, but we can put her back into her bed and pretend as though Natalie took her own life after dinner this evening. You can say you found her in the morning after you went to check on her when she never woke. We can act as though when we left here everything was fine, but that Natalie still seemed quite sad over the lose of her dear husband. Everyone will simply assume she couldn't handle the grief and took her own life."

"Arthur, that's a genius idea," said Lucy as she grabbed ahold of Arthur's arm in excitement.

"Arthur, are you really saying that we should lie about this event?" asked Jane, feeling completely puzzled.

"I don't see what other choice we have in this situation," he said. "We can't let Lucy fry for this. We have to do this to help her out."

"Please Jane," begged Lucy. "You have to do this for me. I'll forever be indebted to you two, but I need your help right now."

Jane was totally confused.

"I suppose we don't have any other option," she finally managed to mutter.

Lucy let out a loud breath of relief as she took ahold of Jane and embraced her. "Oh thank you so much, Jane. I simply cannot thank you enough for this!"

They all stared down at Natalie's lifeless body strewn about the kitchen floor.

"Well, I suppose we should move her into her bed now," Arthur said. "I'll get her head, you girls take ahold of her feet. Be careful."

They gently lifted the corpse and proceeded to head toward her bedroom. They placed her in her bed and Lucy positioned Natalie's head comfortably on her pillow. She almost looked peaceful as she lay completely still.

Lucy and the Bigglesworth's stood over her body at the side of the bed. The totality of the situation was really beginning to settle in.

"Wow," Lucy mumbled. "I can't believe she's actually dead."

Arthur and Jane each took ahold of Lucy's arms to provide her with some comfort. She twisted her head toward Arthur and then back around toward Jane. They were genuinely risking everything to keep her out of trouble. They truly loved her.

"Thank you, my loves," she sweetly whispered to her guests. "You have saved my life this evening and it hasn't gone unnoticed."

Jane lifted her head and gave her a soft kiss on the cheek. "Don't even mention it, sweetheart. We're in this one together."

"I concur," said Arthur.

Lucy was touched by their sentiment, but she was also blithely aware that the scene of Natalie's death was only halfway prepared.

"Will you two do me a favor and go sweep up the broken glass from the vile? We need to place the broken glass on the floor in here as if she dropped the vile on the floor after she consumed its contents. And I think I'd like to have a moment alone with my dearly departed sister."

"Surely, my dear," said Jane. "Take your time. We will go take care of the rest."

Lucy watched as the Bigglesworths quietly took each other's hand and exited the room. While Lucy wasn't entirely certain what would ultimately occur between she and her lovers, this incident had surely brought them closer. Closer to what exactly, well, that had yet to be determined.

Lucy sat down on the side of the bed and sweetly caressed her older sister's hair. In that moment she wished they had more moments like this, moments of sisterly love, compassionate and soft moments.

But so much of their relationship had been filled with venom and animosity. Natalie's raging jealousy had made it impossible for them to ever have a genuine sisterly bond. Even her last words to Lucy were scathing and hateful.

But the cause of this catastrophe was her own doing. She had brought death to her own doorstep.

Lucy bent down and brushed Natalie's hair behind her ear to whisper one final goodbye to her sibling.

"You're right bitch, I win. Haters never prosper."

She sent Natalie out into the heavens the same way they had functioned through life. That was the only way to do their relationship any form of real justice. No frills. No false formalities. No superfluous and phony tears.

That's the only way Natalie would have wanted it.

PART TWO

THE HIGGINS CLAN

CHAPTER ONE

"Rupert! Emily! Get your asses in this kitchen before your breakfast gets cold! I didn't fry up these eggs for the sheer hell of it!" screamed Mary Higgins as she scuffled about the kitchen of her household.

"I swear to the Lord almighty, Baxter, if you don't help me get these miscreant children of yours into this kitchen to eat breakfast before their studies I'll be serving *your* sausage for breakfast tomorrow!" she barked at her husband who sat quietly at the dining room table a few feet away from her.

"Oh bloody hell Mary, will you kindly zip your lips," he said as he placed his coffee mug on the table. "Kids! Get your asses in here before your mother lays a goddamn egg!"

The scene playing out within the confines of this quant cottage was the typical morning mayhem for the Higgins clan. Subtle and subdued, they were not.

In fact, according to folk legend, the Higgins clan were the main inspiration behind the popular 90's sitcom *Roseanne*; the only significant difference between the infamous Connor family and the Higgins' was that the latter bunch were far more brash and insensitive.

But Mary and Baxter did an excellent job at putting up a perfectly pious front for the rest of their neighbors. They quoted scriptures, led prayer circles in the community, and even hosted a weekly Bible study in their home. To the rest of the colony they were the ideal Christian family, but if anyone could see what they were like behind closed doors they would have been shocked and appalled.

"Would you two politely calm the fuck down?" Emily, one half of the fraternal twin teenagers that made up the rest of the family, said as she came into the kitchen and took her seat at the table next to her father. "You two are quite aware of how long it takes for me to get my hair just right in the mornings. I'm going for an Eva Mendes look today and these brunette tresses needed to be tended to, *mother*."[62]

Mary let out an annoyed sigh of disapproval.

"I figured you were going for a *Spaniard*-inspired look considering you're wearing those unseemly and ghetto doorknocker earrings, which you certainly will take out of your ears before you leave this household.[63] And why, pray tell, do you care what the hell your hair looks like my dear daughter?" questioned Mary as she placed the plate of eggs and bacon down in front of her daughter. "You're putting on that lovely bonnet that I sewed for you last week before you go to your studies. What difference could it possibly make what your hair looks like underneath it?"

"You know I don't like that bonnet. It's far too constricting; a bitch can barely breath in the damn thing."

"Excuse me, young lady? We aren't raising some hoodrat harlot who runs the streets without a bonnet. I'll be damned if any daughter of mine makes it onto *Teen Mom: Colonial Edition*.[64] Put on the fucking

---

62   Ryan Gosling's baby mama was one of Emily's style icons and she consistently tried to emulate her.

63   W.A.S.P. Translation: Doorknocker earrings are an urban style staple. Just as the name implies, these gold (typically gold-plated) are usually the size of massive door-knockers that you would typically find at the entry way of old English houses and/or castles. The bigger the better. See any Jennifer Lopez music video for example.

64   Mary is referencing the ultra popular MTV series Teen Mom in which various young ladies get knocked-up by their ill-equipped boyfriends and are forced to deal with the hardships of life all whilst trying to find a prom dress that will fit them in their third trimester.

bonnet before the neighbors start talking," her mother demanded.

"I agree with your mother," Baxter added as he eyed his daughter over the top of his morning copy of the village newspaper, *The Pilgrim Pride*. "You're not some common floozy running around here with your hair all out for everyone in the village to gaze upon. Why look at that young hussy Lucy Skeezabeth; she's always running around these colonial streets looking like a common streetwalker with her hair gallivanting in the wind. No daughter of mine, I tell you that much."

"I find her quite pretty," Emily said under her breath as she scooped up a forkful of eggs.

"Oh, pretty? Is that so?" questioned her mother. "We shall see just how *pretty* she is once she gets the clap from spreading that coochie of hers all over town; or when she finds herself knocked up and downgraded to 'baby mama' status after a one-nighter with one of those *Jersey Shore* fellas.[65] I can't even begin to tell you the stories I've heard about that little slut. Why just the other day…"

"Okay, okay, okay," Baxter interrupted as he folded up his paper and placed it down on the table. "You shall reserve that idle chatter and gossip for later on in your day when you're amongst those hags you deem to call *friends*; this isn't the type of conversation our teenage daughter should be privy to."

Mrs. Higgins rolled her eyes and scoffed off her husband's reprimanding as she took her seat at the table to eat her own breakfast. Besides tending one of the largest and most plentiful gardens in the village, she was also the town equivalent of TMZ. There wasn't a shred of town news she didn't know about and proudly disseminate to anyone with functioning ears.

Mary was a short and stocky woman in her late 30's. At one point in her life, many many years ago, she had been quite pretty; she had big chestnut colored eyes, sleek auburn hair, and a petite and slender frame

---

65   Jersey Shore, another shining example of why Valtrex continues to be prescribed in boat loads during the summertime.

that was the envy of many-a-big-bitch in her small town back home. But sadly, the hardships of pregnancy and childbirth had brought her hips to the point of no return and there was no going back.

Those big chestnut eyes now looked a bit vacant; that sleek auburn hair now seemed a bit stringy and lifeless; and that enviable petite and slender frame was replaced with a figure not dissimilar to that of Danny Devito.

A stunner she was no longer.

Since birthing her twins, Emily and Rupert, she had strangely transformed into one of those women who no matter how much preparation she put into herself there was always something amiss about her appearance. You couldn't ever really put your finger on exactly what it was, but you could just tell something was…off.

The bitch just looked kind of *sloppy*.

As for Baxter Higgins, he was a relatively handsome former military man in his early 40's. He carried himself with a stern stature and, like most militant figures, had a bit of a cold personality. At over 6-feet tall he quite literally towered over his petite wife. Baxter was all business, all the time; to see him crack a smile would be an once-in-a-lifetime occurrence.

His no-nonsense personality made him a bit of an axe-wound to be around for long periods of time so he wasn't exactly "Mr. Popular" amongst the other colonizers. But while he wasn't winning any awards for his shining personality, he happened to be the best hunter in the village. His military skills and training had become an asset that everyone in the colony couldn't live without, quite literally.

"Emily, what is taking your brother so long this morning? Where is he?" Mary asked her daughter.

"How the hell should I know? He's probably in his room whacking it again. You know he barely leaves that room of his since he discovered the wonders of cocoa butter," Emily sarcastically quipped as she took a sip of her orange juice.

"Oh, for Christ's sake Emily! Language please, young lady," Mary said.

"Honestly Emily, what would the Lord say about that mouth of yours?" Baxter asked his daughter. "You know it's a sin to speak in such a manner."

"It's a sin to say that Rupert's in his room choking his chicken? What part of the Old Testament is that from?"

Mary lowered her head and shook it in annoyance.

"Huhhhhhh, the joys of these wondrous teenage years," Mary said as she turned to face her husband. "They don't warn you about them in those *fucking* parenting books now do they? Where was the chapter in *What to Expect When You're Expecting* entitled 'Your Child's Going to Turn Into a Sarcastic Little Shit at 13, Be Prepared.'"

"Enough Mary, you're not making it any better speaking like that," said Baxter.

"Hmmmmmmm," Emily triumphantly muttered under her breath as she glared at her mother and smiled.

Just then, Rupert finally made his grand entrance as he casually meandered into the kitchen.

"Good morning everybody. What's all the yelling about?" he said as he nonchalantly took his seat at the table.

"I've been screaming like a bloody banshee for you to get your butt in here to eat your breakfast before you're late for your studies," his mother said. "Now you're going to have to hurry up and shovel it down."

Rupert took up a forkful of eggs and placed them in his mouth before immediately spitting them back out on to the plate.

"Gross mom, these eggs are cold!" he bellowed out.

"Oh heavenly father, save me from murking this boy in his sleep!"[66] Mary yelled out as she raised her head to the sky as if she were

---

66   W.A.S.P. Translation: Murk is a popular street term that is used to mean "kill," "murder," or "bust a cap in your ass."

speaking directly to God himself. "Why do you think I've been telling you to come eat for 10-damn minutes? There's nothing nastier than cold eggs. Go make yourself a bowl of Lucky Charms and be done with it. Why I bother cooking for you heathens is truly beyond me."

"Maybe your eggs wouldn't be so cold if you hadn't spent the last half hour locked in your room polishing your musket," Emily snapped at her brother.

"Emily! Enough of that," Mary demanded. "But now that we're on the topic, what is this talk of masturbation in my household? You know that's a sin and I had better not find out nothing of that sort is happening in this Godly home."

"Are we really discussing this over breakfast?" Baxter asked his family. "How about a little decorum and tact? Rupert, no respectable girl is going to want to marry a man who spends his free time stroking his bologna. Keep it in your pants, son."

"Yeah, whatever," said Rupert as he poured his bowl of cereal.

As you could probably already tell, even though 15-year old Emily and Rupert were fraternal twins, they couldn't have been more different from one another if they tried. Emily was feisty and had the kind of quick-witted personality that would have made *Mean Girls* Regina George look like Taylor Swift. She was the kind of girl that incited equal parts fear and amazement in the other girls throughout the village; while they loathed and despised her, at the same time they wanted to be just like her.

Upon entering her teenage years, Emily had been overtaken with a strange fascination with stereotypical "urban" culture. While the young Emily of yesteryear was fond of ribbons and lace, teenage Emily only wanted to be adorned with large hoop earrings and neon colored nails. Over her modest grey blouse she wore a layered arrangement of various gold chains and she refused to leave the house without her Amy Winehouse-esque "cat-eye" makeup fully drawn on.

Needless to say the rebellious transformation she underwent as she entered young adulthood certainly confused her conservative parents. What had happened to the innocent little princess they had raised? One minute she was Hannah Montana and the next minute she was Miley Cyrus; she had seemingly went from good girl to hood girl practically overnight.

While Emily was busy pretending to be J.Lo (circa the *In Living Color* "Fly Girl" days), Rupert had crossed over into his teen years going into a completely different direction. He was a reserved, quiet, and some would even say timid young man.

Similar to his father, he certainly wasn't a social butterfly; though, that was the only similarity the two of them shared as Rupert was far too sensitive to be interested in his father's love of the hunt. He went about his days reading various books about history and science, and he had a tender love for poetry. He even kept a small bright-red journal with him at all times where he would secretly write about his feelings and his day-to-day activities.

To his parents he had become an enigma over the years. They never knew how to read their son and the man he was evolving into. They had to press and prod to get any answers out of him, but his nonchalant demeanor never seemed to care much about anything they had to say.

Was he depressed?

Was he a secret genius?

The strangest thing about Rupert's personality is that it seemed to be an odd aphrodisiac to the teen girls throughout the colony. You might assume that being the "loner" amongst the village would almost demonize him to his peers, but it actually seemed to do the exact opposite. Though he never entertained them, practically every girl, and even some of the older women, had a massive crush on the elusive Rupert. The mysterious vibe he exuded seemed to make him smoldering and artistic to the opposite sex of the village (and one very *curious* male baker.)

Though he was the antithesis of the traditional colonial male, it certainly wasn't diminishing his sex appeal to those around him.

"Alright now," said Mary as she scooped up her children's plates and bowls off the table. "I have carrots to tend to this morning and you two need to be making your way to your studies. Let us make haste."

"Huh, what's the point of going to our studies out here in this *new world*," Emily rebuffed. "What are we going to do with this crap Mr. Teeter is teaching us anyway? Do you think I'm going to get secretarial work out here in the middle of fucking nowhere?"

"It's not about that Emily, it's about the fact that your father and I aren't raising you to have the IQ of a speed bump. We're paying good money for you to have these lessons and you will take full of advantage of them," lectured Mary as she placed the dishes into the basin and turned back towards her daughter. "Besides, I don't see your brother complaining about his lessons, do you? I pray to our heavenly father that some of his love for knowledge rubs off on you one day."

"Oh please, the only reason Rupert loves his studies so much is because no one else talks to him so his books are the only company he has. I actually have friends and my girls and I don't feel like spending our entire day stuck in a classroom learning useless information."

"Your girls?" asked Baxter as he leaned in and placed his elbows on the table. "And who, pray tell, are these *girls* you speak of? Those two hounds who follow you around and obey your every word?"

"If you're referring to Lisa and Elizabeth, than yes, those are my girls."

"Sweetheart, you really must get better friends out here," Mary interjected. "Lisa Stein has got to be one of the ugliest girls that God has placed on this Earth. I'm fairly certain her parents pulled her straight out of the Thames River with that horrific trout mouth she has. And don't even get me started on that Elizabeth Rondell; maybe it's just me but I get some *serious* carpet-muncher vibes from her."

"You sound ridiculous," said Emily as she rolled her eyes in annoyance.

"I'm simply stating that between that haircut of hers and the masculine nature in which she tends her family's garden, I get nothing but Jody Foster realness from that young lady," Mary said as she raised her hands to the air and shrugged her shoulders.

"Whatever, those are my ride-or-die bitches and I like them. Besides, it's not very *godly* of you to be judging others like that now is it?" Emily snapped back towards her parents.

"Emily, don't talk back to your mother like that," Baxter answered. "There's nothing ungodly about your mother wanting you to have good friends around you, just not the ugly and dykey ones is all."

Rupert let out a small laugh under his breath.

Emily reached out and slapped her brother on the arm. "What are you laughing about? At least I have actual friends!"

"Yeah, two disciples who hang at your every word," he said softly. "Congrats."

"Alright, alright, alright," Baxter boomed. "Enough of this nonsense. Go get your books and make haste to Mr. Teeter's cabin for your studies. And make sure you both come home right afterward today; there's much that needs to be done around the house before the weather gets too unbearable outside. These winds are getting colder and colder each day and we need to make sure we preserve as much of our food as we can before the snowfall begins."

Rupert and Emily proceeded to grab their things and make their way towards the cabin door.

"Uhm, excuse me young lady, aren't you forgetting something?" Mary questioned her daughter before she made it out of the doorway. "Here's your bonnet, let me tie it on you before you leave."

Emily snatched the bonnet out of her mother's hands, "I'm not a child, I can tie my own damn bonnet, mother."

"Well go right ahead, but you aren't leaving this household until you put it on your head. And hand over those ghetto earrings while you're at it; you aren't going out there looking like some common Compton chola girl."[67]

Emily knew she could huff and puff all she wanted, but in the end her mother would ultimately win the argument. She threw the shabby bonnet on her head and handed over her favorite earrings before she stormed out the door to catch up with her brother.

"Baxter, those children will be the death of me," Mary said as she walked back into the kitchen and began wiping down the dining room table.

"They certainly are a handful, but I suppose that comes with the territory," he muttered in a monotone response.

"What are your plans for the day? Are you going out on another hunt this afternoon?"

"Yes, I must. Like I said to the children, we must stock up on as much food as we can. We don't know how severe the winters are out here in this new land and we must be prepared," Baxter said. "Hopefully I shall be able to get a few big scores today out there in the wild."

"Just be careful, there has been many savage sightings over the last couple weeks and I don't want you running into any trouble while you're out there. You know I don't trust those beastly native creatures," Mary said.

"I know Mary, I know. Don't fret my wife, those natives and their menial weapons are no match for my musket and I. If it were up to me we would eradicate all of them before they cause any more trouble for our colony, but sadly the rest of our fellow villagers are a bit, shall we say, *pussy*."

"You don't have to tell me," Mary agreed. "Why do you know just the other day I was conversing with that spoiled bimbo Jane Bigglesworth and she had the audacity to tell me she allowed one of the female savages

---

67   W.A.S.P. Translation: A Chola girl is a young Latina, usually based out of California, who has very thin eyebrows, heavy make-up, lots of piercings, tons of jewelry, and is a hardcore gang-banger. For example, see any Fergie music video.

to behead and pluck the feathers off a chicken she was preparing for dinner!"

"No!? She allowed one of them to actually touch her food?"

"Yes! That was my reaction as well. I tried to tell her that she should refrain from doing such things as she doesn't know where their demonic and dirty hands have been. Why, between you and I, I've heard stories that they even wipe their asses with those gross hands of theirs. So unseemly, isn't it? I'm not saying they should use Charmin like we do because, lets be frank, I highly doubt they'd even know what to do with it, but they live amongst the leaves so you'd think they would make the most of them for their toiletry needs."

"I fully agree, but talking sense to those liberal Bigglesworths is a fruitless endeavor. Why just the other day in a counsel meeting do you know her husband Arthur proposed that we extend an invitation to the neighboring savages to have a celebratory meal with us to *thank* them for allowing us to colonize on this land? Could you imagine such godless blasphemy? I'd sooner invite Flava Flav over for tea and biscuits before I'd take part in such foolery! Not in this Godly household, I tell you that much."

"Preach that shit, that's right," Mary excitedly agreed.

"Anyway, enough of this silly chatter about irrelevant bitches, let me get my belongings together and make my way out for the hunt."

Mary walked over to her husband and softly embraced him. She planted a tender kiss on his cheek, "Let the Lord bring you back home to me safe and sound. Be safe out there, Mr. Higgins."

"I always do, my dear wife. Now get out there and tend to that garden of yours. We have much to prepare ourselves for."

Meanwhile, while the Higgins parents were engaging in a rare showing of affection towards one another, Rupert and Emily were slowly making their way across the village to get to their studies.

"I *so* don't feel like going to class today, Rupert," Emily whined to her brother as they walked along. "Especially with this fucking milkmaid bonnet upon my damn head. I look like Heidi in this ugly thing."

"Yeah, mom's strongest suit certainly isn't crocheting. It looks a bit...dilapidated," Rupert agreed.

"That's a nice way of saying it looks like a rickety piece of shit. It looks like its part of the Jessica Simpson Colonial Collection."[68]

"Pretty much."

"The saddest part is my hair actually looked really cute today. I was serving Eva Mendes realness to the Gods, I swear. A bitch can't express herself under such stringent conditions. Do you feel me?"

"Yeah, whatever."

In all honestly, Rupert couldn't give a shit about his sister's pitiful plight of the day. He had completely zoned out and wasn't really paying any attention to what she had to say about her ridiculous hairstyle. His gaze was fixated on the woods in the far distance. He stared off towards the trees and carefully surveyed every detail as if he was in search of something as they strolled along.

He tried to concentrate as hard as he could, but his sister's inane banter was like the annoying buzzing of an eager insect that was just begging to be smashed with one mighty blow.

But just as he was about to politely tell her to shut the hell up, he finally caught a glimpse of what he had been hoping for. There, in the distance, amongst the rustic and decaying trees, he saw the radiant glimmer and shine of a mirror reflecting rays of sunlight off of it.

It was the signal he had been waiting to see all week.

Finally.

A feeling of eager happiness and anticipation began to rush throughout his body. The sudden flooding of excitement gave him such

---

68   All jokes about the quality of her clothing line aside, the fact that the woman who was once most famous for asking whether canned tuna was "chicken or fish" is now running a billion dollar fashion empire just goes to show you that miracles can truly happen in America... if you're a blonde-haired, blue-eyed, big-breasted Texan, of course.

a euphoric high that he briefly found himself getting a semi-boner right there in the middle of the trail. But sadly, this joyous feeling was very short-lived. He was quickly jolted back to reality where his sister was still rambling on about her failed hair styling situation of the morning.

"I'm just saying, a woman should be able to wear her hair just as she pleases..." Emily continued with her diatribe.

Rupert knew he was going to have to shake his sister off so he could make his way towards the shining beacon in the distance. There was no way she could find out where he was sneaking off to; it was out of the question.

"Yeah, I agree," Rupert interrupted her before she could continue. "Oh shit, it seems that I've forgotten my English notebook back at home. You go on ahead and I'll meet you there. Please tell Mr. Teeter that I may be a few moments late today."

"Isn't that your English notebook right there under your math book?" Emily skeptically questioned as she eyed the books in her brother's hands.

"Oh no, that's a different one..." he replied, trying to work his way around his lie.

"Mmmmm, if I didn't know any better I'd think you were trying to skip out of class today," Emily said as she came to a halt and stared her twin brother in the eyes. "But since I know you're the type of raging loser who gets wet off math equations and poem verses, I'm fairly sure you aren't even remotely cool enough to attempt such a thing. Go ahead, run along. I'll tell him you'll be on your way shortly."

"Thanks," Rupert said as he turned around proceeded to walk back towards the cabin.

When he got far enough away, he turned and peered over his shoulder to make sure his sister was completely out of sight. He couldn't see her; but just to be safe he jumped behind a massive tree that stood along the trail.

He peeked around the side of the tree. The coast was completely clear; Emily was nowhere to be seen.

Rupert began stealthly maneuvering towards the shining signal in the distance. He ran from tree to tree in an attempt to stay as covert as possible; the last thing he needed was any of his fellow villagers spotting him en route to where he was about to go. He knew that no good could come from it.

He sprinted, darted, and ducked until he finally reached his destination.

As he stepped into the densely wooded area his sense of smell was enveloped with a familiar scent that he immediately recognized; he closed his eyes and took in the spicy scent of nutmeg and pumpkin. It made him feel warm and tingly inside; it was as if he had stepped into Starbucks during Autumn.

As he made his way closer to the area where he first spotted the prismatic signal he could smell the scent getting intensified. He knew he was heading in the right direction. Then, seemingly out of nowhere, he heard the crinkling and crushing of dried leaves to his left.

He spun his head in the direction of the noise to find a teenage Native American girl coyly hiding behind one of the giant trees. Though he couldn't see all of her, he could spot the small mirror she was holding in her delicate hand.

Rupert began to make his way towards her direction, but just as he began to get closer to her she took off running faster than a woman realizing she's going on a blind date with Bill Cosby.

He chased behind her like a predator running down its prey, trying not to lose her amongst the wilderness. He clutched tightly to his notebooks as he watched her smooth raven-colored hair disappear and then reappear behind every twist and turn.

She was certainly fast, but he refused to give up the chase.

He had been waiting too long for this.

But no matter how quick he ran, no matter how fast he dipped

and dodged between trees, it was becoming more and more
she wasn't about to be taken without a fight.

Rupert knew he was hot on her trail because her sc‹
dancing in his nostrils, but in the blink of an eye she had suddenly seemed
to vanish into thin air.

He came to a halt.

There was no sight of her at all.

He was completely confused and bewildered.

He had to act fast and move before he lost her for good. His
intuition told him to make a sharp right and start running like an illegal
Mexican trying to make their way out of Arizona. And that's exactly what
he did.

He had to catch up with her before it was too late.

He could feel himself getting closer, but where was she?

Why was she playing this strange game of cat and mouse, anyway?

Then, out from behind one of the trees, came a sturdy straight-
arm that caught Rupert right in the chest. The stealthy attack completely
clotheslined the poor boy and knocked him right onto his back, sending
his books flying through the air. The wind was knocked right out of him.
He lay on the ground with his eyes closed and rocked back and forth in
agony. He attempted to shake off the pain and get his bearings, but before
he could he felt someone straddle and lay atop of him.

As he slowly opened his eyes he saw the stunningly beautiful face
of his prey staring down at him.

"Well, hello there," the mysterious native girl flirtatiously said.
"Now don't tell me a strong and strapping young fellow like you was
brought down by little ole' me? Can it be true?"

Rupert smiled through the sharp pain pulsing throughout his
chest as he reached up and grabbed ahold of her face to bring her in
for a kiss. It was an intense lip lock. It was the kiss of lovers who have
been longing to see one another. It was that Ryan Gosling and Rachel
McAdams in *The Notebook* type of shit.

They lay on the ground of the forest and kissed each other for what felt like a millennia (but in real time it was about three minutes. Bitches got places to go and soil to till; they don't have time to be making out in the woods all day as if this were a Danielle Steel novel.)

She raised her head up and looked down at her conquest. "So how have you been, mister Rupert?"

"How have I been?" he sarcastically responded as he placed his hands behind his head and lay back so that he could stare up at the exotic native goddess. "How do you think I've been, my beloved Princess LaQuintia? It's been almost two weeks since I've gotten to see you. I've been patiently staring off towards these woods every morning with hopes of seeing you shine our signal for a meeting. Where have you been?"

"Oh, you know boss bitches like myself have much to attend to before the first snow of the winter," Princess LaQuintia said with a smirk. "My *annoying* father has left me in charge of making sure all of our tribe's maize is properly stored away and that the various meats are cured. It's such an annoying task, but I guess it must be done. The joys of being the only daughter of the chief of the tribe; people think I run around everyday 'painting all the colors of the wind' like fucking Pocahontas, but I've got real shit to do."

"This is true. I suppose it's just one of the many privileges of being the princess of a native tribe," he said in a mocking tone.

"Oh hush, you know I hate that ridiculous title. It sounds so pompous and entitled; who do I look like, Gwyneth Paltrow? I'm a trill ass bitch in these wilderness streets![69] You know I don't like people to think I walk around these woods with a silver spoon up my ass. I plant my own corn and kill my own wild turkey just like every other regular ho in that tribe," she said rather defensively.

---

69   W.A.S.P. Translation: Trill is an adjective that is the combination of "true" and "real." When LaQuintia refers to herself as a "trill ass bitch" she's basically saying that she's the realest bitch around.

"I know, I know. I'm just joking a little to get a rise out of you since I haven't gotten to see you in so long," Rupert said reassuringly as he rubbed her exposed thigh.

She looked down at his hazel eyes and smiled at him.

"You must know that even though I have been extremely busy there hasn't been a day that's passed where I haven't thought of you. I've missed you so very much Rupert," she said as she leaned down and planted another kiss on her lover's lips.

"I've missed you, too. I don't think I can survive like this. Not seeing you for weeks at a time is quite torturous. When I'm not attending my studies or indulging in my writing, I find myself spending all my free time in my bedroom having erotic thoughts about you and 'polishing my pony.' I've used so much lotion over the last few weeks I'm seriously considering buying stock in Jergen's to start making some of my money back."

Princess LaQuintia let out a deep laugh as she rolled off her prey and lay down next to him on the woodland ground.

"I know. Trust me it's torture for me too, Rupert. But it's just hard to get away without being noticed at the moment. No one can know about our rendezvouses or else it would cause nothing but drama amongst our people. I don't even want to imagine how my father would react if he found out that I let a colonial boy get a piece of my native nookie. Chief Wailing Badger would be none too happy."

"Yes, I know you're right," Rupert agreed as he turned on his side and began to run his hand through her dark hair. "I'm sure my parents would lose their shit too if they found out, but at some point they're all going to have to find out and deal with it, aren't they?"

"I suppose so," she answered.

"I want to be with you and that's all I've ever wanted. Ever since that very first summer day when we encountered each other in these very woods, I knew from that first moment that it was destiny that brought us together. It was serendipity."

"Oh, you artistic types and your emotions," LaQuintia said with a dramatic eye-roll in an attempt to rile him up. "I don't know how much *destiny* was really involved, but I *do* know that I wanted to see what sex was like with a white guy. And seeing as how Justin Timberlake is busy boning that wench Jessica Biel these days, I figured you would have to suffice for the moment."

Rupert propped himself up on one arm and looked down at his mysterious lover, "Oh, is that so?"

"Yep, I just wanted the dick. But you had to go ahead and catch feelings," she jokingly quipped as she winked at him.

He knew she was only joking, but he decided to take advantage of the situation and give her exactly what she claimed she wanted. He rolled on top of her and whispered in her ear, "Well, if that's what you're after then go ahead and take it."

LaQuintia opened her legs and immediately began to fiddle with his belt so she could remove his pants. She leaned in close and seductively whispered, "Let's make it quick, I've got some bacon to cure back at the village."

Forty-five minutes later, Rupert quietly entered Mr. Teeter's cabin and went straight to his seat towards the back of the classroom.

"Excuse me Mr. Higgins, but is there a reason you've come to class so late?" questioned Mr. Teeter as he gave Rupert a stern glare.

"I'm sorry about my late attendance sir, I informed my sister to tell you that I had to run back home to get my notebook that I mistakenly forgot to grab this morning."

"And it took you *that* long to grab a notebook? Let me ask you a question Rupert, does it say 'dumbass' across this forehead of mine? How stupid do you think I am?"

"No sir, I don't think you're stupid at all," Rupert politely answered as he hung his head down in shame after being called out for his lying.

"I expect that this won't happen again, young man. Now open up your notebook and begin your daily writings."

"Yes sir, I shall."

"And Mr. Higgins…"

"Yes, sir?"

"You might want to run a brush through your hair before you come to class next time. I'm not sure if I want to know why, but you seem to have twigs and grass in your hair for some odd reason."

"Oh my, I'm sorry sir," he said embarrassed as he brushed his hair with his hands to remove the debris from his woodland tryst.

From across the classroom Emily Higgins eyed her brother with an accusatory stare. She couldn't tell exactly what her brother had been up to, but she knew that something was surely amiss. His behavior this morning was truly out of character, and one way or another she was going to find out what was going on.

CHAPTER TWO

After her family had filed out for the day, Mary spent much of her morning doing exactly what any other colonial matriarch would: she tended her beloved garden, tidied up the cabin, and met up with her girlfriends to gossip and talk *mucho* shit about her neighbors.

"I'm telling you Ester, something is quite fishy in that Skeezabeth-Williams household," said Mary. "Don't you find it a bit odd that Edward 'buys-the-farm' and then a matter of days later Natalie follows suit? Something very devilish is occurring in that house, mark my words."

"I don't know, Mary," Ester rebutted. "I think the sheer sadness of losing her husband brought poor Natalie to the edge and she couldn't handle it, the poor soul."

"Oh pish posh, Ester! It's common knowledge that she barely even liked her husband let alone would she be willing to take her own life from losing him. I'm surprised we didn't see her running the streets singing Pharell's "Happy" after that poor bastard bit the dust. Trust me, my gut is never wrong about these kind of situations; why, I was the first one to call bullshit on that whole Tom Cruise-Katie Holmes union, you know? I know when I'm being bamboozled."

This was a typical conversation between Mary and her pack of gossips. Every day, after their household chores had been completed, she and Ester Smith, Theresa Mills, and Lydia Collins would get together in the center of the village and discuss what was occurring around the colony. They would watch the passers-by as they sipped their coffee and whispered the latest news to one another.

"I bet that hussy of a sister, Lucy, had something to do with it," whispered Lydia. "There's something about her that I've never trusted. You can never trust the ones that let their hair flow free like that with no bonnet. It's immoral if you ask me; she may as well be running around without any pantaloons on with her beaver on full display."

"Why, that's exactly what I was telling my daughter Emily this morning," Mary interjected. "That Lucy Skeezabeth is a bad influence on the young girls in the village. Do you know that Emily tried to walk out of the house this morning *without* a bonnet on her head?" The other women at the table let out an audible gasp. "And if that wasn't bad enough, she tried wearing some huge, horrifically ghetto Hispanic-looking earrings. I just want to know at what point did my daughter turn into Selena Gomez? It's simply immoral if you ask me."

"Well, speak of the devil…" Theresa whispered to the rest of the group as she used her eyes to direct the rest of their attentions to the road directly behind them. They all casually turned their heads to see Lucy Skeezabeth coming up the trail carrying a wicker basket full of fresh fruits and vegetables.

All of the women threw cutting glances in Lucy's direction as she drew nearer and nearer to them until, finally, she wandered right up to their table to greet them.

"Hello there, ladies," said Lucy. "And how are you all on this glorious day?" Lucy asked.

"Greetings Lucy," Mary said. "It is surely great to see you out and about despite the horrible events that have occurred in your household as of lately. How are you holding up, dear thing?"

"I'm doing quite alright at the moment, thank you for asking," Lucy answered in a condescending tone. She knew that none of these women gave a single fuck about how she was coping with her sister's death considering none of them even bothered to come to the cottage to offer their condolences. "I decided to find solace in knowing that Natalie and Edward have been reunited in the afterlife and can now spend eternity together. It's a *beautiful* thing when you really sit back and think about it."

All the women at the table shook their head in an agreeing manner as they pretended to fain interest and compassion toward a girl that none of them could stand.

"Well, dear thing," Lydia said. "You know that if you need anything from the rest of the village you can always come to us for help. Please don't ever hesitate to ask us."

"That's certainly very sweet of you, Mrs. Collins. Your offer simply warms my heart. As a matter of fact, now that you've mentioned it, I could *really* use some help chopping some firewood for these chilly evenings we've been having. Why don't you send your husband, the glorious Mr. Collins, over to my house later today to help me split some wood? I've seen the way he works his axe and I know he can handle working some wood with me."

Lucy purposely drenched her request in sexual innuendo. She knew that everyone at that table thought she was a raging tramp so she figured if she was going to be labeled the town harlot than she was going to live up to the title to the fullest extent.

All of the women at the table went completely silent as they turned toward Lydia Collins with stunned glances. How would she respond?

"Oh, my husband? You want my husband to come over? Oh, oh, uhm, I see," Lydia became so flustered with embarrassment that she began stammering over her words trying to figure out what to say. "Well, uhm,

I shall ask him if he can do that for you once he returns home from the hunt this evening. You see he's out with Mr. Higgins today trying to stock up on some meat before the weather gets too harsh, and usually he's very tired after such a day so I can't say for certain that he'll be able to do that today..."

"Oh, I see," Lucy said with a sarcastic smirk. "Well, whenever he has a free moment just send him over my way. I'd be more than happy to pay him for his services. Anyway ladies, if you'll excuse me, I must make haste and return home. As always, it's been such a delight to catch up with all of you."

They all gave their fakest cordial goodbyes as Lucy made her way down the trail toward her cabin.

"Oh-my-fucking-gosh," Ester said after Lucy was out of earshot. "I cannot believe she said that to you, Lydia. Surely you're not even thinking about letting your husband go to her home all by himself, are you?"

"Bitch, are you crazy?" Lydia snapped. "I wouldn't allow my husband to be within 500 feet of her cabin by himself. That would be like sending a lamb into a lion's den. How dense do I look to you? That's exactly how Jennifer Aniston lost her husband to that sex hussy, Angelina. She can go chop her own damn wood for all I care."

"I just can't believe the sheer nerve of her to ask you that! And in such a manner as well," Mary said in response.

"I know," said Lydia. "I was just trying to be nice to her, but I wasn't really expecting her to *actually* ask for help!"

"The sheer audacity of her," said Theresa. "If she wants a man to come help her chop some damn firewood than she should go find herself a husband like a respectable young lady."

As the group of ladies continued their ranting and raving about Lucy's ridiculous request they failed to notice that Captain James Todd was approaching their table from the east side of the village.

"Greetings ladies," said the captain as he politely removed his hat and addressed them in the most gentleman-like manner. "How are the most beautiful women in the village doing this glorious morning?"

All the women at the table seemed to light up from within upon catching a glimpse of the elusively handsome, and very single, Captain Todd. All of them except Mary Higgins, that is.

"Why Captain Todd, where have you been?" asked Ester. "I feel as though it's been an eternity since we've got the chance to socialize with you. I've barely seen you at all over the last few months since we all got off that god-awful ship."

"I know, and I feel quite awful for my long absence. I've just been so busy getting myself settled in these new surroundings," the captain responded. "You'll have to excuse me for being so anti-social lately. I suppose I'm also trying to become accustomed to life on land after spending so many years commanding a ship and living on the seas."

"Oh yes, that must be quite difficult," said Ester.

"Yes, it has been," he said. "I never thought when I decided to hand over the reigns of the ship to my second-in-command and disembark the ship with you all that it would be such a culture shock for me. I've felt a bit like a 'fish-out-of-water.' But I realized if I didn't get out of that lifestyle and start interacting with people again I was going to go full Shia LeBeauf and start losing my grasp on reality."[70]

"So true," said Theresa as she and the other ladies shook their heads acquiescingly; all except Mary Higgins, who sat at the table completely silent and stared into her coffee cup. Never once attempting to make eye contact with the captain.

"But we really must see you more often, Captain Todd," said Lydia. "Why my husband, Mr. Collins, was just asking about you the other day. You two had quite the 'bromance' going on when we were out at sea and I'm sure he'd love to catch up with you, as well. In fact, it's actually fantastic timing running into you today. I was planning on throwing a

---

70   If at any point you begin to show up to events wearing a paper bag on your head like ole' Shia did then it's about that time to really start evaluating your relationship with sanity.

small dinner party at our cottage next week and it would be quite splendid if you could attend, what do you say?"

Mary's fixation on her coffee cup finally broke and she shot Lydia such a scorching glare it could've melted the ice around Bill O'Reilly's heart. It was the kind of look a parent gives a child when they're misbehaving during church service. It was the kind of look that tacitly says, *Wait until we get home. Your ass is grass!*

Unfortunately for Mary, her heated stare went completely unnoticed because the rest of the women at the table were completely enamored by the presence of the devilishly handsome Captain Todd.

"Oh that sounds great, I'd be happy to attend. Thank you for the invitation, Mrs. Collins," the captain politely answered.

"Fantastic, I'll have an invitation sent your way tomorrow with all the details," said Lydia.

"I'm looking forward to it," Captain Todd said enthusiastically. "Well ladies, I must sadly bid you farewell. I have more than a few errands to run today before it gets much colder outside. I hope all of you have a great day."

All of the women at the table gave the captain a cheerful goodbye as he made his way toward the center of the village; all of them except Mary of course, who gave a cold and careless wave as he departed.

"Now ladies, that is one fine specimen of a man," said Ester as she emphatically pretended to fan herself from the heat vapors that had overtaken her from the captain's presence.

"Bitch, who are you telling?" Theresa agreed. "I'm afraid to stand up off this chair because I know there's going to be a puddle left behind because of that man. His sheer presence makes a bitch hella moist!"[71]

They all let out a loud burst of laughter. All except Mary, who sat there and rolled her eyes at the crude joke.

---

71   W.A.S.P. Translation: I would give a detailed explanation as to what it means when Theresa says that she's "hella moist" because of the captain's presence but I'm fairly certain it's pretty self-explanatory enough. And I'm quite certain my mother would wash my mouth out with soap if I even attempted to.

"Tell me about it," interjected Lydia. "You ladies know I'm a devote Christian woman, but that's one man I wouldn't mind creeping between the sheets with. I'd sacrifice my eternal and peaceful slumber in the heavens for a roll in the hay with that sexy mofo."

"You got that right," said Theresa. "What about you, Mary? Don't you think he's hot as hell?"

"Me?" questioned Mary very offensively. "Firstly, I'm a married Christian woman who fully respects her vows so I don't look at other men in that way. Let's have a little decorum, ladies."

The rest of the women at the table glanced between each other and hung their heads in shame from their reprimanding.

"Secondly, any man that is his age and still lives the single lifestyle throws up some major red flags in my opinion. He's either got some major commitment issues or he's secretly a raging homo. That's probably why we haven't seen him in so long; he's probably been prancing and dancing around his cottage in feathers and Louboutins like Johnny Weir.[72] Either way, there's no reason a group of godly women should be getting wet over a man like that. Plus I hear he's a big fan of the drink as well so who wants to deal with that?"

"Well, in all fairness, he is a sea captain," said Ester. "Show me a sea captain who isn't a lover of the drink and I'll show you an impeccable Asian driver; it just doesn't exist."

Mary rolled her eyes in annoyance. "Oh please Ester, how do you think it is that we first hit land all the way up here and not our original destination further south in Virginia? Clearly the man was slizzard on that sizzurp when he was making his trajectory. We may as well have let Lil' Wayne steer the damn ship."[73]

---

72   One must really love Johnny Weir, the ultra-flamboyant figure skater. He really has no shame whatsoever. He looks like the by-product of a love affair between Lady Gaga and Liberace.

73   Lil Wayne is allegedly an avid fan of the notorious "sizzurp" drink, which consists of Promethazine with Codeine syrup, fruit-flavored soda, and a Jolly Rancher. Who needs a Martini with a fresh olive when you can get wasted on a glass of Nyquil with a cherry-flavored hard candy as garnishment? Oh the things rich people do.

"I suppose there is a bit of truth to that," said Ester. "But the man is still handsome. You have to admit that much."

"He's no Bradley Cooper, that's all I'll say about the matter," Mary replied. "And Lydia, I cannot believe you invited him to the dinner party. What are we going to do with a raging drunk attending our gathering? Why stop at Captain Todd, maybe you should invite Snookie and J-Wow while you're at it. Why don't we go all out and have Tara Reid host the damn event."

Mary's extreme distaste for the captain bewildered her friends. What had he done to piss her off so wholeheartedly? They had never seen her act so seething over a matter.

"Well I don't think he's that bad," Lydia said defensively. "I don't think I've ever seen him belligerently drunk and he's never been anything but sweet and humble to my husband and I. I don't really see the big deal about him attending the dinner."

"I have to agree with Lydia," said Theresa. "He's always been extremely pleasant to my family as well. And, just between us girls, I can only hope he's a raging queen like you suggested; my hair has been so dry and lifeless lately, maybe he'll know a good conditioning treatment to give it some va-va-voom!"

Mary shook her head in complete disgust.

"Mary, where is this coming from?" asked Ester. "I don't think we've ever seen you so vehemently against an individual before."

At that moment Mary knew she had played up her distaste for Captain Todd far too strong. She knew that by behaving the way that she had was only putting a spotlight on the type of relationship the two of them shared. She had to water down the situation before her friends began to raise questions that needn't be brought up. There was far too much to lose to allow that to happen.

"Oh it's nothing in particular," she answered very nonchalantly as she raised her coffee cup to her lips. "I suppose I may be exaggerating the situation a bit; please excuse my poor attitude. You must forgive me. I barely know the man, but I'm always a bit leery of those sea fellows. They always seem to be a bit ungodly if you ask me. But I suppose I should give him more of a chance."

The other women at the table seemed to be relieved that their friend had lightened up a bit about her opinion of the poor captain.

"Well I'm glad to hear that. I think it'll be interesting to have a sea captain over for dinner. Imagine the stories he'll have to share!" Lydia said excitedly. "I'm sure our husbands will love that."

"Indeed," said Theresa.

"Yes, I'm sure it'll be quite interesting," Mary agreed in an attempt to convince her friends she was open to the prospect of learning more about their newly invited guest.

Little did the rest of the ladies at the table know, but Mary already knew everything there was to know about the mysterious Captain Todd.

CHAPTER THREE

The day seemed to be never-ending for poor Emily Higgins. She placidly stared out the window of Old Lady Smith's cabin completely uninterested in her daily sewing class. Every afternoon, after their general studies with Mr. Teeter, she and her brother, Rupert, both attended trade courses that their parents thought would best suit them for career paths in the new world. Rupert went to a carpentry class where he practiced his woodworking skills and Emily attended a sewing course with Old Lady Smith.

Like most teenagers being forced to partake in classes for careers neither one of them truly wanted, Emily and Rupert basically put zero effort in attempting to learn their respective trades.

Emily knew that learning a trade like sewing would make her a huge commodity in the colony, but she just couldn't give a shit to be brutally honest. Not only did she find the entire act of sewing to be completely inane, but Old Lady Smith was basically the oldest living creature on the planet and her teaching style was anything but engaging for a teenage girl.

It was a daily occurrence for the old woman to fall asleep

midsentence or for loud elongated bursts of flatulence to escape her without even realizing she was doing it. The poor girls had been in the class for weeks and so far the only skill they'd managed to master was the art of putting the thread through the head of needle.

The only saving grace about taking the class was that Emily got to take it with her girls: Elizabeth Rondell and Lisa Stein. If Emily was going to be bored to tears than at least she'd be bored to tears with her two best friends.

Elizabeth, who was seated immediately to her left, reached out and whacked Emily on the arm to get her attention. "You know how I know there's no God?" she whispered.

"How's that?" Emily asked.

"Because if there was a God there's no way he would allow this old bag to continue torturing us with this class," she said as she placed her hands together in mock prayer. "Please God, she's ready to come home. Take her now."

Emily covered her mouth to contain her laugh from echoing throughout the room; not like it would have mattered much anyway, Old Lady Smith's hearing was so bad you could land a Boeing 747 in her backyard and she wouldn't flinch an inch.

"You're horrible," Emily said.

"Oh please, don't act like you haven't thought the same thing," Elizabeth giggled. "It's not my fault she was born during the Paleozoic period."

Emily reached over and playfully smacked her on the leg to shut her up. She could always depend on Elizabeth for a good laugh, even during the most inappropriate moments. But after what her parents had said about her earlier this morning she couldn't help but look at her a bit inquisitively today.

I wonder if Elizabeth really is a lesbo, she wondered as she looked at her butchy friend. *I've never really thought she could be until today. Not that I care either way; it's her personal life and she's still my friend so I'll always accept her, but I must say I am a bit curious now. Maybe people just think she is because she's built kind of like Rosie O'Donnell and her hair always looks a bit frayed and disheveled under her bonnet. And I suppose her hands are always a bit rough like she never moisturizes after gardening. And she doesn't really sit much like a lady; in fact, I've seen cross-country truckers who sit more elegantly than she does. She's also a bit obsessed with that plaid flannel dress she always wants to wear. By golly, Elizabeth actually is dykier than a Home Depot beauty queen! How didn't I notice this before?*

"What are you staring at?" Elizabeth asked.

The question took Emily by surprise. She didn't realize she was grilling Elizabeth so hard, "Huh? What do you mean?"

"You're looking at me like I have a third tit growing out of my shoulder. What's wrong?"

"Oh, it's nothing. I suppose I'm just daydreaming a bit. Old Lady Smith is boring me to tears today."

"You think you got it bad? Take a look at Susan Landon over there," she said as she pointed across the cabin towards Susan who was fast asleep in her chair with a long strand of drool leaking out of the side of her wide-opened mouth. "I haven't seen a bitch sleep so hard since I took my narcoleptic grandmother to see *Lincoln*. Snooooze."[74]

The two girls giggled under their breath.

"And even worse, look at little Suzy Homemaker in front of you," Elizabeth said as she pointed to Lisa Stein who was listening intently to Old Lady Smith's directions and clearly trying to get more out of the class than her two friends behind her. "Hey Lisa, how's the sewing going up there? You finally figure out how to do a cross-stitch yet?" Elizabeth teased.

"Eat me, bitch," Lisa responded without even turning around to fully acknowledge the shade Elizabeth was throwing. "You're just jealous."

---

74   The cure for insomnia; Steven Spielberg's *Lincoln* is a two-and-a-half-hour snoozefest that will knock you out quicker than an Ambien smoothie.

"Jealous?" Elizabeth said with a laugh. "Jealous of what? Jealous of the skills that Old Lady Smith is imparting on you? At the rate this old bitch is teaching you'll be able to sew your own dress by 1992."

Emily and Elizabeth knew that Lisa took their sewing class a lot more serious than they did. She fully intended to learn as much as she could about the trade so that she could become an asset in the colony and make her family proud. And as much as she loved her friends, she wasn't going to let their jokes sidetrack her from mastering the craft; especially since she knew she wasn't exactly the *prettiest* pilgrim in the land. If she ever had a chance of finding a good husband she was well aware that she had to bring a lot of supplementary talents to the table in order to make up for her lack of physical appeal. She figured becoming a master seamstress, learning how to bake a succulent-tasting chicken, and acquiring the skills to suck a dick with the same suction and gusto as a super-powered Dyson vacuum cleaner would provide her with the qualities needed to nab herself a good man to put a ring on it.

"Will you please hush Elizabeth, I'm trying to listen. You don't see me interrupting you when you're learning about mulch or whatever it is that you like."

"Mulch? Bitch, when do I ever learn about *mulch*?"

"Shhhhhhh, zip the lip," Lisa reprimanded as she finally turned around and stuck her index finger up to her lips to illustrate the universal symbol for *please shut the fuck up*.

"Alright, alright, alright, I got it," Elizabeth finally conceded as she put her hands to the air to surrender.

Emily couldn't help but laugh at her friend's interaction. They may not have been the most conventional group in the colony, but they certainly were funny and that's exactly what she needed at this moment in her life.

After her exchange with her parents earlier this morning all she could feel was immense stress. That's actually all she ever felt these days since they landed in this new world. Her family didn't understand her and she was convinced they never would. She was certainly the black sheep of the Higgins clan and everyone knew it. As if the daily rigors of being a teenager wasn't hard enough, now she was dealing with being ripped away from golly ole' England and thrown into uncharted territory where she was being forced to colonize a new settlement full of weirdos. What kind of bullshit was that about?

And while she loved Elizabeth and Lisa, she still couldn't help but miss her old friends and their life back home. But thanks to her insanely religious parents, she was now stuck in the middle of nowhere with no access to the things she loved (i.e. electric blue nail polish, cheap gold-plated accessories, a nearby MAC store, etc.) and the only home she'd ever known.

But there was no use crying over spilt milk. There wasn't much she could do about the situation at this point. Her parents had already made the decision and they couldn't care less about how she felt about it she thought to herself as she redirected her attention back towards the window.

As she stared out towards the woods her eyes caught a glimpse of someone in the distance. It was a boy. She could see that the he was attempting to be stealthy as he made his way deeper and deeper into the woods, peering around with each step to verify that no one had seen him.

Who the hell is that? she thought to herself as she squinted her hazel-hued eyes to make out the face of the mysterious figure.

Wait, is that…is that Rupert? Why it is him! Where the hell is he going? Now this is really strange, first he comes to class late this morning with shrubbery littered throughout his hair and now he's running off into the woods when he's supposed to be in his carpentry class learning how to make a birdhouse or whatever the hell it is those boys make in there. I have to figure out what that dipshit is up to before he gets himself into major trouble.

"Excuse me, Mrs. Smith," Emily bellowed as she stood up from her chair and placed her needle and thread back into her sewing basket. "Will you please excuse me early today, ma'am? I completely forgot I was supposed to go home early this evening to help my mother prepare for the winter storage."

Old Lady Smith peered around the cabin trying to figure out which young lady in the class was addressing her; she was horrible at distinguishing voices and since she had become blind as a bat she had no idea who was talking to her. "Who said that? Who needs to leave early?"

"It's Emily Higgins, Mrs. Smith. Over here ma'am, by the window," she responded as she waved her hands through the air as if she were directing a plane in for landing.

"Oh yes, Emily Higgins. Alright dear, you may leave a little early today. But don't forget to practice what you learned today when you get home, young lady."

"Of course, ma'am. Thank you."

Elizabeth and Lisa looked at Emily suspiciously. They knew when their friend was full of shit.

"Is everything okay?" Elizabeth leaned in closer and whispered to her friend.

"Oh yeah, it's all good. I just forgot that I promised my mother that I'd help her today. No biggie," Emily answered as calmly as possible. She didn't want to raise any red flags amongst her friends so she had to play it cool, but she needed to hurry up before Rupert's trail went cold. "But anyway, I'll hit you ho's up later tonight."

Emily grabbed her sewing basket and headed towards the door. She waited until she heard the door close all the way before she took off running like a bat out of hell towards the direction she last spotted Rupert.

I have to find that little asshole, she thought as she swerved between massive trees scattered throughout the woods. *He's going to get himself in major trouble, I can just feel it with every fiber of my being.*

Emily slowed down a bit once she reached the area she last laid eyes on her brother. She looked around in every direction, but he was nowhere in sight. She had been too late.

Shit! You slow ass bitch, you lost him! She scolded herself as she hung her head with the same disappointment and shame usually reserved for the proud Asian students who received "B's" on their report cards.

But then it caught her eye.

Out of the corner of her eye she caught a glimpse of a small red notebook lying open on the ground.

Emily rushed over to the book and lifted it off the ground. It was Rupert's journal. The same journal he never left the house without. The same journal he fiercely guarded with the same devotion that a fat person guards the cheese biscuit basket at Red Lobster. Wherever he was off to it was pretty clear that it must be important if he hadn't noticed he had accidentally abandoned the written extension of his soul.

Emily was tempted to flip the little red book open and start reading about every secret feeling her twin brother had ever put down on paper, but she wasn't finished with her mission-at-hand just yet. She tucked the journal deep into the bottom of her sewing basket underneath a plethora of fabrics and started off again further into the woods closest to where she found the book.

Emily ran for what felt like an eternity.

She peered in every direction looking for Rupert. She seemed to be searching for the one thing that was impossible to find; she felt like Tori Spelling in search of a reputable feature film role. It just wasn't materializing for her.

She went deeper and deeper into the dense forest until she finally had to stop to catch her breath and rest. She leaned against one of the massive tree trunks that seemed to be growing uncomfortably closer and closer the deeper she went into the wooded labyrinth.

As she bent over and placed her hands on her knees to focus on her breathing she began to hear something strange in the distance, it sounded like the crunching of dried leaves. *What the hell is that?* she thought as she stood up and concentrated all her attention on the area where the sound had originated.

O-M-G, what if it's a fucking bear? What if I came out into this damned woods trying to protect my idiotic brother and end up getting eaten by Smokey the Bear? This is why bitches should just mind their own business! I should have just kept sewing my little bonnets and aprons in Old Lady Smith's cabin like a proper colonial girl, but no, a bitch had to get all adventurous and head off into the woods like I was Bear Grylls or something.

Emily continued to scold herself as she slowly and cautiously made her way towards the noise. She knew that she should probably be heading in the opposite direction just in case it was a bear or some other flesh-hungry predator ready to devour her, but her curiosity had been peaked and she had to know what it was.

As she got closer she could hear the rustling noise of the leaves getting more intense with each step. It wasn't until she was within a few feet of the commotion that she realized this may not have been the smartest idea; she tightly grabbed ahold of her sewing basket and squeezed it as a way to release some of the fear and stress that was beginning to bubble out of her body. Right in front of her she could see a bed of leaves and foliage moving about, but a tight grouping of trees prevented her from seeing exactly what was causing the movement.

Emily backed up to one of the larger trees to keep herself concealed from the mysterious culprit. As she gradually began to peek around the side of the gigantic tree trunk she realized it wasn't a blood-thirsty bear making all the ruckus, in fact, it actually wasn't an animal at all she quickly learned. Rather, it was two people ferociously making out with one another right there on the grounds of the forest.

Emily carefully surveyed the couple. She could immediately surmise the female involved was a native girl based on her clothing (or lack thereof), but she had to focus her vision to see who the male pawing at the girl like a badger in heat was.

That's when Emily's jaw dropped in shock.

"WHAT THE FUCK DO YOU THINK YOU'RE DOING,

RUPERT?" Emily yelled as she came out from behind the tree, completely disrupting the woodland tryst.

Rupert and Princess LaQuintia shockingly stared up at Emily as she bombarded into the illicit love-nest the two of them had created. They had been so certain that they had snuck off into the wilderness without being noticed; the last thing they had anticipated was being caught, especially by Rupert's sister of all people.

"Emily, what the hell are you doing out here?" Rupert questioned as he rose to his feet.

"Oh no, you're not the one *asking* questions right now Rupert! You've got some explaining to do, buddy! Have you lost your fucking mind, dear brother? Don't you realize how bat-shit crazy mom and dad are going to go when they find out you're gallivanting around the wilderness with some savage slut like her?" Emily said forcefully as she pointed at Princess LaQuintia who was still sitting on the ground rearranging her suede skirt back into place. Needless to say she was none to happy to be spoken about in such a disparaging manner.

"Excuse me, what did you call me?" Princess LaQuintia asked as she rose to her feet and stepped toward Emily. "I don't know who you think you're talking to bitch, but I'm not the one to play with!"

"Don't test me, Sacagawea!" Emily snapped right back at her. "My brother may have the hots for you, but that doesn't mean I won't pull a Chris Brown on you and beat your ass right here in the middle of the forest!"

"Oh hell no!" said LaQuintia as she raced toward Emily ready to come to blows with the twin sister of her lover.

Rupert rushed between the two girls in an attempt to break up the impending *Jerry Springer*-esque brawl that was about to ensue. Normally he wouldn't have dared to interfere with a potential girl fight (especially one where his sister might have some sense knocked into her), but he knew his shameful secret had caused this and he couldn't help but feel guilty.

"Girls, girls, girls! Chill the hell out!" he yelled as he scooped up LaQuintia and pulled her away from Emily. "Nobody is fighting anybody!"

"That bitch started it," said LaQuintia as she gave Emily a death stare from over Rupert's shoulder.

"No hussy, you started it by seducing my innocent brother with your native voodoo magic!" Emily venomously bellowed at her opponent. "We know all about the evil magic you and your people practice! What kind of ungodly coochie-worshiping spell have you put this poor boy under?"

"Emily, that's enough!" interrupted Rupert. "She didn't seduce me with voodoo magic. She's a good woman and I love her very much."

Emily stared at her brother in disbelief. In that moment she didn't recognize her own twin at all. He had seemingly become a stranger to her.

"Love her? Rupert, do you hear yourself?" she questioned. "She's a *savage*, how can you say you love such a lesser being?"

"Emily, dear sister, that's such a ridiculous thing to say. Princess LaQuintia is one of the most pure and beautiful people I've ever met and I know you would feel the same way if you got to know her a bit. I beg of you to give her a chance," Rupert pleaded as the tears began to well up in his eyes.

"Princess? Oh, so you went ahead and found yourself a savage princess, did you?" Emily said sarcastically. "What's she the princess of, exactly? Corn? Maybe she's the trail-mix princess? Where's your turquoise crown, your majesty?"

"No bitch, I'm the princess of ass-whoopings so keep talking shit if you want a royal beatdown!" LaQuintia quickly snapped back.

Emily didn't like Princess LaQuintia but she respected her gangsta qualities. Had she not been whoring around with her twin brother in the middle of the woods she might have been a girl of Emily's own heart.

"Emily, please stop it. I'm being serious, I truly do love her. We've been secretly seeing one another for months now and I'm quite convinced that the beautiful princess is my soulmate. We've wanted to tell everyone, but we both know how much dissension it would cause between our respective communities. I know you may not understand it at this very moment, but please believe me when I say that she and I are meant to be together."

Emily eyed her twin up and down trying to figure out what kind of game he was playing at. *He can't honestly expect me to believe he loves this nature jezebel, does he? There's no way he's being serious. Doesn't he realize the kind of rift this would surely cause for the colony?* A million thoughts were racing through her head as she tried to make sense of all the information that had just flooded her senses within the past few minutes. And as much as she wanted to believe there wasn't a chance in hell that her brother could be in love with a native girl, she could see in his tear-filled eyes that he was telling the truth.

"Rupert, I just don't understand what's going on," Emily said as her eyes darted back and forth between him and his lover. "How did this even come about?"

"Well, Princess LaQuintia and I first came across each other in these very woods one scorching hot summer day when I was taking a scenic walk towards the shore to enjoy the breeze," Rupert began as he reached out and grabbed ahold of his lover's hand. "I encountered LaQuintia collecting some fruits and berries for her tribe and while I knew we had always been told to steer clear of the natives, much like an Italian turning down carbs, I just simply couldn't do it. I had to introduce myself to her. And from that moment on our friendship began to bloom. We began to secretly sneak off and meet each other in the woods where we would talk for long hours at a time about any and everything in our lives. Before we knew it our friendship evolved into love and we couldn't resist being together. I know this is hard for you to comprehend right now Emily, especially since our differences are stacked so strongly against us, but you must please try to understand that we're very much in love."

Emily knew her brother was being forthright and honest, but he wasn't the one she was necessarily worried about. "And what about you, *princess*?" she asked as she locked eyes with LaQuintia. "Do you feel as strongly about my brother as he of you?"

"Very much so," she calmly answered as she gave Rupert's hand a tight squeeze. "You must understand we didn't expect this to happen, but we aren't ashamed that it has."

"You know your little love story is quite beautiful and all, but do you two realize what could occur if you continue down this road?" Emily asked as she threw her sewing basket down on the ground and crossed her arms across her chest. "Life isn't some romantic comedy like in the films where a young Matthew McConaughey would be cast to play Rupert and, presumably, an intensely spray-tanned Kate Hudson would be chosen to play you, Princess LaQuesha…"

"Actually, it's LaQuintia," the princess snarled.

"Whatever your highness, you're missing the point," Emily said. "Rupert, you know our parents would go on a holy rampage if they ever found out you where shacking up with a native girl; they'd lose their shit! And *LaQuintia*, while I don't know enough about your culture to be certain, I'd assume your father, the chief of a tribe, would be none too happy finding out his daughter had been getting felt up by some hormonal teenage white boy in the middle of the woods. And by the way, real *classy* there princess."

"You're exactly right, I don't disagree at all," said LaQuintia. "But Rupert and I already know that, which is why we've worked so hard at keeping our relationship such a secret. We don't want the ignorant and racist bigots like yourself to try to rip us apart."

"Racist? Me, a racist?" Emily said, shocked. "Please, I'm the furthest thing from a racist. My ex-boyfriend, Dondrell, was from Trinidad, thank you very much. And my brother can date who he damn well pleases for all I care; as Rupert will fully attest to, I had no problem when he got caught finger-banging that Filipino foreign exchange student at last year's homecoming dance. I have no problem with the swirl, but what I *do* have a problem with is a potential sister-in-law with no sense of breeding who walks around barefoot like some sort of prehistoric cavewoman."[75]

"That's not fair Emily, you don't even know her to make those kinds of ridiculous judgments," Rupert defensively chimed in.

"No Rupert, she's right," said LaQuintia as she released Rupert's hand. "This is exactly why I never wanted us to go public with our love. No matter how much we hope and pray, our respective people will never bless a union like ours. What hope do we have if your own sister is so vehemently against us? Maybe, much like the great love between J.Lo and Ben Affleck, or more commonly known to the general public as 'Bennifer,' our love was only meant to last a limited amount of time."

Rupert was shocked. He hadn't expected LaQuintia to throw in the towel so easily. "What are you saying?"

"I'm simply saying that maybe it was a blessing from the Gods that your sister discovered us today," she said. "Maybe we should take this as a sign that our time together should come to an end before greater conflicts begin to ensue."

"I can't believe you're saying such fuckery, LaQuintia!" Rupert exclaimed. "How can you just decide on a whim like that to end our glorious relationship?"

"No Rupert, she's making the smartest decision possible," Emily interrupted as she tried to convince her brother that this would be the best possible outcome for everyone involved.

"Emily, with all due respect sister, please shut the fuck up!" he yelled. "LaQuintia, please, you know within the confines of your heart that this is wrong. You can't let the fear of ignorance tear us apart. The bond we've created is stronger than that."

"But that's just it Rupert, I don't want what we've created to

---

75   W.A.S.P. Translation: The "swirl" refers to those individuals engaging in an interracial relationship. See Nick Cannon and Mariah Carey, John Legend and Chrissy Teigen, Khloe Kardashian and (insert random NBA player name here).

become tainted and tarnished by the unjust forces of the world, and as much as we like to think it won't, just like your sister says, it's a foolish idea to think it won't eventually turn us against one another. It may not happen today, or tomorrow, or even next year, but at some point our differences would make it too hard to function any longer and I care far too much about you to ever let that happen," LaQuintia said as she gently stroked his cheek and planted a kiss on his forehead. "I'm sorry my love, but I must go now. This hurts far too much to prolong it any further."

LaQuintia turned on her heels and ran off further into the woods. Rupert and Emily watched as she disappeared amongst the trees and seemingly out of their lives, forever.

Emily walked over to her brother and placed her hand on his shoulder, "I know it hurts a lot right now dipshit, but trust me this was the best thing that could have happened."

Rupert sharply shrugged his sister's hand off of him. He turned around and glared at her with the type of pure disdain that was only comparable to the way John Boehner looks during one of President Obama's State of the Union addresses.[76]

"This is all your fault, Emily! I shall never forgive you for what has transpired in these woods today. Thanks to your meddling the love of my life is now gone and I'll never see her again."

"I know you don't understand it right now, but my meddling has surely saved both you and your lover's lives. In time you'll see that it was for the best."

Rupert wasn't trying to hear any of that foolery at the moment. He scooped up his notebooks off the ground and ran back toward the colony. The way he was feeling at the moment, if he never heard his sister's voice again it would be far too soon.

As Emily stood there all by herself in the middle of the forest she began to fiddle with the thick gold nameplate necklace that adorned

---

76   Doesn't John Boehner's face remind you of a villain in *Harry Potter*? It always seems like he has stank face like he just took a fresh whiff of fart.

her neck and contemplated what had just occurred; while she knew it had to be done, she couldn't help but feel a bit guilty after seeing how hurt Rupert had become over the situation. She had seen him break-up with random chicks in the past, but he had never reacted in such a way. Maybe he did in fact love the native princess. *Could that even be possible?* she wondered.

Whatever, she thought to herself as she shrugged with indifference and grabbed her sewing basket off the ground to proceed with her walk home. She couldn't distinguish if she felt bad because she had aided in the breaking of her twin brother's heart or if it was because her nerdy sibling was actually getting laid more often than she was these days.

CHAPTER FOUR

Nearly five days had passed since Mary Higgins' awkward interaction with Captain Todd in front of her friends, and now it was the night of Lydia Collins' dinner party. It was the event she had anxiously wanted to avoid for the better part of the week. But it was something she couldn't run from any longer. She and Baxter were going to have to attend this dinner and sit across from the man who had the capability to not only ruin her Christian reputation but also demolish everything she had worked so hard to build. Every single move of the evening needed to be meticulously planned out to avoid any potential surprises.

Mary stood in front of the mirror in her bedroom and gripped tightly to the cross around her neck. She closed her eyes and began to pray.

Dear Lord, please give me the strength I need to get through this evening. You know that I live my life in your service and always try to be the best Christian woman possible. As I prepare to head out in the world this evening and face the consequences for the sins I have partaken in, I ask you to watch over and protect me from the evil temptations the devil may put before me. I may have faltered in the past, but it only made my faith stronger. I continue to ask for your forgiveness and allow for me to continue to serve you; and if you were willing to give Robert Downey Jr. so many chances that should be a breeze. Amen.

Mary opened her eyes and stared at her reflection. *I can do this,* she thought to herself. She gently smoothed out her gray dress and made sure her bonnet was placed perfectly center on her head. She looked every bit the proper pilgrim wife. It was time to go now.

She walked out of the room and into the kitchen where Baxter and the kids were waiting for her.

"Have you finally finished pampering yourself in there?" asked Baxter as he looked up at his wife as she entered the room.

"Yes, I'm ready. How about you two?" she asked as she gave her children an inquisitive look. "Have you children brushed your teeth and washed up? I won't have kids of mine going to a dinner party smelling like the cast of *Duck Dynasty*."[77]

"Do you honestly think I'd step out the house looking *and* smelling anything less than amazing, mother?" said Emily as she blew a bubble with her chewing gum and fiddled with the assorted gold rings that adorned her fingers.

"Lose the chewing gum, Britney Spears. You aren't leaving this house chewing on that shit like a cow grazing in the meadow. And what about you, Rupert?"

"Yeah, I'm clean," he carelessly answered without even lifting his head up to make eye contact with his mother.

"Rupert, I know you think this whole teenage angst thing you've got going on is cute, but I expect you to at least attempt to be social this evening," said Mary. "You've barely spoken four words over the past week and it's getting to be a bit trite. I've been biting my tongue but I must ask if something in particular is bothering you, son?"

Emily turned her head and shot her brother a look of concern.

---

77   Otherwise known as the cousins that Santa Claus wants nothing to do with.

She was the only one in the room who knew the reason why Rupert was acting like his puppy had just got ran over by an AmTrak train. He had sunk into a depression since the woodland demise of his relationship with Princess LaQuintia and had barely spoken to anyone over the past few days.

"Give him a break, mother," Emily said as she came to the defense of her twin. "He's just on his period, leave the nerd alone."

Mary and Baxter exchanged a suspicious glance. They knew something was going on with their children; Emily would rarely miss an opportunity to throw Rupert under the bus for her own amusement, and the fact that she was now seemingly coming to his defense set off a multitude of red flags.

"Whatever the reason is, I also expect you to take the stick out of your ass for the evening and try to be personable," said Baxter. "While I find these dinners to be the equivalent of a colonoscopy sans any lube, it's important to your mother so I want nothing but the best behavior out of the two of you, understood?"

Rupert and Emily both shook their heads in compliance with their father's request.

"Alright then, let's be on our way. We don't want to be the last ones to arrive," said Mary. "And Emily, I expect that you'll remove those earrings before you leave this house. We're going to a dinner party, not a Quinceanera."

When the Higgins clan arrived at the Collins home nearly everyone had already arrived for dinner, everyone except Captain Todd.

Mary breathed a temporary sigh of relief. *Maybe he decided not to attend the dinner after all?* She thought to herself as she graciously socialized with the other attendees. *Maybe the dear lord answered my prayers and gave him Bird Flu or cholera. Oh, how ideal would that be!*

But Mary knew not to get too excited just yet; Lydia told her the captain had promptly RSVP'ed to the invite she had sent over to his cabin and that he was probably just running a little late.

So with the prospect that he still might show up, Mary went about her business as to not draw any more attention to the subject of the missing captain. She stayed close to her husband and kept a close eye on her children to make sure they were behaving like the well-behaved kids she had taught them to pretend to be.

"Lydia, I must say the cabin looks spectacular and these hors d'oeuvre's you've prepared are quite delicious," Mary complimented the hostess as she sampled all the savory treats she had laid out for her guests. "I'm going to have to steal the recipe for those deviled eggs from you before the night is over. Aren't they just splendid, Baxter?"

"Yes, they're very good, but I think I'm more impressed with this gin and tonic," her husband said dryly as he took another swig from his glass.

"I'll second that," said Lydia's husband, Sam. "Half the reason I married her was because she's a licensed liquor wench."

"You hush your mouth, Samuel Collins," said Lydia with a giggle. "I had to pay my way through university one way or another and bar wench's get paid a pretty penny in tips. I paid for my B.A. by mixing Long Island Ice Teas and I'm proud of it."

Sam planted a kiss on his wife's cheek. "She's the best, isn't she? Who would have ever thought I would have met my saintly wife while she was slinging drinks at the local pub? And who says you can't turn a ho into a housewife?"[78]

"Oh pish-posh to that philosophy, Mr. Collins," said Lydia. "There's nothing in the good book that says a woman can't be a godly woman in the streets and a ho between the sheets."[79]

"Amen to that," he said as he gleamed with pride at his wife.

Mary chuckled at the couple's playful banter. She wondered why

---

78   Just look at Christina Aguilera.
79   Mother Theresa's most famous mantra. No, totally kidding. Don't quote me on that.

she and Baxter never had that kind of lighthearted relationship where they could flirt with one another in public. While she felt P.D.A. was incredibly tacky and unseemly, especially for a good Christian woman like herself, she sometimes felt a little innocent flirtation between them would be quite nice. But she knew who Baxter Higgins was, and she knew that wasn't the type of man she married. His stern demeanor had never posed a problem for her during their marriage, but there were certainly moments where her mind would wander and she'd wonder what life would have been like had she made different decisions; moments where she'd wonder which direction her life would have gone in had she followed her heart and not her head.

It took a boisterous knock on the sturdy wood door to bring Mary back to reality and out of her romanticized thoughts about a life unlived.

"Looks like our missing captain has finally arrived. Will you please excuse us while we let him in," Lydia said excitedly as she and Sam made their way towards the front door.

Mary swallowed hard as she watched the captain enter the cabin and greet the hosts of the evening.

Fuck! I knew it was too good to be true. You couldn't have just given the bastard a case of leprosy for the evening? She thought to herself as she raised her eyes to the sky as if she were having a one-on-one conversation with God. She grabbed the gin and tonic out of her husband's hand and proceeded to gulp it down until the glass was empty. Mary knew she was going to need a minor buzz to get through this dinner.

Baxter looked at his wife in amazement. "Since when does my wife drink alcohol? I thought you hated booze?"

"Hey, even Jesus needed a wine buzz every now and again," she said as she handed him back the empty glass and scurried off to go chat with Ester.

As the two ladies made superfluous small talk about everything from how lovely Lydia's living room rug was to how yummy her deviled eggs were (though they both snidely agreed under their breath that she had been far too liberal with the dill this time around), Mary made sure she was always within an earshot of Captain Todd. She stealthily monitored the enigmatic figure out of the corner of her eye as he worked the room and mingled with the other guests. It seemed as though everyone in the room was clamoring for the opportunity for some face time with Captain Todd; he seamlessly went from conversation to conversation, charming each and every person in the room with various anecdotes of his past and the time he spent out at sea. If Mary hadn't been utterly paranoid about his motives she would've been thoroughly impressed with the man's social skills that's for damn sure.

There even came a *very* brief second where Mary actually wished she were conversing with Captain Todd rather than to be suffering with the current discussion she was enduring. She had been enjoying a perfectly nice, and shady, conversation with Ester about how dated Lydia's window treatments looked, when Timothy, Ester's husband, interjected himself into their discussion and proceeded to wax poetic about his love for the oak flooring and all the wonders of the miraculous wood material. While Mary loved Ester, and thought of her as one of her dearest friends, she found Timothy to be drier than a box of Triscuits.

Just then, seemingly out of nowhere, Mary began to feel a rush of dizziness overtake her. She wasn't sure if it was the gin and tonic she had guzzled down earlier, the anxiety of her entire family being so close to Captain Todd, or trying so hard to fain interest in Timothy's ridiculous wood monologue, but she knew she needed to step away from the crowd for a moment to get her bearings.

"If you two would please excuse me, I'm going to run to the ladies room for a second," she said as she stood up from the living room couch and made her way towards the restroom.

Mary assumed she had exited the room in the most ladylike fashion, making sure no one noticed she was en route to the bathroom; but there was one pair of eyes in the room that had clocked her movements just like the way an NBA player spots a blonde-haired groupie who's D.T.F. during All-Star Weekend.[80]

Mary stepped into the bathroom and leaned against the counter as she closed her eyes and took in several deep breaths. After a few minutes of calm silence the dizzy feeling began to subside. She opened her eyes and looked at herself in the mirror. Beads of anxiety-induced sweat had begun to form on her temples.

Get your shit together, bitch! She thought to herself as she wiped her forehead. *You got this! You got this! No weapon formed against you shall prosper!* She stood up straight and took in one final big breath before she reached for the door handle and swung it open to find the man of her dreams/nightmares waiting on the other side.

"Captain Todd, what are you doing?" Mary said, startled, as she stood frozen in the doorway.

"Oh would you cool it with the whole 'Captain Todd' bullshit, Mary. You can kill the false formalities when none of your friends are around," he softly said to her as he leaned in closer. "You know you can call me James, just like you always used to."

Mary had been trying to play it as cool as she could up until this point, but now Captain Todd was getting too close for comfort. She quickly grabbed ahold of his well-toned arm and pulled him into the bathroom and closed the door behind them.

"James, I don't know what kind of game you're playing at lately, but you and I have had an agreement and you know damn well what you're doing right now is against the rules."

Captain Todd hung his head in sadness. He looked like a child that had just been scolded for coloring on his bedroom walls with crayons.

"Don't you think I know that, Mary?" he solemnly muttered. "Don't you think I'm aware that you and I are supposed to be pretending

---

80   NBA All-Star Weekend: the holy mecca for gold-diggers from sea to shining sea.

as though we're complete strangers? Don't you think I know that I'm supposed to behave as though I don't love you? Like I haven't loved you every single day for almost 20 years."

"Oh sweet Jesus, James. Do you even hear yourself right now? Have you been washing your meds down with bourbon again? I think I forgot how bloody emotional you are."

"Don't make fun of me, Mary. You know that I love you. You know that I've always loved you. And I also know that you feel exactly the same way about me."

"James, I most certainly do not."

"Is that so?" he questioned. "I don't believe that for a second. I saw your reaction aboard the ship when you first spotted me at the helm before we took off from England. I know that look very well. It was the look of love. I know that because it's the same way I look at you every time I'm in your presence."

"Listen James, a part of me will always have feelings for you. The week we spent together in Devon was magical, but you knew that I was already betrothed to marry Baxter back then. The brief affair that we engaged in was nothing more than a pre-wedding fling; you were nothing more than a jump-off, boo.[81] I was weak, and sadly I let my faith waiver and allowed the evil influence of adultery take over me. But it was a mistake James. A mistake that I regret every single day of my life."

"But how can you say it was a mistake when fate has seemed to reunite us almost 16 years later?" he asked as he reached out to grab ahold of her hands. "Don't you see Mary, this is the universe bringing us back together after all these years apart. It's God's will being done."

Mary yanked her hands out of his and looked up at him with fire in her eyes. "Don't you ever say that you and I are God's will; God had nothing to do with what transpired between the two of us. If anything, it's

81   W.A.S.P. Translation: A "jump-off" is a mistress or gigilo that one keeps on the side for strictly sexual purposes whilst you're in a relationship. Which, in turn, makes you a low-class skuzz-bucket for having a "jump-off" in the first place.

Lucifer putting us to the test to see if we'll falter all over again."

Captain Todd stared deep into her eyes. He could see the hatred brewing in the once jubilant, chestnut-colored eyes he had loved to get lost in. The guilt of what happened between them had obviously been haunting his lover for far longer than he realized. It had changed her. Just like the way Aretha Franklin clings to the last succulent, all-white meat drumstick in a bucket of KFC, he could see that Mary now clung tightly to her faith as a means of retribution for what had gone on between them.[82]

"Well Mary, if that's how you truly feel then I shall leave you be; the last thing I've wanted to do is hurt you with my presence," he calmly said to her. "If you tell me that Baxter Higgins is the one that you truly love I shall leave you alone forever."

"Yes James, my husband is the one that I love and he is the one that I will always love. I'm sorry if that hurts your feelings, but it's the truth."

"I understand," said Captain Todd as he slowly shook his head in compliance. "Does Baxter know the truth?"

Mary placed her hands on her hips and squinted her eyes in annoyance. "Seriously? Are you being for real right now? Why would Baxter know about what occurred between us? I've spent my entire marriage keeping our *brief* affair a secret from him and that's how I plan on keeping it."

"I wasn't referring to that, Mary. Let me rephrase my question, does Baxter know that Emily and Rupert aren't his children?"

Mary's jaw dropped.

A flood of emotions washed over her, she couldn't believe what she had just heard. She had never felt this much pure, unadulterated anger coursing through her body before.

"What did you say to me?" she said as she reached out and grabbed ahold of Captain Todd's shirt. "I cannot believe you would ask

---

82   Aretha isn't about to let that bad-boy go. Don't even try it.

me such a ridiculous question."

"Mary, do you think I don't see myself in those children? How bloody dense do you take me for?" he asked as he removed her grasp on his shirt. "The moment I saw those kids board the ship it was like staring at myself in a mirror. I know you got pregnant shortly after you and Baxter wed, and since you and I were together the week prior it's highly plausible that I could be the father of the twins. Those are my children aren't they Mary?"

Mary Higgins was speechless.

She couldn't believe she was being asked the one question that she had spent the last 16 years denying to herself; she refused to believe that God would be vengeful enough to punish her in such a harsh way for a sin she had felt so guilty about committing.

But ultimately, Mary had always known that what Captain Todd was saying was indeed the truth. Every time she looked into her children's eyes she saw him. She saw him in Emily's rebellious spirit. She saw him in Rupert's pure, unfiltered emotion. The very characteristics that drew her to him in the first place would end up being the same traits that would haunt her on a daily basis as she watched her children grow into adulthood.

"Listen to me very closely James," Mary calmly said as she walked right up to his face. "I don't know what you *think* you know about my family, but you're so unbelievably wrong. Baxter Higgins is, and always will be, the father of my children. I'm not sure what you're trying to do by making claims like that but for your own good I would cease such foolery."

Captain Todd could see that she was fuming with anger. "Mary, I wasn't trying to upset you, but I need to know if…"

Mary reached up and slapped him across the face with such an almighty force that it would have made *Dynasty*'s Alexis Carrington gleam with pride. "God damn you, James! What did I literally *just* say to you? I let you smash my goodies to smithereens once or twice without a rubber and now you think you can come claim stake on my children some

16 years later? I think not, playa! Now I won't tolerate anymore of this ridiculous conversation and I don't want it ever brought up again."

Captain Todd was shocked that his beloved Mary would actually strike him in such a manner. He had always remembered her as being a soft and caring creature; it was evident that he had struck a nerve with his claims.

"You can deny it all you want Mary, but I want a paternity test to determine the truth," he said.

"A paternity test, how dare you ask such an asinine request?" Mary venomously spewed at him. "This isn't the fucking *Maury* show, James. You'll sooner see Paris Hilton win a Pulitzer Prize before I grant you the opportunity to put my children through such an ordeal."

"You can fight it all you want Mary, but we both know the truth and I *will* be a part of my children's lives whether you like it or not. You've kept this dark secret from everyone for all these years and for that you should be ashamed of yourself," he said. The last thing Captain Todd wanted to do was to resort to threats, but this situation had played out very differently than he had originally anticipated it would. He had naively thought his love for Mary would be reciprocated upon their reunion, but she was making it abundantly clear that she had no intention of bringing their relationship back to life. "I'm going to give you 48 hours to make it happen or else I'm going to Baxter with the information myself."

Mary looked at him in disbelief.

The world she had worked so hard to keep together all these years was crumbling to pieces in a matter of minutes.

She turned her back to the captain and leaned against the bathroom counter with her head bowed. The dizzy feeling was coming back to her. Mary had to breath deeply to regain her composure before this conversation went any further.

"Listen Mary, I don't mean to upset you but I think I have a right to…"

Mary knew that Captain Todd was speaking to her, but at a certain point it all just started to sound like static. All she could see was black. She had never been so angry in her entire life. At that moment the rage had overtaken her. There was no way she was going to allow him to destroy her family.

Mary reached out and grabbed ahold of the heavy metallic soap dish that lay next to the basin; she mustered up every molecule of strength she had and swung it around with such force that when the blow struck the captain on the temple it caused him to fly backwards and bang his head on the corner of the metal bathtub.

As she stood there in complete silence, still holding the blood-splattered soap dish, she stared down at the lifeless body of her one-time lover. Several minutes passed before Mary was able to bring herself back to reality and realize what had just occurred. As she knelt down next to Captain Todd's body she began to viciously shake him, hoping that she had simply knocked him unconscious, but when she spotted the expanding pool of blood forming around his head she knew that his fate had been sealed.

Good lord, what have I done? She thought to herself as she stood up and backed away from him. *I've just killed a man. I've just killed the father of my children. Sweet Jesus, what if someone heard the commotion?*

Mary reached for the door handle and cracked it open just far enough to make sure no one had heard the scuffle. She eyed the vacant hallway and saw no one. From the living room she could hear that Lydia had just put on a Lil Jon record so there was no way anyone in there could've possibly heard any noise from the bathroom over that loud ass mess.[83]

She closed the door behind her and went into immediate panic mode. *What the hell am I going to do? Dear lord, how did I let this happen?*

---

83   People do realize that Lil Jon is basically just yelling at them in every song, right? Like, you're actually paying money for a song where a man is yelling at you at the top of his lungs. Like, quite literally, yelling at you.

It wasn't me who did this horrific act. It was the devil! He took over my body once again! God, how could I have been so weak to let him influence me all over again. I'm a good Christian woman, you know that lord!

As Mary stood in the bathroom next to the dead body of the man with whom she shared her darkest secrets with and bartered with God over the sin she just committed, she came to the realization that there was no way anyone in the other room was going to understand her rationale for what had just occurred.

There's no way I'm going to be able to get out of this situation without being hung from a tree, she thought to herself as tears began to stream down her cheeks. *I need to come up with a plausible excuse for why I had to strike him. But what? What could I possibly say to justify killing this imbecile? There's no way anyone can find out the actual truth as to what connected the captain and I.*

She placed her hands together and began to repeat the "Our Father" prayer over and over. Mary always did this when she was concentrating on something very intensely. She felt the prayer gave her insight into situations that she normally couldn't see.

That's when the answer came to her.

It was the perfect solution to her problem.

Oh, that's genius! She thought to herself as she giddily jumped up and down with triumphant excitement. *There isn't anyone who wouldn't believe the story I just concocted.*

Mary turned toward the bathroom mirror and ripped the bonnet off her head. She grabbed ahold of her hair and began to run her hands all through it in order to make it look messy (messier than it *usually* already looked). She ran her hand across her mouth to smear her lipstick along the side of her face. Next, she grabbed ahold of the top of her white, buttoned-up blouse and forcefully tore it open, exposing her bra.

As she stared at her disheveled appearance in the mirror she began to wonder just how good of an individual she actually was. She walked around under the guise that she was this honorable Christian woman, but in reality she had done some deplorable things in her life. And now she was about to commit another despicable act to cover up the others.

What are you doing, bitch? She questioned as she reached out and harshly slapped herself across the cheek. *This clearly isn't the right time to be having this internal struggle. The lord will see you through this dark moment and you shall persevere. No evil shall take you under, Mary Higgins! Now let's do this shit.*

She took one final deep breath and reached for the door handle. She flung the door open and raced out into the living room where the other party guests were still casually mingling.

"Help me! Someone please help me!" Mary wailed as she scanned the room looking for Baxter.

Everyone in the room let out an audible gasp when they laid eyes on Mary in her distraught state. Baxter spotted his wife from the kitchen and ran to her aide.

"Mary, what the bloody hell happened to you? Are you okay?" he asked as he scooped her up in his arms.

"It was that madman! It was that *drunk* sea-loving madman, Captain Todd! He followed me into the bathroom and tried to force himself on me!" she yelled out so everyone in the room could hear.

"Mary, are you saying Captain Todd tried to rape you?" asked Ester as she took ahold of her friend's hand to comfort her.

"Yes! Yes, he did indeed try to molest me! I tried my damnedest to push him off me, but I knew from the look in his eyes that he meant business. Finally, after begging and pleading for him to stop, I grabbed ahold of the bathroom soap dish and whacked him across the head with all my might. I think I knocked him unconscious."

Everyone in the room looked on and listened in horror. No one could believe that such a frightening act had occurred right under their noses.

"I'll kill the bastard," said Baxter as he released his wife and ran toward the bathroom.

Mary attempted to cover her exposed chest by pulling the ripped sides of her blouse together.

"You poor thing," cried Lydia as she ran to her friend with a blanket. "Here you go, put this around yourself and come have a seat by the fire. I can't believe such a thing could happen to you in my home. I feel so guilty for inviting him, you were completely right about him, Mary."

"I tried to warn you that he was no good, Lydia. My intuition about these situations is never wrong," said Mary as sat on the couch next to her friends and continued to give such an amazing performance that it made Jodie Foster's work in *The Accused* look like community theater.

"Here you go mom, drink this up," said Emily as she handed her mother a glass of water. "Are you okay?"

"I'll be fine my dear daughter, I'm just thankful to the lord almighty that I was able to stop that evil creature before he was able to really hurt me. God kept me safe this evening."

"I just cannot believe the audacity of the man," said Theresa as she rubbed Mary's back. "You knew exactly what he was about Mary, you hit the nail on the head last week when you were warning us about his drunkard ways. I bet that's why he was late this evening, he was probably getting hammered at his house before he came over for dinner."

"He didn't seem drunk to me," interrupted Rupert.

Everyone in the room turned their heads and glared at him in shock. As Mary eyed her son inquisitively, wondering why he would try to refute her claims, she could see the accusatory eyes of Captain James Todd staring back at her. In that moment she wondered if she would ever be able to look at her children again without seeing the face of their father reaching out through them for silent retribution. It had already been hard enough watching her kids evolve into miniature forms of him, how would she be able to survive seeing him shine through in their personas now?

"Why of course he was Rupert! How can you say such a thing?"

Mary questioned him. "The man attacked me in a drunken stupor, I could smell the Belvedere all over his breath when he came up behind me; it took me a minute or so before I realized it wasn't Chelsea Handler trying to get frisky with me."

"I wasn't trying to imply anything, I'm simply saying he didn't seem to be acting drunk to me," he repeated.

"Okay Rupert!" Emily barked. "Jesus, we heard you the first time, just shut up about it!"

Mary grabbed ahold of her daughter's hand to tacitly thank her for the support. She squeezed out one more tear and let it run down her cheek for effect. As everyone continued to shower her with support, Baxter walked back into the room with a ghastly look painted across his face that sent an eerie silence throughout the cabin. It was a look that no one in his family had ever seen before.

"Father, what have you done?" asked Emily, frightened, as she pointed to his blood-stained hands.

"There was nothing to be done, daughter. It seems as though the deed had already been done before I even got to him," he calmly muttered as he made his way towards his wife. "Mary, the devious scoundrel was already dead when I entered the bathroom. When you hit the captain over the head he must have fallen back pretty hard and banged his head on the side of the tub. I felt for a pulse, but the blow must have killed him immediately."

The entire room gasped in shock.

"Are you telling me there's a dead man in my bathroom?" Lydia tearfully asked. "Dammit, I just got that rug from Crate & Barrel! I surely hope he didn't make a mess; blood is so difficult to get out of fabrics. Come along Sam, we must inspect the damage."

As the hosts of the event hastily made their way to the bathroom, Mary decided to take her performance into overdrive.

"Baxter, are you saying that I murdered a man?" she bellowed as she raised her hands to her mouth in horror. "You're saying that I killed him? That cannot be true, I'm not a murderer! Oh sweet Jesus, what have I done?"

Baxter embraced his trembling wife, "Mary, you were only protecting yourself from being violated. You didn't murder anyone, my dear wife."

But no amount of reasoning seemed to comfort the distraught "victim" of the night; Mary knew she was laying it on pretty thick at the moment, but she continued to shake and wail like her life depended on it (which, in reality, it kind of did).

"Rupert and Emily, please take your mother home and put her to bed," Baxter said to his children. "We need to remove that lecherous captain's body and there's no reason for your mother to suffer through that as well, she's already had enough trauma for one evening."

As the twins gently took ahold of their frantic mother and led her out of the Collins cabin, the rest of the attendees began to grab their belongings and file out as well. The evening had certainly gone to pot fairly quickly and no one really wanted to stay and mingle after what had taken place; nothing quite kills the vibe of a dinner party more than an attempted rape and violent murder.

"I haven't seen a dinner party end so violently horrible since that time Oscar Pistorius invited us to his beach condo for that Super Bowl shindig," Ester whispered to her husband as they exited the house. "But at least his deviled eggs weren't so dill-y."

It only took Emily and Rupert a matter of minutes to whisk Mary through the village and into their cabin. They didn't live particularly far from Lydia and Sam Collins, but the children didn't want any prying eyes catching a glimpse of their mother while she was in such a fragile state so they took her on a shortcut through the woods. Neither one of them had ever seen their mother so disturbed before, clearly the news of Captain Todd's death by her own hands had sent Mary into an emotional tailspin.

"Mom, would you like anything to eat or drink?" asked Emily as she walked her mother to the mahogany rocking chair in the living room. "I can bring you some biscuits or juice if you'd like?"

"No thank you," Mary answered through her tears. "I just need to be left alone right now. Please go into your rooms and leave me be until your father gets home."

Emily and Rupert stared at one another, not quite sure if they should leave their mother by herself at the moment.

"Are you sure you want to be alone right now, mom?" Rupert asked. "Maybe we should get you out of those clothes and into something else."

"No, I want to be left alone," she softly muttered once again.

"Well, I think we should at least get you..." Emily tried to say before the hurricane of emotions blew through the room.

"GODDAMN IT! WHAT DID I JUST SAY? I WANT TO BE LEFT ALONE!" Mary screamed as she rose out of the rocking chair and began flailing her arms violently through the air. She knocked over candles, threw books in the air, and kicked an end table so hard that it sent Emily's sewing basket clear across the room and scattered all the objects within along the floor.

At first the chaotic outburst was just part of Mary's perfectly-crafted "victim act," but she found that unleashing all that anger really did make her feel better. The release made all her anxiety and stress fade. The more crazed she became, the more at ease she began to feel. She yelled louder, she kicked harder, she punched stronger; every release felt better and better.

Mary had gone full Joan Crawford in *Mommie Dearest* and she loved it.

Unfortunately the scene didn't exactly make Emily and Rupert feel the same. The twins looked on in shock as their mother seemed to lose her grasp on reality. She had become unraveled right in front of them and there was nothing they could do about it.

It took several minutes for the ravaging of their living room to finally cease.

Mary stood in the center of the wreckage, breathing heavily, and looked around at the damage she had done. *Oh shit!* She thought to herself as she raised her eyes and met the horrified looks that were plastered across her children's faces. *Maybe I took this one a little too far.*

"I'm…I'm…I'm very sorry, my beautiful children," Mary softly said as she slowly walked back to the rocking chair and sat down. "I'm very sorry you two had to see that. I'm simply stressed is all and I'd like to be by myself for a while. Please go to your rooms and I shall see you in the morning. I'll hear nothing else this evening. Go to bed."

Emily and Rupert sure as hell weren't going to put up a fight this time after seeing how close to the edge their mother was; they both silently removed themselves from the living area and went to their respective bedrooms.

Mary sat in silence and quietly rocked back and forth in her chair. *I did it! I did it! I did it!* She exclaimed from within. *There isn't anyone in the village who won't believe my story. I'll putter around the village looking sad and dismayed for a few days just to solidify my story, but after that it'll become yesterday's news and the village will forget all about it. Oh thank you lord for helping me get through this horrible situation. You are my savior and I shall be forever in your debt. And while I know it's because of your guidance and love that I was able to weave such a convincing tale, even you have to admit my acting was pretty darn convincing! Cate Blanchett, who? She doesn't have shit on me!*

A deviously gleeful smile spread across Mary's face.

She was proud of herself.

In her heart she knew that what she had done was wrong, but she was convinced that her love for God was going to see her through it all. Though, as she looked around her living room, she knew that there was one thing that God wasn't going to be able to help her with: cleaning up the mess she had just made throughout her home.

I suppose I'll leave the mess a little while longer until Baxter gets home so he can see just how upset this experience has made me. That should add an extra layer of believability to the story, she thought as she scanned the room, examining what she had done.

Then Mary noticed something at the base of her rocking chair.

It was something strangely familiar that seemed to be jumping out and begging to be noticed. She squinted her eyes and saw that it was a red notebook.

Is that the same red notebook that Rupert always carries around with him? She thought to herself as she bent over and picked it up off the floor. *Where did this come from? Rupert usually guards this diary with his life. He would never just leave it sitting out in the open here in the living room.*

The red notebook had still been sitting at the bottom of Emily's sewing basket when her mother punted it like a field goal across the cabin and sent it flying out of its hiding place. With all the commotion that had ensued that day in the woods when Emily discovered Rupert with Princess LaQuintia, she had completely forgotten that she had taken up his diary and placed it at the bottom of her basket.

Emily had every intention of giving the notebook back to Rupert later that day, but she had become preoccupied trying to recreate Beyonce's make-up look from the "Drunk in Love" music video and it kind of just slipped her mind. Teenage girls do have priorities, you know?

But now it was too late.

The book that housed all of Rupert's secrets and feelings had fallen into the hands of his mother.

Mary reached down and picked up one of the fallen candles off the floor. She placed it on the end table closest to her and lit it to illuminate the room. She got cozy in the chair and opened the book to the first page.

This should be an interesting read, she thought to herself.

CHAPTER FIVE

Knock, knock, knock.

Three gentle taps landed on Rupert's bedroom door the following morning.

"Yes?" he said as he lowered the book he had been reading.

"It's me, can I come in?" Emily said, quietly.

"Yeah sure, come in."

Emily quickly entered the room and closed the door tightly behind her. She was already completely dressed in her most modest, freshly pressed gray dress and white blouse buttoned all the way to her neck. After the events she had witnessed the night before, she figured it was in her best interest to dress as conservatively as possible today as to not ruffle any of her mother's feathers. But that didn't stop her from tying a white bandana, adorned with sparkly crystals, around her head of wavy tresses that had been placed in curlers during the night.

"Well, that's an *interesting* look you're going for," Rupert said, sarcastically.

"Are you referring to the bandana? It's hot, isn't it?" she said as she gently tussled her hair. "I was shooting for the J.Lo look at the VMA's when she was still in her 'urban' phase and letting Diddy take rides on her 6 train. Anyway, it's cute right?"

"Yeah, whatever. What's up?" he asked as he raised his book back towards his face.

"I just wanted to come in and see how you were doing this morning. Last night was pretty intense, wasn't it?"

"Yeah, I suppose it was," he said as he let out a loud yawn and continued reading.

"I just can't believe that mom actually *killed* someone. It's just nuts to even try to comprehend," Emily said as she took a seat next to Rupert on his bed. "And then that outburst she had when we got home. She just totally spiraled out of control. I haven't seen a woman snap like that since Celine Dion lost top-billing to Mariah Carey at *VH1's Diva Live!*[84] Rupert, I wasn't expecting mom to lose her shit like that."

"Yeah, I know. It was pretty strange."

Emily turned and stared at her brother in a questioning manner. "Why are you so nonchalant about this situation? Call me crazy, but I'd assume you would show a bit more concern after your mother was attacked."

Rupert huffed and lowered his book once again. "I don't know what you want me to say Emily. Of course it's a horribly shitty thing that happened, but mom is okay, thankfully. Anyway, like I said last night, I'm still not convinced that Captain Todd was drunk. I saw the way he was acting last night and he wasn't maneuvering like a drunkard. Something about the whole story just seems a bit off to me."

"What do you mean?"

Rupert turned toward his sister and looked her right in the eyes. "Emily, think about it, what kind of idiot is going to try to attack a woman in a house full of people? Even if he was drunk, which I'm fully convinced he wasn't, he wasn't dumb enough to think he could get away with

---

84   Diva's don't play that "supporting role" bullshit.

something like that. What was he going to do after he got done attacking mother in the bathroom, sit down with all of us at the dinner table and enjoy a plate of short ribs and rice?"

Emily knew that everything Rupert was saying was true. Now that she had time to stew over the situation she realized there were more holes in her mother's story than in Courtney Love's pantyhose.

"Well, what do you think actually happened then? Do you think mom purposely killed him?" she whispered as she anxiously bit her lower-lip.

"Emily, I don't presume to know the answer to either one of those questions, but I know that it all seems a bit fishy to me. We both know that mom is a godly woman and I don't see her as some vicious killer, but I feel like we're certainly not being told the whole story."

The Higgins children sat in silence for a moment.

Could their mother really be devious enough to intentionally kill a man like Captain Todd?

But why? What could have possibly motivated her to murder someone?

Their minds were blank; neither one of them could think of any plausible reason as to why their mother would do such a thing.

"What a damn mess all this has become; and to be honest, I'm not sure if I really want to know all the gory, factual details of it all," Emily said, breaking up the silence. "Truth be told, after her explosion last night I'm even a bit nervous to go out there into the kitchen by myself. That's the main reason I came in here this morning because I want you to go out there with me. It's going to be so awkward and I don't want to do it alone. Please come with me?"

Rupert could see in his sister's demeanor that she was telling the truth. He could read the tension all over her face; and as much as he was still pissed off about his twin's meddling in his romantic endeavors, he didn't like to see her so worried.

"Yeah, I'll go with you," he said, casually. "I want a Pop-Tart anyway."

The two of them picked themselves off Rupert's bed and walked out of the room, side-by-side. As they entered the living room, which they had last seen completely trashed just hours before, they discovered it looking immaculate once again. Every book was placed back in its right spot, every candle had been put back to their upright position, and every table had been moved back to their proper locations; it was as if their mother's tantrum had never even occurred. The sight of the perfectly manicured room sent an eerie chill through the children.

"Oh, well there the sleepyheads are! Good morning," Mary happily announced from the kitchen. "I was actually about to go wake the two of you up. I've prepared a delicious breakfast for my family."

Rupert and Emily slowly walked into the kitchen to find their mother cooking away at the stove and their father, seated in his usual chair, with a cup of coffee in his hand. The whole scene seemed strangely ordinary to the twins; after the shit storm of events that transpired the night before they certainly weren't expecting to awake to a morning like this.

"Have a seat you two, I've got fresh bacon and eggs for you," Mary said. "Would you like some toast as well? I can heat some up if you'd like."

"Bacon and eggs is fine, I can do without the carbs," said Emily as she apprehensively took her seat. "But how are you feeling today, mother?"

"Oh, I couldn't be better my dear daughter. I slept like a baby last night and I woke up feeling so renewed and full of vitality. The lord has given us a brand new day and for that I am happy."

The children curiously looked at one another and then to their father. They needed tacit reassurance from Baxter that their mother was doing okay, to which he gave them a half-smile and a nod as if to say, *It's all good in the hood, don't worry.*

"Okay mom, as long as you're feeling okay," said Emily. "But please let me know if you need anything and I'll be happy to help."

"Well, that's very sweet of you, but I'm fine and I really don't want to discuss the happenings of what transpired last night any longer," Mary said as she placed the breakfast plates in front of her children. "It's not something I choose to keep reliving. I simply want to go back to normal life, is that understood?"

Rupert and Emily shook their head in agreement.

"Fantastic, now everyone eat up before it gets too cold."

Everyone began to quietly eat their breakfast. The Higgins household was usually never this solemn in the mornings; it was strange for Mary not to be screaming for the kids, or Emily not to be ribbing Rupert for something, or Baxter to be huffing and puffing out of annoyance while he tried to read his morning paper. It was as if the family had been invaded by Scientologists and replaced with drones of their former selves.

But just like a romantic relationship with John Mayer, times of solace in the Higgins household had an expiration date.

"So how are you feeling today, Rupert?" asked Mary as she took a swig of juice. "You've been awfully quiet this morning my dear son."

"I'm fine, just a bit tired after last night."

"Are you *sure* that's all?" she said with a wide smile plastered across her face as she prodded some more.

Rupert looked his mother in the eyes. "Yes, I'm sure. What are you trying to get at mom?"

"I'm not trying to get at anything Rupert, I'm simply asking if there's anything your father and I need to know about?"

"If there was anything you *needed* to know then you *would* know about it," he slyly snapped back at her.

"Hmm, that's an interesting response," said Mary as she pulled Rupert's red notebook out of her apron pocket and threw it on the wooden kitchen table. The thud of the book reverberated through the room.

The kitchen fell silent as everyone's eyes were glued to the mysterious book; Emily nearly choked on her scrambled eggs when she realized her mother had found the hidden notebook, Rupert was completely dumbfounded that his mother had it because he was under the impression he had lost it in the woods.

"Mary, is that Rupert's journal?" asked Baxter, completely confused.

"Why yes it is, dear husband," she said with a smirk. "That surely is our sweet and innocent little Rupert's journal."

Rupert's eyes were burning with anger. He couldn't believe his mother had the audacity to invade his privacy like this.

"Well why do you have it Mary?" Baxter asked.

"That's a good question Baxter," she said as she took a seat across from her son. "While I was cleaning the living room last night I came across this little red notebook. It piqued my curiosity because I didn't recognize it at first, but after I started flipping through the pages I realized it was our dear Rupert's diary. And believe me when I tell you, it's *certainly* a page-turner. I was 45-minutes into my reading before I realized it wasn't a new installment of *50 Shades of Grey*!"

"I can't believe you read my journal!" Rupert yelled as he stood up and grabbed the book off the table. "I'll never forgive you for this! You are really wildin' out for this one, mother!"

"Rupert Higgins, I suggest you sit your ass down right now before I whip the holy-ghost out of you!" Mary yelled as she banged her fist on the kitchen table. Her mood had suddenly turned toxic; she had gone from Betty Crocker to Russell Crowe in the span of three seconds. "No son of mine will continue down this sinful road you've been secretly wandering for months! This type of perversion shall not be condoned in this holy household"

Baxter looked at his wife in awe; he had never seen her be so forceful before. "Mary, what in the world is going on? What are you talking about?"

"Why don't you tell your father what I'm talking about, Rupert," she said.

"It's none of your damn business you meddlesome witch!" he

burst out in response.

Emily couldn't believe what she was witnessing. While part of her couldn't help but feel guilty considering she had left the notebook in her sewing basket for so long, forgetting to return it to Rupert, but she also wanted to get her own ass out of her mother's line of fire.

"Uhm, I'm not sure if I need to be here for this conversation so I'm going to go back to my room to practice my needlework and…" Emily said as she tried to casually leave the kitchen.

"Not a chance in hell, sit your ass back down in that chair, muchacha!" Mary barked. "We're about to lay some fundamental ground rules for this household young lady and you need to hear them as well!"

"Would someone please tell me what the hell is going on right now?" Baxter asked again.

"Well Baxter Higgins, I hope you're prepared for this, it seems as though our son as been engaging in a sexual relationship with a neighboring native girl!"

Baxter's jaw dropped. He couldn't believe what he had just heard. "What did you say?"

"Oh you heard me, Baxter. As if engaging in pre-marital sex wasn't bad enough, Rupert has decided he's going to take the express train to hell by sticking it to some *dirty* native creature who's not even worthy to scrub our delicates!"

"You don't know what you're talking about mom, Princess LaQuintia is a saint and I love her!" Rupert yelled.

Mary stood up and reached across the table and planted a hard slap with the back of her hand to her son's cheek. "You got a bitch fucked up if you think any son of mine is going to *love* some native skank with no house-training! I'll be damned, Rupert Higgins!"

Baxter stood up to calm his wife down; with everything that had happened over the last 12 hours the last thing he wanted to do was get her overly worked up.

"Rupert, how long has this disgusting affair been going on?" he asked his son as he led Mary back to her seat.

"It went on for a few months, but it's over now. Emily discovered us together in the woods last week and we were forced to end it after that," Rupert said, solemnly.

Mary and Baxter now focused their attention on their daughter.

"You knew about this too, Emily?" Mary asked, disappointed. "You knew that your twin brother was engaging in such a sinful act and you didn't say anything to your father and I?"

Emily bowed her head in shame. "Yes, I found out about it last week, but Rupert promised me that it was over so I didn't see a need to bring it up and cause any potential drama."

"Potential drama? Emily, your brother's eternal soul is at stake and you chose not to bring it up to avoid 'potential drama'?" asked Mary. "Don't you see the devil is trying to bring your brother down a path of sin by sending that enchantress to blacken his soul."

"O.M.G. mother, can you chill out with the dramatics?" Rupert chimed in. "LaQuintia and I were having sex, we weren't sacrificing babies to Lucifer asking for eternal life. And she wasn't an enchantress, if you actually took the time to get to know her I'm sure you'd see that she's a great girl..."

"I surely won't get to know her! No native hooker shall *ever* set foot into the Higgins household! I'd sooner let Justin Bieber drive a kindergarten carpool than allow her into my home, young man!"

"Rupert, son, what are you thinking?" asked Baxter. "A good Christian boy like yourself cannot be dealing with a female savage. It's simply beneath us, dear boy. Don't you see how this could destroy our families reputation?"

"As if I give a shit about your stupid reputation? You two care more about what others think of us than our own happiness. And you, you're the worst one," Rupert said, pointing to his mother. "You walk around this village wearing your faith like a badge of honor and looking down at everyone when in reality you're the worst of them all! You boast about being the most godly woman in all the land, but we both know that you're anything but that!"

"And what is that supposed to mean?" Mary asked, shocked that her usually timid son would have the gull to call her out in such a manner.

"You might be able to fool the rest of these idiots in this village, *mother*, but I know what really went down in that bathroom last night!"

Mary's face went white in terror.

Could Rupert actually know what happened last night? He did voice skepticism when she said that Captain Todd was drunk, but how could he have possibly found out what really occurred?

"Rupert, you don't know what you're talking about," Mary said, trying to divert the attention back on her son. "I haven't seen such a poor deflection technique since President Bush used that whole 'weapons of mass destruction' nonsense to justify invading Iraq. Don't try to turn the tables on me because your secret has been uncovered, young man."

In truth, Rupert actually had no idea what really went down in the Collins bathroom the night prior; he did know that his mother was lying though. He was bluffing and putting on his best poker face as a means to throw her off and see just how much he could rattle her. He wanted to push her far enough to break her and get the truth to come forth. And he could tell by her facial expression that it was already working.

"Yeah, whatever you say mom," Rupert said, cool and calmly. "But just remember that God see's *everything* and no matter how many prayers you say you'll never be able to get back in his good graces after what you did."

"Rupert, what aren't you telling us? What do you know that we don't?" Baxter asked, more confused than ever.

"Baxter, please! Can't you see what he's doing?" Mary interrupted. "The boy is pissed off at me so he's trying to concoct some kind of ridiculous story surrounding the horrific event I had to endure last evening! The devil has surely overtaken our boy. I know that much to be true!"

"Spoken like a true murderer if you ask me," Rupert said,

venomously. "How will you ever sleep at night with the blood of an innocent man on your hands?"

Mary's blood began to boil.

She could feel the blinding, demonic rage coming over her yet again.

She was about to go full Kanye.[85]

"BE GONE YOU UNGRATEFUL LITTLE INGRATE!" Mary bellowed as she grabbed ahold of a plate and hurled it at the wall, smashing it into a million pieces. "I PROVIDE YOU WITH A LOVING AND CARING HOME, AND THIS IS HOW YOU REPAY ME? YOU MAKE FALSE CLAIMS ON YOUR OWN MOTHER! WE ARE THE HIGGINS FAMILY, NOT THE LOHANS, AND I WILL *NOT* PUT UP WITH THIS BULLSHIT! I HAD NO PROBLEM PUTTING AN END TO YOUR FATHER'S LIFE, DON'T THINK I WON'T DO THE SAME TO YOU!"

All the air seemed to be sucked right out of the room. Time seemed to stand still as the family digested the earth-shattering revelation Mary had just unveiled. The world they had always known was now forever gone.

"What do you mean you killed their father?" Baxter asked in complete horror. "What in holy hell does that mean, Mary?"

It took Mary a moment to realize that in her monstrous tantrum she had inadvertently shot herself in the foot.

"What? What are you talking about? I never said that," she said, trying to backtrack.

"Mother, you literally just said you killed our father," Emily said. "Why would you say such a thing? Are you saying that Captain Todd was our father?"

"Emily Higgins, what a fucking preposterous thing to even imply! Of course he wasn't your father, don't be silly."

"Then why did you just say that?" Baxter snarled at his wife.

---

85   Ain't no tantrum like a Kanye tantrum cause a Kanye tantrum don't stop!

"Baxter, I'm sorry, but I don't recall ever saying that. Maybe it was just a slip of the tongue or maybe I just got confused while…" Mary said, still trying to justify her error.

"Don't you dare lie to me, Mary!" Baxter yelled out. "Captain Todd was the one, wasn't he? He was the one you had an affair with before the wedding, wasn't he?"

Mary was dumbfounded; had Baxter known about her indiscretion all these years? Had he known about the paternity of Rupert and Emily all this time as well? One thing Mary was for sure of was she no longer had the energy to harbor these secrets any longer. The guilt had broken through the levees and flooded out of her.

"How did you know about that?" she asked, weak and defeated.

"Mary, I'm not a fool. Of course I knew there was someone else at one point. You think a man doesn't know when his girl is tricking on the side?[86] Sure I did. But I never thought you could be devious enough to fake a pregnancy and pull the wool over our eyes for all these years. It's truly a sad day in a man's life when he finds out his wife is phonier than Nicki Minaj's ass, tits, and teeth. This entire life we've created is one giant charade, isn't it?"

Mary had never felt so dishonored in her entire life. She had spent so many years, and so much effort, trying to keep all her skeletons hidden in the closet and now, here they were, coming back to haunt her for every indiscretion.

"That's not true, Baxter! The life we've created is one of virtue and love. No matter what any test may say, you are the father to our children. None of you understand the burden I have bared in order to keep this family together," Mary said, tears beginning to well up in her eyes as she frantically searched the room for a comforting face. "Everything I did, I did for the good of our family. I did it to keep us together, don't you

---

86   W.A.S.P. Translation: "Tricking on the side" refers to the act of being a trampy trollop and screwing around behind your boo's back.

understand that?"

"Mom, you killed a man; a man who was apparently our biological father. How can you possibly try to justify that?" Emily asked, frightened and heartbroken from what she just learned.

"He was going to expose our secret to the entire colony! That drunkard sinner was going to tell everyone that I was a harlot who birthed bastard twins and then lied to my husband about their paternity; of course I had to stop him before he ruined us!"

"You mean before he ruined *you*?" Rupert said, coldly. "It was never about us, it was always about you and your sanctimonious image you had to uphold. God forbid you weren't viewed as the perfect Christian specimen; you were actually willing to kill another human being to keep up that image. I never want to see you again."

Rupert ran to his bedroom and slammed the door shut behind him. Emily stood up from her kitchen chair to chase after him, "I can't believe this, our entire lives have been one giant lie. I don't think I'll ever be able to forgive you for what you've done."

"YOU DON'T UNDERSTAND! NONE OF YOU UNDERSTAND THE STRUGGLES I HAVE ENDURED TO KEEP OUR FAMILY TOGETHER!" Mary wailed as the tears began to run down her cheeks. She grabbed ahold of Baxter and wrapped her arms around him, "Please forgive me, Baxter. I know I have done a wicked thing and for that I must seek penance, but you must understand that it is you who I love. It is you who I wish to spend eternity with. You do know that, don't you?"

"I can't even look at you right now Mary," said Baxter, refusing to reciprocate her embrace. The full levity of the situation still hadn't sunk in to Baxter's brain yet; he was still functioning in a state of suspended disbelief. "I don't know if I'll ever be able to look at you again after this treacherous lie you've kept all these years."

"Oh Baxter, please don't say such a thing! You must forgive me, you simply must! I know it was a horrible dishonor to keep this from you all these years, but no matter what any test says you're the father of our children and you always will be. Do you hear me, you'll always be the father of our children."

"Don't you think I know that? Of course I am. There isn't a test on this earth that could tell me otherwise, but that still doesn't excuse the lie, Mary. I feel like I don't even know the woman I'm married to any longer," he said as he pushed her off of him, releasing himself from her grasp.

"Are you going to leave me? Please say you won't, I don't know if I can handle you divorcing me, my love."

"You probably should have thought of that 16 years ago when you built our entire lives on a foundation of lies, shouldn't you?" he said as he started to exit from the kitchen.

"But we can't get divorced Baxter, God will never forgive us! And what will the neighbors say?"

He stopped dead in his tracks and turned back to his wife, infuriated.

"You turn your family's life upside down and you have the audacity to care about what the neighbors will say if we get divorced? My God, maybe Rupert was right about you."

Mary was left speechless. She had no other cards to play. Up until this moment she had always been able to manipulate any situation to get what she needed out of it, but it seemed as though her time for calculated maneuvers had come and gone.

"Will you tell the colony the truth about what really happened to Captain Todd?" she asked.

He looked at her with a blank expression. "I may hate you with every fiber of my being at the moment, but I don't want to see you burned at the stake for your hideous deeds. Your secret is safe with me."

"So you do still love me?"

"That's not what I said, Mary. I can't be in your presence at the moment because I'm afraid for what I might say or do," Baxter said as he grabbed ahold of his musket and made his way towards the front door. "I'm going out for a hunt to clear my mind."

Mary watched as her husband walked out of the front door. She didn't know if she'd ever see him again or if he'd simply disappear off into the wilderness forever.

An unearthly silence lingered over the Higgins cottage; not a single sound could be heard. The family had finally imploded and she didn't know if they would ever be the same again. She solemnly took a seat at the kitchen table and put her hands together in prayer; she knew what she needed to do to find some solace.

She began reciting the "Our Father" prayer once again. She repeated it over and over, waiting for the lord to give her a way out of this messy predicament. She kept praying and waiting, but no answer ever came to her. No answer was ever going to come.

No prayer was going to dig her out of the hole she had dug for herself. She stayed in her state of continuous prayer for hours; it wasn't until Baxter came home at nightfall, after taking the whole day to collect his thoughts while hunting, did someone finally notice that Mary had been sitting at the table all day, praying by herself.

Baxter tried to get his wife's attention upon his return, but everything he said fell upon deaf ears. She was staring off into space and quietly muttering the prayer over and over again. It didn't take Baxter long to realize that his wife had completely snapped. The stress of it all had finally broken Mary Higgins. She had tried to keep everything together for so long that it finally became too much for one to handle. The false façade had finally cracked. It was as if her mind had just slipped away during her petition for guidance; she just sat at the table, emotionally vacant and reciting her prayer.

This was how Mary Higgins would spend the rest of her days.

Whenever anyone in the village would ask the family what had happened to their matriarch, they would tell them that the stress of

Captain Todd's attack on her had just been too much for her to handle. That she mentally slipped away doing what she loved the most: praying. They had made the decision to protect their mother's Christian image from the dark reality of her deeds.

But, sadly, with all the commotion that went on in the Higgins household on that fateful day, there was one event that went largely unnoticed until hours later when the sun began to set.

Emily, concerned with how her brother was dealing with the trauma she inadvertently caused, entered Rupert's room to check on him.

But no Rupert would be found in the empty bedroom, only an opened window and a curtain billowing in the chilly wind.

Rupert was gone.

PART THREE

THE SUCYAMAMA TRIBE

CHAPTER ONE

It had been almost a week since Princess LaQuintia had been forced to turn her back on her one true love, Rupert Higgins, and the harrowing feeling of lose had yet to begin to subside. She knew her hands were tied in the matter and she had no other choice, but that still didn't make her feel better about the situation. In reality, LaQuintia had wanted to pull a Mayweather on Rupert's sister and snuff her out with a quick jab to the jaw, but she knew that wouldn't have fully rectified the ordeal.[87] But it certainly would have made her feel a whole lot better today.

LaQuintia had barely spoken to any of her fellow tribesman since she returned from the woods after she was forced to make that heartbreaking decision. Practically every member of the Sucyamama tribe could see that something was clearly bothering their beautiful princess; ladies would come to her, and in the most caring fashion, inquire as to what was distressing their princess and offer up their services if she needed them for anything.

But she wouldn't dare let anyone know what the real cause of

---

87   Fighting is certainly never the answer, but sometimes a punch is just necessary.

her pain was. So in true LaQuintia fashion she decided to come up with colorful lies in order to mask her grieving demeanor.

"Oh you're very sweet to ask, but I am fine. I think I just had a bad serving of bacon recently and my stomach has been unrelenting. I've got more gas than Chevron this week and it's made me quite cranky."

"No, I'm not sad, but I appreciate you checking up on me. My period hit this week and I'm having a heavy flow, it's made me a bit bitchy for the last few days."

"Please excuse my generally unpleasant attitude I've been exhibiting as of late, I'm just a bit tired of seeing Kim Kardashian's ass every time I turn around. Between the sex tape, the leaked nude selfies, and that *Paper* magazine spread, I'm just at my wits end with the world lately."[88]

These lies seemed to keep the majority of her loyal tribesman at bay, but there were those that knew her better than most and they weren't buying it one bit.

"Okay LaQuintia, it's time for you to fess up," said Raindrop Twerk, LaQuintia's best friend and most trusted companion in the Sucyamama tribe, as they were tending to the cornfields near the edge of the woods. "I know something is up with you and I know it's got nothing to do with your bowels or Kim K's succulent derriere. What's wrong, girl?"

"Why Raindrop Twerk, whatever do you mean?" asked LaQuintia as she attempted to deflect her best friend's blunt questioning of her behavior.

"LaQuintia, cut the crap. It's me. I need you to be honest with me about what's going on with you," she lovingly said as she sat down on the chilly soil next to the princess. "We've been best friends for many moons. You and I skinned our first deer together. You and I planted our first seeds together. Hell, we even made out with one another that one time those boys dared us to for a handful of wild berries. We know everything there

---

88   I'm fairly certain I've seen Kim K's bare ass more often than I've seen my own at this point.

is to know about one another, which is why I want you to be honest with me and let me know what's really going on?"

LaQuintia stared at her best friend in her deep brown eyes and she knew that she couldn't lie any longer. All the emotions she had been bottling up inside since she left Rupert in the woods were about to boil over and she couldn't contain the tears anymore.

"Oh Raindrop Twerk, you're right. I can't keep it from you any longer, there has been something dreadfully bothering me for the past week, but I'm so terribly afraid to utter it from lips."

Raindrop Twerk took her friend into her arms and gently brushed her hair with her hands. "LaQuintia, you know you can tell me anything. I hate to see you so distraught like this, what's causing you such grief?"

Princess LaQuintia raised her head off of her friend's shoulder and wiped the tears from her eyes. "If I tell you this secret you must promise to keep it only between us. No one else in the tribe can know about this, do you understand?"

"Of course, LaQuintia. You know my lips are sealed."

"Well, okay then, I'll be perfectly honest with you. I've been keeping the intimate company of a boy lately."

Raindrop's face lit up with shock and awe.

"A boy? What boy? How could you keep such juicy information from me? I bet I know who it is, it's that beefcake Fellatious Falcon isn't it? I knew I saw him giving you some come-hither looks lately. Is it true what they say about him and his oral skills? Why, I believe it was that big-breasted girl Full Moons Nightingale who told me that when he went down on her she thought her coochie was going to start emitting smoke signals because he was going at it so ferociously."

"No, no, no, you've got it all wrong," LaQuintia said as she grabbed ahold of her friend to reel her back into the conversation. "Jesus, it's nothing like that Raindrop Twerk. I've been seeing a boy, but he's not exactly part of the tribe."

"What do you mean he's not exactly part of the tribe?" Raindrop

Twerk questioned as she cocked her head to the side trying to figure out what her friend was talking about.

LaQuintia leaned in closer to her friend and gently whispered, "I've been seeing a white boy named Rupert from the colony across the woods."

"Huhhhhhhhhhhhhhhhhhhhh," Raindrop Twerk gasped aloud as the initial shock of the news hit her like a freight train.

LaQuintia immediately reached over and covered her friend's mouth, "Jesus Christ woman, calm down. Try to keep your composure, your drawing attention our way."

Raindrop Twerk turned her head to find a gang of other Sucyamama tribeswomen halting their harvesting work to peer in their direction to see what all the commotion was about.

"I'm sorry, please forgive me LaQuintia, but you have to understand when your best friend drops a bomb that she's been rolling in the sheets with some Zac Efron-looking bastard from across the woods it's going to cause such a reaction."[89]

LaQuintia let out a soft chuckle. Raindrop Twerk was always good for bringing a smile to her face and making her laugh.

"But I don't understand why you're so sad LaQuintia, what happened? Is this Rupert not very well endowed in the trousers? I've heard that about those white boys," Raindrop asked.

"No, it's not that at all. He and I had been secretly meeting in the woods for months now; we would walk, talk, and even enjoy some sexy time together, but last week we were discovered by his sister and I was forced to call off our romantic trysts out of fear of what might happen if either one of our colonies discovered about us. It's been eating me up inside since then; I just miss him so."

"Oh LaQuintia, I'm so sorry," Raindrop said as she leaned in once

---

89   Zac Efron: who would've ever thought the little lesbian looking boy from *High School Musical* would grow up to become sex personified in human form.

again to embrace her royal friend. "I know that must have been very hard for you to do, but I think you made the right decision. I mean you know I'm very open-minded, but what did you think would come of this situation in the end? You know your father wouldn't let you have any kind of future with a boy like that. He would sooner trust a Sony Pictures executive with his life story than allow his only child to engage in an interracial relationship with a Caucasian boy."[90]

LaQuintia took in a deep breathed and exhaled, "I know, I really did think we had a chance though. I can't even begin to tell you how hard it was to leave him behind. I can still see the look of sheer disappointment and anguish written all over his face as I said my final goodbye. I'm not sure if I'll ever be able to shake myself of that image."

"I know what you mean, that's exactly how I felt when I had to end things with Hung Horse last summer. Do you remember how heartbroken he was when I told him we were through? I mean the sex was amazing, but we both knew there was no way a bitch like me was going to stay committed to man with a fucking mullet. I still shudder inside when I think of that haircut."

"Oh yes, I remember that well," said LaQuintia as she shook her head in agreeance. "I'm sure I'll be okay. It's simply been a tough week trying to navigate through my daily life while holding onto such sadness, but I feel so much better now that I've been able to speak about it with someone. Thank you so much, Raindrop."

"Of course, that's what having a bestie like myself is for," she said as she embraced her friend one more time. "And you know if you want to talk about it any more that I'm always here for you."

"I know, and that's why you're my main bitch," LaQuintia said as she smiled at her best friend. "But anyway, back to work. We have to get

---

90   That's really saying a lot about the situation at hand considering, thanks to the valiant efforts of North Korean hackers, we now know that the executives over at Sony Pictures are basically the worst people on earth. It's a pretty sad day when North Koreans can somehow manage to make someone else look more unscrupulous than them.

this corn taken care of before the winter winds begin to pick up their pace. I'm already beginning to freeze my nips off."

Both of the girls began to rub their arms in order for the friction to provide them with some warmth.

"I agree," said Raindrop. "Let me run to your teepee and get your fur shawl so you don't get any colder. I'll be back shortly and then we can talk some more if you'd like?"

"That sounds like a plan, thank you Raindrop Twerk." LaQuintia said as she watched her friend begin to run off towards to the village. She really was thankful to have a friend like her that she could trust implicitly; she already felt a million times better just getting the secret off her chest.

Princess LaQuintia then began to refocus her attention on the crops as she took ahold of a nearby ear of corn and placed it in her basket. As much as she hated these daily chores she knew it was what had to be done in order for the tribe to make it through another harsh winter. But just as she was about to reach for the next ear of corn a small pebble flew from the woods and landed right at her feet.

"What the hell?" LaQuintia said as she peered towards the direction of the woods to see who, or what, had thrown the rock her way. Just then another small rock came hurling her direction and landed a mere few inches away from her. Princess LaQuintia threw down her basket full of corn and stomped off towards the woods,

"Who dares throw rocks at the princess of the Sucyamama tribe?" she called out as she crossed over into the wooded terrain in search of her assailant. She looked all around, but to no avail. There seemed to be no one in sight. "Oh so you're all big and bad when I can't see you, but as soon as you're confronted you run off like a little bitch! Grow some balls and stand up for yourself; you must be a Democrat!"

But just as she was about to turn around and head back to her corn duties, a figure ran up behind her and quickly grabbed ahold of her and placed their hand over her mouth in order to block her screams.

"Shhhhhhhh don't freak out, it's me," whispered the sweet and familiar voice into her ear. She turned around to find Rupert standing there with a bag full of clothes strapped to his back.

"Oh Rupert, I've missed you so much," said LaQuintia as she embraced her true love and planted a kiss on his lips. "But what are you doing here? You're insane to be coming down here after the ordeal with your sister last week. Aren't you afraid she's going to blow up our spot if she finds out you came out here to see me?"

"I'm afraid the cat's already out of the bag, my love. My family has already found out about our love affair. And believe me when I tell you, bitches was *trippin'*."

LaQuintia covered her mouth in shock. "No, they couldn't have? What did they say to you? Your parents must have been livid."

"Yeah, my mother lost her shit and kinda went nuts. But I'm fairly certain she was holding on by a thread anyway since she murdered a guy who may have been my biological father last night at a dinner party."

"What the fuck?" questioned Laquintia as she squinted her eyes and tried to digest the information Rupert had just given her. "I thought all you white people were supposed to have your shit in order; turns out you're more ghetto than we are!"[91]

"Yeah, go figure right? That's the deep dark secret no one is supposed to know. But I just had to see you, LaQuintia. This last week has been torture; nothing but pure agonizing torture without you. So I snuck out of my window when the shit really started to hit the fan at my house and I came to be with you. I couldn't bare going another day without seeing your beautiful face."

"Oh, you always were such a sensitive boy," she replied nonchalantly as she placed her hand on his cheek. "But I can't even lie, I too felt the same way. I've been walking around the village like a cranky bitch all week long. Someone even had the audacity to say I was behaving

---

91   Shhhhh, keep it on the downlow. No one's supposed to know that.

like Katherine Heigl, that's how you know how miserable I've been without you."[92]

"Well, I must say it's comforting to know you've had a tough time dealing with the situation as well," said Rupert as he turned away from LaQuintia. "I was a bit flabbergasted when you so quickly threw in the towel on us last week when Emily discovered us. I thought you were more of a down ass bitch than that."

LaQuintia quickly grabbed ahold of Rupert and turned him around to face her, "Oh Rupert, you must understand, I was only trying to spare you from being hurt. I couldn't bare the thought of your sister spilling the beans and your parents punishing you. I refused to let that happen, not for me. I couldn't allow it. I only made that decision because I thought it would be what's best for you, had I known the despair it would have caused you then I wouldn't have put you through that. Please forgive me?"

"I've already forgiven you, my dearest LaQuintia," said Rupert as he took ahold of her face and planted another kiss on her lips. "But I'll be damned if I lose you again. Let's run away together LaQuintia, just you and I against the world."

LaQuintia looked at Rupert in the eyes with equal parts shock and excitement. "Are you serious, Rupert?"

"Why, of course I'm serious. It's the only way we'll ever be able to actually be together. There's no way either one of our families are going to let it happen so we have to do it for ourselves. What do you say? Are you down for an adventure?"

"Rupert, you know that I want to be with you more than anything in the world, but where would we go? Not only that, but winter is approaching and we'll be doomed if we're roaming these lands alone in the dead of the season. I don't think you realize just how intense these

---

92   It's quite interesting to see how fast Katherine Heigl went from being the next Sandra Bullock to becoming the next Molly Ringwald in the span of what seemed like 3 hours, isn't it?

winter months can get out here. These lands get more frosty and frigid than a blowjob from Anna Wintour."

"Well then what do you propose that we do? I ran away from home and I refuse to go back to that den of falsities and lies. There's no way they would allow us to be together and I can't be separated from you like that ever again. I just won't be able to survive."

LaQuintia ran her hands through her hair and closed her eyes to think. She had to come up with an alternative plan for her and Rupert to be together. Just then, like a bolt of lightening, a brilliant idea struck her.

"Oh my god, what a fool I am. I have the perfect plan!"

Rupert was wide-eyed with excitement, "Well what is it?"

"My father had a massive tree house built when I was a child for us to frequent during the summer months, but it's been years since we've gone there. My father tends to tire of things quite easily so after a few summers he virtually abandoned the place. Why don't you go there and hide out for awhile and everyday I can come bring you food and drink and we can be with each other in the privacy of our little home. It's less than a mile or so along the tree line of these woods; if you go east you're bound to run right into it. What do you say?"

"I think it's a great plan LaQuintia, but I can't stay hidden away there forever. Eventually we're going to have to move out of there."

"Of course, but at least we can wait out the harsh winter months there and it'll give us time to come up with a better plan of where we can run off to. Oh Rupert, please say you'll agree?"

Rupert could see in LaQuintia's eyes that she wanted him to comply with her plan. He knew it was probably the best chance they had in order to keep their love, and their bodies, alive during the impending winter. "Surely I agree, my love. I think that's probably the best plan we have at the moment. I'll go there now and you can join me later?"

"Yes, for sure. I'll bring you some food for dinner. Luckily the whole village is busy in preparation for the Festival of the Dancing Deers that's taking place in a few days. I don't think anyone will notice if I sneak off with a bag full of treats for you."

"That's perfect LaQuintia," said Rupert as he embraced her once again. "I'm just so thrilled to see you once again and know how bright our future is."

Just as they were about to kiss once again, they could hear a voice in the distance. "LaQuintia! LaQuintia where are you? Where you at bitch, I have your shawl!"

LaQuintia had gotten so wrapped up in her reunion with Rupert that she forgot that Raindrop was coming back to help her continue her work with the corn.

"Shit, I forgot Raindrop Twerk had gone off to bring me my fur shawl," LaQuintia quietly said.

"Wait, her name is Raindrop Twerk?" asked Rupert with a smirk. "I bet the boys must *love* her."

"Yeah don't bother asking about that one. Her mother was a big fan of Three Six Mafia when she was born, hence the name."[93]

"I got you," said Rupert as he shook his head in an understanding fashion.

"But you must go now, please hurry. I don't want her coming in the woods trying to look for me. As I said, you must follow this tree line east for less than a mile and you'll find our refuge awaiting you. Go, please hurry."

"I shall see you shortly my dearest LaQuintia," said Rupert as he planted a quick kiss on her cheek and took off for the tree house with his bag of belongings.

LaQuintia fixed her hair and hastily made her way out of the woods and back towards her friend.

"There you are, I thought you ran off on me," said Raindrop as she proceeded to place the shawl across LaQuintia's shoulders.

"Oh no, not at all. You know when nature comes calling a bitch

---

93   With such classy song titles as "Pussy Got Ya Hooked" and "Put Cha D. In Her Mouth," how could any mother not just love the tunes of Three Six Mafia?

has to handle her business. That's the last time I eat Pizza Hut buffalo wings for lunch, I swear," replied LaQuintia as a means to cover-up her secret whereabouts. "My booty is on fire today."

"I totally feel you on that one," agreed Raindrop. "So, I don't want to pry into your business, but if you wanted to talk some more about this situation with Rupert, I'm all ears. Sometimes it's good to get all those emotions out and talk them over with a someone."

LaQuintia turned to face her trusted friend and gave her a smile, "You know Raindrop, I think things are already beginning to look up."

CHAPTER TWO

"What do you mean we won't have the guacamole ready for the Festival of the Dancing Deers?" bellowed Chief Wailing Badger as he pounded his fist on the ground in front of him. He and his festival organizers all sat cross-legged on the soft earthen ground within the chief's large teepee in the center of the village. "What kind of sick fucking joke are you playing on me with that bullshit? We can't have a celebration without any guacamole to dip the corn chips in! Sultry Snow Owl, I thought you were in charge of all the dips to be procured; what is the story behind this foolishness of no guacamole?"

Sultry Snow Owl swallowed hard and began to sweat from her temples. "Well chief, it seems as though the avocados haven't been as plentiful this year as we had hoped. We may have enough for a small amount of guacamole but certainly not as much as we need for everyone at the festival."

"This is extremely disheartening news, Sultry Snow Owl," said the chief as he glared his trademarked look of disappointment in her direction. "I don't care what or who you have to do in order to get more avocados, but it needs to be done. You can ride down to Tijuana and bang Cheech and Chong in exchange for a bag of them for all I care, but get it taken care of. Do I make myself clear?"

"Yes chief, I'll see what I can do," replied Sultry Snow Owl as she hung her head in shame.

This time of the year was extremely stressful for the Sucyamama Tribe. The Festival of the Dancing Deers was the tribe's annual celebration to show appreciation to nature for providing them with enough food and materials in order to survive through the harsh winter months. This was their way of giving praise to their surrounding environment for giving itself to them in order to flourish and keep the Sucyamama lineage alive.

So, needless to say, Chief Wailing Badger always strived for pure perfection when it came to the festival. Every year he assembled the most qualified team of tribesman to assist him in coordinating each facet of the festival. So as one might imagine, hearing news that guacamole may not be ready in time for the festival, which was set to take place in three days, was certainly not the news the chief wanted to be hearing.

"Now that we've discussed the dip debacle, let's get a status on the live entertainment," said Chief Wailing Badger as he moved right along and changed topics. "Pervy Panther, how are the dancers faring with their rehearsals so far?"

"They're working very hard sir and the dance is certainly looking more on-point after each and every run-through," said Pervy Panther as he attempted to make sure he stayed on the chief's good side after the thorough reading he just gave Sultry Snow Owl. "I think this will surely be one of the finest and most spirited routine's in recent memory."

"Is that so?" questioned the chief as he squinted his eyes and looked Pervy Panther up and down.

"Why yes sir, certainly. You don't have reservations about the dance, do you?" he asked.

"I've been hearing rumors around the tribe that you had a bit of trouble during yesterday's dress rehearsal. Would you care to explain that?"

Pervy Panther bit his lip in terror. "Well chief, I wouldn't say we had *trouble* yesterday as that sounds a bit exaggerated, but we just had a sizing issue with one of the young ladies outfits. We have to let it out a bit before the night of the festival."

"You wouldn't happen to be talking about that rather plump girl, Jazzy Jaguar, would you?" asked the chief.

"Why yes sir, that's the young lady I'm referring to. She was simply having a tough time getting into the skirt. But I'm sure once..."

"Listen here, Pervy Panther," said Chief Wailing Badger as he lifted his hand to interrupt the tribe's dance choreographer. "I told you that I had misgivings about Jazzy Jaguar being part of the dance routine when you first informed me of who was in the line-up and you assured me that it wouldn't be a problem. Now here we are, only three sunsets away from the night of the festival, and you're telling me little miss thick'ems can't fit into the chosen ensemble? That's unacceptable. I don't care if you have to lather her big ass in Crisco and use a tow truck to get that skirt around her hips, but get it done. Do I make myself clear?"

"Crystal clear, chief," said Pervy Panther as he shook his head in compliance.

"And finally, the last item on the agenda, the wine selection for the evening. River Rat, how is that going?"

"It's going quite well so far, chief," said River Rat as he sat up straight and proud to deliver his update on the procurement of wines. "I've been able to get 10 cases of Barefoot Moscato so far, and I'm working on trying to secure another 10 cases of Merlot but I'm still negotiating that deal."

"So you're telling me that all we have so far is some cases of Barefoot *Moscato*?" the chief disdainfully questioned.

River Rat took a deep gulp before he responded. "Yes sir, that's correct."

"River Rat, this is the Festival of the Dancing Deers, not a fucking middle school prom. Moscato? We may as well serve Mike's Hard Lemonade while we're at it!" the chief yelled. "This is a classy affair. I want you to scrap the Moscato and replace it with enough Pinot Grigio and Chardonnay to knock out an Irish army. I don't care if you have to crush the fucking grapes yourself like Lucy and Ethel, but get it done."

"I understand, sir" River Rat responded.

Chief Wailing Badger scanned the circle of coordinators that were sitting on the ground in his teepee. He sincerely hated to do what came next, but he knew it must be done for the sake of a prosperous festival. "Now listen up people! I'm pretty sure you all know the importance of the Festival of the Dancing Deers and what it signifies for our tribe. With that being said, all you motherfuckers now have three days to work out whatever final kinks you may have for your respective responsibilities. All I know is I better see guacamole next to the chips, a big bitch dancing her ass off in a showcase of gratitude for our land, and some wines that *didn't* come from the $3 bin at Wal-Mart, is that understood?"

The group agreed in unison.

"Fantastic. Now everyone except Bottom Bear be on your way and go take care of your business," commanded Chief Wailing Badger.

The group immediately got up and removed themselves from their fearless leader's living quarters. All except Bottom Bear that is.

"Huhhhhh Bottom Bear, what am I going to do with these fellow tribesmen of ours? They give me such a headache," said the chief as he closed his eyes and began to rub the temples of his head. "Don't they realize how important this night is and what it means for the tribe? I just want everything to be perfect, but they drive me insane with these ridiculous problems. Can't they see just how stressed they make me?"

Bottom Bear stood up off the ground and walked over towards his chief.

"I know chief, I can see just how stressed you truly are," he said as he came up behind him and began to massage his shoulders to relieve some of the anxiety.

"Sometimes I think you're the only one who does," said the chief as he brought his hand down on top of Bottom Bear's and tilted his head upwards so that their eyes met. "I don't know what I would do without you to keep me levelheaded."

Bottom Bear leaned down and planted a kiss on Chief Wailing Badger's lips. "Well, fortunately for you sir, you won't ever have to worry about that."

The secret affair had been going on for years.

Longer than either one of them could even really remember anymore.

Chief Wailing Badger originally didn't even know he could have those kinds of feelings for another man; with the exception of the occasional tingle in his trousers whenever he would see Jared Leto on the big screen, the chief had never questioned his sexuality before. Not in the slightest.

The man was devastatingly handsome: the pure definition of tall, dark, and handsome. He looked like a cross between Joe Manganiello and Chris Hemsworth; in other words, he got more Sucyamama ass than toilet seat.

In fact, the great chief had been known for his womanizing ways during his younger years and had developed a bit of a player reputation. It was nothing out of the ordinary to see the young chief going on multiple dates a night and bringing various ladies back to his teepee after last call. He had the kind of virility and stamina that would have made Robin Thicke look like Housewife Barbie.

But Chief Wailing Badger's days of bachelorhood were numbered after he caught the first glimpse of the woman that would be his first true love. Her name was Cooter Cat. She was the princess of a neighboring tribe and she was flawlessly gorgeous in every way possible. She had hair so black and shiny it looked as if it had been grow right from an onyx stone. She had skin so luminous it looked as if rays of sunshine were exuding from within her. She had a body so immaculately perfect that it made Gisele Bundchen look like an ideal candidate for Hydroxycut. In conclusion, bitch was da bomb!

And Chief Wailing Badger knew it as soon as he laid eyes on her. He knew that one way or another she would be his lady.

The chief began to woo the beautiful princess with words of romance and trinkets of his affection. But Cooter Cat would not be an easy victory for the chief. She had heard a plethora of stories about his Casanova ways and she refused to become just another notch in his belt until she knew exactly what his intentions were with her.

It took weeks for Cooter Cat to be open up to the prospect of going on a date with the chief, and even longer before she allowed him to steal a kiss from her supple lips. Needless to say, Chief Wailing Badger was in his own personal hell; while he loved Cooter Cat with every fiber of his being, he had never had to work so hard for some tail in his entire life and it was slowly starting to affect his health. The poor guy was blue-balling more severely than Nick Lachey when he was engaged to virginal queen Jessica Simpson.[94]

But in the end his hard work and determination eventually paid off. After a full year of dating, Chief Wailing Badger and Cooter Cat were married in a lavish affair that brought the two neighboring tribes together to celebrate the union. It was the beginning of what should have been a fairy-tale love story of the ages.

Sadly, as with most good things in life, their union would be short-lived.

A mere three months after their union, it was announced that the chief and his wife would be welcoming their first child into the world. The tribes rejoiced at the prospect of a young prince or princess running around the villages and carrying on the legacy of both lineages.

---

94   Poor Nick Lachey; by his wedding night those balls must've been the same hue as Papa Smurf's.

But while everyone on the outside rejoiced, those on the inside were getting increasingly worried as the pregnancy progressed. Cooter Cat was having an extremely difficult time carrying the child and while many kept assuring her that the pregnancy would get smoother and become easier over time it only continued to worsen each month.

Then the night finally arrived, after months of sheer torture Cooter Cat finally went into labor. Par for the course, the labor was just as miserable as the previous nine months of pregnancy. Cooter Cat suffered through 17 hours of excruciating pain during the labor of her first child, but at the end of it she had given birth to a healthy seven-pound baby girl who would be named LaQuintia. Sadly, Cooter Cat would not live to hear her daughter's first cry on earth. With the last push to bring LaQuintia into the world, Cooter Cat released her final breath and passed over to the spirit world the same minute her daughter was brought into ours. It had simply been far too much for poor Cooter Cat's body to handle and she gave in to the pain.

After Cooter Cat's death the chief was left utterly inconsolable. He felt as if he would never love again; certainly not the same kind of love that he had possessed for Cooter Cat. And now, on top of the crippling grief, he was left as a single father with an infant daughter to raise on his own; an infant daughter who looked like the spitting image of her breathtakingly beautiful mother. There were moments where Chief Wailing Badger couldn't even look his own daughter in her eyes because the feeling of grief and sadness she gave him was just too much to bare.

Luckily for her, LaQuintia had two tribes looking over her every want and whim. Everyone knew that Chief Wailing Badger wasn't in the right frame of mind to take care of this poor child like the way she needed to be cared for so each and every tribesmen stepped up to make sure that Princess LaQuintia always had someone around to play with her and tend to her every need. And no one was more helpful and attentive than the chief's second-in-command, Bottom Bear. After Cooter Cat's death, he bent over backwards to ensure that father and daughter were looked after.

There was nothing that he wouldn't have done for the both of them; and this type of devotion certainly didn't go unnoticed, especially to Chief Wailing Badger.

It wasn't until late one summer night, nearly two years since the untimely death of his wife, that the internal passion and fire within Chief Wailing Badger would become reignited. The rain was pouring down outside his teepee and as per the usual routine Bottom Bear entered the dwelling to make sure that all was well with the chief and princess before he returned to his own teepee to retire for the evening.

The princess had already been tucked away in her bed and the sound of the rain had quickly lulled her to sleep. Feeling quite lonely this particular night, Chief Wailing Badger invited Bottom Bear in to sit by the small fire in the center of the teepee and converse for a while over a glass of Chardonnay. While this invite wasn't completely out of the ordinary, Bottom Bear was the chief's most trusted advisor after all so he routinely spent a lot of one-on-one time with the leader of the tribe discussing nearly every facet of the village, but there was something different about this particular evening. The conversation didn't have anything to do with the status of the crops, or how the other tribesmen were dealing with the summer heat, or how the tribe hussy Skanky Snake was pregnant for the fourth time with a different baby daddy, but rather the conversation was geared towards Bottom Bear's personal life.

"Tell me Bottom Bear, why have you never been married after all these years?" questioned the chief.

"Well that's certainly an interesting question, sir," remarked Bottom Bear as he stared toward the top of the teepee, attempting to avoid eye contact with the chief. He took a swig of his wine. "I guess I just haven't met the right person yet, that is all."

"The right *person* you say?"

"Yes, that's correct. The right person," he reiterated.

"You know Bottom Bear, now that I think of it, I don't think I can ever recall you even dating a girl. Not even when we were younger. Has there not been one single young lady in the tribe that you've had your eye on after all these years?" the chief inquired.

Bottom Bear stared across the fire at his fearless leader and wondered what exactly he was prying at? The chief had never been this inquisitive before, especially not when it came to personal matters like this.

Could it be possible that the chief knows about me? Bottom Bear thought to himself. *No, it's simply impossible. There's no way the chief could possibly know that I'm gay. But what if he does? And more importantly, what if he knows about my feelings for him? There's no way I can let him know, just play it cool Bottom Bear.*

"Well, of course there's been someone I've had my eye on over the years, but I haven't really pursued it," said Bottom Bear.

OMFG what the fuck kind of response was that you idiot? That's your idea of playing it cool? You might as well just put on your Madonna cone bra and start Voguing through the village now because everyone is going to find out your gay!

"Is that so?" the chief questioned as he locked eyes with his trusted confidant and smirked. "I think that's silly. If you have feelings for someone you should tell them. What's the worst that could possibly happen?"

Uhmmmm, how about you and the rest of the tribe string me up by my feet and take turns wacking me until I burst like a fucking piñata? Yeah, that's definitely the worst that could possibly happen.

"Yeah, I guess you're right. Maybe one of these days I'll act on it, who knows," Bottom Bear responded as casually as he could.

Chief Wailing Badger then stood up and walked over to his friend and sat down in front of him. "You know I've seen how attentive you've been over the past two years with Princess LaQuintia and always going out of your way to make sure that I am okay. I just wanted to let you know how much I truly appreciate it. I don't think anyone has ever cared for me the way that you have Bottom Bear and I just wanted you to know that."

Bottom Bear tried his hardest to keep his eyes in contact with the chief's, but it was all a bit too much for him to deal with and he could feel his composure slipping away from him. He averted his gaze towards the fire and slowly sipped at his wine before he mustered up enough courage to respond. "It's truly been my honor, Chief Wailing Badger. You know I would do anything for your and the princess."

The chief let out a small laugh and smirked, "I'm very aware of that, Bottom Bear." Then he leaned forward and grabbed ahold of the back of Bottom Bear's head and pulled him in for passionate kiss on the lips.

Bottom Bear was in complete shock.

Could this really be happening right now? he thought.

He was completely torn: on one hand he wanted to kiss the chief back just as passionately as he was kissing him (after all, this was the only person he had ever truly loved), but on the other hand everything was happening so fast that he had no time to really compute what was occurring.

Feeling totally panicked, Bottom Bear pushed the chief away, "Chief Wailing Badger, what are you doing? Why are you kissing me?"

The chief smiled and placed his hand on Bottom Bear's knee; he had anticipated something like this might occur and he knew some coaxing may be necessary. "Listen Bottom Bear, it's totally okay. I've known about your secret for quite some time now and I just want you to know you're safe and you have nothing to worry about. You don't think I haven't noticed the way you look at me when we're on the hunt for wild turkey's, or the way you're always making sure my clothes are laid out for me the night before a big tribal meeting, or the way you're always the first to volunteer to give me a shoulder rub after a stressful day. I mean I'd have to be pretty damn blind not to notice you're gayer than a Jonas Brother at summer camp."

"But why didn't you ever say anything if you've known all this time?"

"That's not exactly my place to say, is it? I figured you would eventually speak to me about it when you were good and ready, but frankly my friend I got a bit tired of waiting so I decided to take the matter into my own hands," the chief said with a laugh.

While it was good to see the chief laughing and smiling again, Bottom Bear still had so many questions. "I'm just so confused right now. Is this your way of telling me that you're gay too?"

"Not exactly," said Chief Wailing Badger as he turned to stare into the fire. "I've never thought of myself as gay, but I will say I did always stare a little too long at those old Calvin Klein ads with Mark Wahlberg holding his junk. And I won't deny that I know every song on the *Glitter* soundtrack. With that being said, I certainly didn't think I would ever want to be *with* a man in that sense, but I've seen the way you've cared for me and my daughter over the past two years during this tumultuous time in our lives, and I've grown fonder of you than I have for anyone else in my life. I love you for what you've given up to make our lives easier, and those are feelings that I simply cannot ignore. It also doesn't hurt that you look like Ryan Reynolds in a leather loin clothe; so I figured I might be open to give it a dabble."

Bottom Bear began to blush. He had been hoping to hear those words stumble from the chief's lips for as long as he could remember. He truly thought he would never see the day when his own feelings of love would be reciprocated. "It makes my heart smile to hear that Chief Wailing Badger, but you and I both know that we could never be together. The tribe would never be willing to accept a gay chief. They would turn on us both."

Chief Wailing Badger knew he was right. The Sucyamama tribe was a fairly open-minded and liberal bunch - they had even recently started to allow some females to accompany the men during their big game hunts, but only the really husky women who none of the men would miss if they died during the expedition - but this was an entirely different ball game. Both men knew that this relationship they were on the cusp of embarking on would most certainly be met with opposition from the rest of their fellow tribesmen.

"I know you're right Bottom Bear, but I refuse to allow the opinions of others to dictate who I engage in a relationship with. What if we just keep it between us and don't tell anyone else?"

"Are you proposing that we engage in a DL relationship?" asked Bottom Bear.[95]

"Well I mean what other option do we have at the moment?" said the chief as he leaned forward and rested his palms on Bottom Bear's knees. "It could be kind of fun anyway. Sneaking around and having a secret to hide from the rest of the tribe, it could be kind of hot too. Don't you think?"

The only thing Bottom Bear could do was smile. He not only thought this day would never come, but he never thought he would see the moment when the chief would put everything on the line to be with him. For the first time in his entire life Bottom Bear felt real joy.

"If this is what I have to do in order to be with you than that's what I'll do," he said as he leaned in and kissed the chief.

And that, ladies and gentleman, is how it all began for Chief Wailing Badger and Bottom Bear; and here we are, nearly 15 years later in the same teepee, and the two of them are still happily, and secretly, together. Through the years their bond had only strengthened. And just like always, the chief came to his boo, Bottom Bear, for advice on all the challenges he faced in his position; his most current and pressing one being the Festival of the Dancing Deers.

"I mean, I wish these fools would just get their shit together," he said in an exasperated tone. "It can't be that damn hard to secure some damn guacamole for the festival, now can it?"

"Relax chief, it will work itself out," Bottom Bear reassured his

---

95   W.A.S.P. Translation: The type of union that Bottom Bear is referencing here is known as a "down low" relationship. This is when two males engage in a sexual relationship behind closed doors, yet still act as though they're straight to the outside world. For reference, please see basically everyone in Hollywood/show business.

partner. "Like that catchy little song from *Frozen* says, 'Let it go, let it gooooo.....'"

Chief Wailing Badger raised his hand and put it over Bottom Bear's mouth. "I love you, but if I hear you sing that fucking *Frozen* song one more time I'm going to smother you in your sleep."[96]

Bottom Bear began to laugh as he removed the chief's hand from over his mouth. "Okay, okay, okay. All I'm saying is don't let it stress you out. You can't let it get to you. The Festival of the Dancing Deers will be a smashing success, you and I both know it."

The chief closed his eyes and let out a loud sigh of aggravation. "I know, I know, you're absolutely right. Anyway, next order of business, have you seen LaQuintia today? One of us needs to have a serious talk with that girl; she's had a pout on her face for the last week and it's starting to affect the morale of the tribe. The princess of the Sucyamama tribe can't be walking around with a frown plastered across her face. She looks downright miserable. You'd think she was working for Martha Stewart the way she's been acting."

"I know, I'm not sure what's been bothering LaQuintia lately," said Bottom Bear as he took a seat next to the chief. "I've tried talking to her quite a few times and she keeps giving me the brush off. I'm a little worried; I don't think I've ever seen her behave like this before, either."

"Whatever it is my patience are wearing severely thin with it. I've got enough things on my plate to deal with and having a moody teenager is the last thing I need to be worried about right now."

"Just give her some time my chief, I'm sure this too shall pass. You know your daughter is just as stubborn and passionate about life as you are, I'm sure once she gets past whatever she's going through all will be back to normal," Bottom Bear said as he took ahold of the chief's hand and gave it a squeeze.

Over the course of LaQuintia's life she had come to look at Bottom Bear as another fatherly figure; since he had been around since

96   Please. No. More. Of. That. Song.

she was born and helped raise her it came as no surprise that she looked at him with a special degree of love and tenderness. But, as the same as the rest of the tribe, Princess LaQuintia had no idea about the real relationship that her father and his most trusted confidant actually had.

"Fucking teenagers," said the chief as he shook his head and returned his partner's hand squeeze with one of his own.

Just then the two men heard a foreign voice coming from outside the teepee; a soft and feminine voice that seemed to be calling out for assistance.

"Excuse me, is anyone around? I could use some help! Where is everyone?"

Chief Wailing Badger and Bottom Bear exited the teepee to find Jane Bigglesworth standing toward the edge of their village with a live chicken in her arms.

"Oh, hello there," she said as she spotted the two men. "Good day to you gentlemen, I am Jane Bigglesworth and I live on the other side of the woods in the new colony. Anyway, I was coming over to see if one of your lovely native ladies would help me with my chicken here. You see I just simply hate cutting the poor little creatures heads off and some of your mamacitas are usually so helpful with doing it for me."

Chief Wailing Badger casually turned his head toward Bottom Bear and whispered, "Did this bitch just call our women *mamacitas*? She does know we're not Mexican, right?"

Bottom Bear had to cover his mouth in order to contain his laughter.

"I do hope it's not too much to ask for, I'm just not really accustomed to decapitation is all," continued Jane.

Chief Wailing Badger raised his hand as a symbol for Jane to stop talking. "It is no trouble at all, we would be glad to help a neighbor in need," said the chief in a most pleasant and welcoming tone. He casually walked over to neighboring teepee and announced, "Fancy Fox, please come help our foreign neighbor with disposing of this chicken's head."

A few moments later, a small and stout woman emerged carrying a razor-sharp blade in her hand. She waddled toward Jane and snatched the squawking bird from her arms without uttering a single word. Fancy Fox raised the blade into the air and in the blink of an eye she severed the chicken's head.

"Oh, how splendid," Jane said as she clutched her hands together and rejoiced. "I simply cannot thank you enough!"

Chief Wailing Badger leaned closer to Bottom Bear to whisper again. "All she did was take a chicken's head off. This uppity bitch is over here acting like Oprah just gave her a new car."

"Shhhhhhh," Bottom Bear said as he elbowed the chief in the side.

"I really hate to be anymore meddlesome than I've already been, but do you think you could pluck the feathers out too?" Jane requested. "You can feel free to keep them if you'd like; maybe save them to make one of those pretty headdresses you people like to wear so much."

"*You people*? Is this white girl for real?" whispered Chief Wailing Badger again.

Bottom Bear knew he had to step in at this point. "Sure, we would be happy to help. Fancy Fox, please take the feathers off the bird for our neighbor."

"Thank you so much, you see I just got a manicure yesterday and I'd hate to fuck up my French-tips by messing around with this filthy chicken."

"French-tips? Who still gets French-tip manicures?" whispered the chief. "Who does this girl think she is, a member of Destiny's Child circa 1998?"

Bottom Bear just turned and stared at his partner with a disapproving look. While part of him wanted to laugh and partake in the joke with the chief, another part of him had something very different on his mind.

"Chief, why don't you invite her and some of the other foreigners to the Festival of the Dancing Deers?" he whispered.

The chief squinted his eyes and looked at him inquisitively. "Have you lost your mind? Have you been smoking that *special* grass that Marijuana Mountain Lion grows over by his teepee?"

"No, I'm totally serious. It would be a good showing of gratitude to invite the foreigners over to witness one of our most important functions of the year. Maybe then some of them will be able to understand our culture a bit more."

"Bottom Bear, I love you and your desire to bring the world together in peace and harmony, but you would sooner see Donald Sterling invite the Wu-Tang Clan over for brunch before I allow those foreigners to attend our festival. I'm sorry, I just won't even entertain the idea."

Bottom Bear frowned and hung his head in disappointment. He didn't care though. He knew it was a good idea even if the chief was too stubborn to admit it. How could they possibly learn to coexist with these new neighbors of theirs if they didn't fully understand their culture?

Chief Wailing Badger turned back toward Jane, "You're quite welcome, we are happy to help if we can. Now you may go."

Jane carefully took ahold of the de-feathered chicken, making sure her newly painted nails didn't come in contact with the bird's skin, and strolled back towards the woods and her cabin on the other side.

"We have to watch out for those foreigners," said the chief as he and Bottom Bear watched the woman disappear into the distance. "I don't like the idea of them just walking into our village any time they want to. I didn't put up much of a fuss when they decided to build their little town on the other side of our woods, but there must be some boundaries set between ourselves and them."

Bottom Bear simply rolled his eyes in annoyance. As much as he loved the chief, he also knew he was wrong on the subject of the foreigners. One way or another he was going to have to convince him that they would have to get to know their new neighbors or else friction was bound to occur. But he would reserve that battle for another day.

As the two men turned around to return to their teepee they were greeted by an exuberant Princess LaQuintia as she and her friend Raindrop Twerk came rushing up to them. "Is it true? Was one of those foreigner women really here in the village?"

"Oh Jesus," said the chief as he raised his hand to his head. "Is that really what has you so excited right now? And how in the hell did you find out about it so quick?"

"I mean it's not everyday a white woman wanders into the village like that. Everyone is already talking about it," she said excitedly as she peered around her father to see if she could still catch a glimpse of the woman who was brave enough to saunter onto Sucyamama soil. Princess LaQuintia thought this could be the kind of progress needed to start helping to bring the two societies together, and ultimately aiding in her being able to be with Rupert publicly.

"Alright, alright, alright," said the chief as he grabbed ahold of his daughter. "Chill out young lady, the woman has already came and gone. She simply needed some help with a fowl. Don't get too carried away over it. But I must say it's good to see the cheerful side of you on display again, I feel as though I've barely seen you smile in the last week. I take it you're feeling better?"

Princess LaQuintia and Raindrop Twerk exchanged glances.

"Huhhhh, yes father," she said nonchalantly. "Everything is totally fine. It's whatever. I'm totally over it. Anyway, Raindrop and I have things to tend to. Bye!"

She quickly planted a kiss on her father's cheek and ran off with her friend back towards the cornfield.

Chief Wailing Badger turned and looked at Bottom Bear, "Fucking teenagers, I swear."

CHAPTER THREE

It had been a hectic three days leading up to it, but the Festival of the Dancing Deers had finally arrived. Every member of the Sucayamama tribe knew just how important this night was for their people and the last thing they wanted to do was disappoint their chief.

So with great determination and hard work, everyone in the tribe worked overtime to ensure that a prosperous festival would take place. And, just as Bottom Bear had predicted, everything seemed to be going off without a hitch.

Sultry Snow Owl had managed to barter with a neighboring tribe for some additional avocados so that enough guacamole would be available; which, by the way, ended up tasting marvelous with the fresh corn chips and fish tacos that were on the menu for the evening.

And, while he hated to do it, Pervy Panther went to great lengths to ensure that Jazzy Jaguar was able to fit into her skirt for the traditional Sucyamama dance of gratitude for the land. He would never admit to it, but word around the tribe was that he put Jazzy Jaguar on the world-renowned "Stage Mom Diet;" the same diet that has been working for decades in Hollywood for clingy mothers who need their underage children to loss weight quickly in order to secure their next gig. Equal parts intense exercise and a strict diet of eight carrot sticks, a shit ton of Diet Coke, and two packs of Marlboro Lights a day had allowed for Jazzy Jaguar to go down three dresses in the span of 72 hours. She may have looked like she was on the brink of mental breakdown, but the bitch looked great in her outfit.

And River Rat ended up really coming through with the wine selections for the evening's festivities. He was able to work out a deal with the elderly wine distributor that allowed him to trade-in the previously purchased 10 cases of Moscato for 12 cases of Pinot Grigio and 10 cases of Merlot. Sure, he may have had to promise his eldest daughter's hand in marriage to the decrepit old man, but at least they got a good wine selection out of it.

Chief Wailing Badger sat at the head of the royal table, Princess LaQuintia and Bottom Bear on each side of him, and looked out towards his people as they celebrated. He had never been more proud of his tribe and he wanted them to know it.

"Attention everyone, attention!" the chief bellowed as he stood up from his royal chair and raised his glass in the air. "I wanted to propose a toast to the tribe this evening! I'm extremely proud to see just how great this year's festival has turned out and I can't thank you all enough for all the hard work that you put into making it a success. Tonight the land that surrounds us can feel just how grateful we are for what it has given us throughout the year and will continue to keep us thriving throughout the impending winter. I know that I've been a bit of a hard-ass over the last couple weeks, some might even say I've been a Scott Disick-sized d-bag for the way I've been acting, but I just wanted my wonderful Sucyamama tribe to experience the best Festival of the Dancing Deers ever! And I can say in all honestly that you've all achieved it this evening!"

The tribe erupted in cheers and applause for their chief.

"With that being said," he continued. "Let's keep the drinks flowing, the plates full, and the party all the way turnt up! And remember, if you succumb to the heat of the moment tonight and you end up bringing a stranger back to your teepee, please be responsible and wrap it up! Yes, I'm looking at you when I say that, Skanky Snake; last thing we need is another one of your bastard kids running around the village. Anyway, party on!"

The tribe let out another round of roaring applause for their beloved chief as he sat back down between the two most cherished people in his life.

"That was a fantastic toast, daddy," said Princess LaQuintia as she took ahold of her father's hand. "I don't think I've ever heard you speak so heartfelt to our people. They, and our beautiful lands, truly know how much appreciation you hold for them."

"Thank you my daughter," he replied as he leaned over to place a kiss on her cheek. "It warms my heart to hear you say such things."

"I agree, sir. I know the tribe loves to hear those words of encouragement from you," said Bottom Bear as he placed his hand on his partner's shoulder. He wanted to embrace him with a showing of affection, but he knew that was out of the question in such a public atmosphere.

"Thank you very much, Bottom Bear. I couldn't have pulled his off without you," the chief replied as he quickly gave his partner a wink that only he could see.

"Soooooooo, anyway guys," LaQuintia interjected as she began to rise from her seat. "I'm going to go find Raindrop Twerk and see what she and the girls are up to. I'll catch up with you later."

"Please don't stay out too late LaQuintia and take your fur shawl with you, it's going to get colder as the night progresses," said the chief as he lifted the shawl off her chair and proceeded to place it on his daughter's shoulders.

"Thanks father."

Chief Wailing Badger and Bottom Bear watched as Princess

LaQuintia ran off to find her friends amongst the crowd of celebrators.

"Well, she certainly seems much better these days than she was last week," said Bottom Bear.

"Yes, I know. She's more jubilant and happy than I've seen her in a very long time. It's a fantastic sight to behold."

"I certainly agree, chief," Bottom Bear said as he picked up his glass and finished off the last bit of wine that lingered at the bottom.

"Be careful there Bottom Bear, don't get yourself too tipsy tonight or someone might be bound to take advantage of you," the chief casually whispered to his partner, making sure he was out of earshot of any other tribesmen.

"Oh, is that so? In that case, maybe I should have another glass," he casually responded with a wink of his own.

"Don't tease me. It's been over a week since we've last been intimate and I've been so stressed out from this damn festival. If you continue to tease I'll just have to take you right here at this table."

Bottom Bear let out a raucous laugh. The four glasses of Pinot Grigio had certainly gone to his head a bit. "Oh hush chief, you'll do no such thing. Sex in public? This is the Festival of the Dancing Deers, not Christmas dinner at George Michael's villa."

"Now there's a man who knows how to have a good time," said Chief Wailing Badger between laughs. "No, but seriously, let's sneak off for awhile. What do you say?"

Bottom Bear looked around and surveyed the crowd of tribesmen in front of them. Everyone in the village was in such a jovial spirit as they celebrated and danced with drinks in their hands. The DJ had just thrown on Rihanna's "We Found Love" and the entire tribe was wildly dancing around like they had all just been slipped a Molly;[97] Bottom Bear knew that if he and the chief were to sneak off for a while this was probably the

---

97   A form of Ecstasy that apparently makes you want to dry-hump anything in sight. Do not ingest one near your aunt's potted cactus because you will try to dry-hump it and it will hurt.

best time to do it.

"Where do you want to go?" he quietly asked the chief. "We certainly can't go back to your teepee, that's the first place people will go to look once they see that you're absent."

Chief Wailing Badger took another gulp of his wine and thought where on earth they could go to get it popping for a while. He had to think quickly before another one of these drunken tribesmen came up to him to discuss their crops again. He loved his people but if he had to hear about one more corn crop this evening he was going to lose his shit. That's when the idea hit him.

"I know, why don't we go to the old tree house down the edge of the woods?" the chief said. "We haven't gone there in ages and it's far enough where no one will come looking for us there. Then when we're finished we can come right back. These fools are so tipsy they probably won't even notice that we're gone."

Bottom Bear was hesitant to traipse all the way to the old tree house, but when he looked into Chief Wailing Badger's eyes he knew that he had to be alone with his love for a while. "Alright, I'll make my way towards the woods now and you follow after me in a few minutes. I'll wait for you at the giant oak then we can make our way to the tree house together."

"Sounds like a plan to me," the chief said with a smile.

Bottom Bear stood up from his seat to make his exit, but before he began to make his way towards the woods he casually leaned over and whispered to the chief, "Bring one of those bottles of Pinot Grigio with you. You know wine does something freaky to me."

The chief turned around with a smirk and watched his partner walk away. While they certainly weren't the most conventional couple in the tribe, the chief really did love Bottom Bear with all his heart.

He waited a few minutes before he nonchalantly grabbed ahold of a nearby wine bottle and proceeded to sneak off towards the woods without anyone at the festival seeming to notice.

Meanwhile, about 30 minutes later, Princess LaQuintia, having grown tired of her friends and their sloppy drunken behavior, walked back to the royal table and noticed that both her father and Bottom Bear were absent.

Where the hell are those two? she thought to herself as she found an empty table waiting for her upon her return. *They're always sneaking off together to discuss strategies or whatever else it is that they care to talk about. I'm bored out of my mind now. Maybe I should just call it a night?*

That's when an idea came over the princess.

How silly of me! I know what I shall do with the rest of my evening! I'll pack up some of this delicious food and wine into a nice basket and bring it to out to the old tree house for Rupert to feast upon. He deserves to enjoy some of this great food as well. I've been so busy getting ready for the festival that I haven't had the chance to go check on him today. Everyone else is so wrapped up in their celebrating that they won't even notice that I'm gone.

So that's exactly what the young princess decided to do. She grabbed ahold of a nearby basket and began to fill it with meats, vegetables, pastries, chips and guacamole, and pretty much anything else that was within reach. She peered around the festival grounds to ensure that no prying eyes had locked onto her suspicious behavior; the last thing she needed was one of her fellow nosey tribesmen clocking her moves and going back to spill the beans to her father.

So with that in mind, Princess LaQuintia stealthy made her way towards the woods with her basket of treats in hand, consistently looking over her shoulder to ensure that no one was following behind. When she finally crossed over into the densely wooded forest, she took one final look behind her and then began to run towards the tree house. The sheer excitement of getting to see Rupert had put a spring in LaQuintia's step; she was sprinting through those woods with a pace that would've left Jackie Joyner-Kersee out of breath.

A little less than 10 minutes later, Princess LaQuintia finally reached the base of the old tree house. As she was about to climb the wooden ladder to enter the small living quarters above, she began to hear a funny noise from within the house.

What the hell is that noise that's coming from within the tree house? she thought to herself as she set the basket down on the ground. *It sounds like a loud grunting of some sort. Oh sweet baby Jesus, what if a creature is in there feasting on Rupert? Oh no! Am I too late?*

Princess LaQuintia quickly proceeded to climb up the ladder as fast as her limbs could carry her and when she finally reached the top she burst through the door with all her might, ready to come to blows with the dangerous beast that awaited her within.

Unfortunately for her, the type of *blow* she would be encountering inside that treehouse was of an entirely different nature. It had taken her eyes a moment to fully comprehend what she was witnessing, but when they finally did it was certainly an earth-shattering revelation for the poor princess. There they were, Chief Wailing Badger and Bottom Bear, the latter on his knees in front of the former, performing the kind of *job* that so many years later would make Monica Lewinsky a household name.

The brazen interruption had caused quite the commotion within the small tree house. Upon LaQuintia's entry, Chief Wailing Badger quickly sprang up off the small bed and pushed Bottom Bear to the side as he pulled up his suede pants. "LaQuintia! What in God's name are you doing up here? You're supposed to be down at the festival!"

LaQuintia was in complete shock. The sight of seeing her father engaging in such acts with Bottom Bear had rendered the princess momentarily speechless.

"Answer me when I'm speaking to you, young lady!" the chief demanded as he smoothed out some of the loose strands of his ponytail that had come undone during this sensual tussle with Bottom Bear.

LaQuintia looked up at her father and a sudden rush of burning anger came over the young princess. "How dare you speak to me in such a way after I've just witnessed what you two have been up to? I cannot believe you father! How long have you been living this lie of yours?"

"LaQuintia, listen to me," said the chief as he walked toward his daughter and placed his hands on her shoulders. "Bottom Bear and I have wanted to tell you about us for years now, but, in all honesty, we've just been afraid."

"Your father is right, LaQuintia," Bottom Bear interjected. "We've wanted to tell you for so long, but we just didn't know how you would react. The last thing we wanted to do was hurt you or have you find out under these very unfortunate circumstances."

LaQuintia's eyes darted back and forth between her father and the man whom she had grown to love like an uncle. "How long has this been going on?"

Chief Wailing Badger and Bottom Bear exchanged a glance before the chief softly answered, "Since you were about two years old."

LaQuintia's jaw dropped. "Oh you two are really wildin' out right now! You're telling me that you've been playing 'Hide the Salami' for nearly 15 years now and neither one of you had the balls to tell me the truth? This is some straight-up bullshit, I swear!"

"Watch your mouth, young lady," said the chief. "I'm sorry about what's gone down, but I'm still your father and in the words of Aretha, you will R.E.S.P.E.C.T. me."

"Jesus Christ, you and your divas," LaQuintia said with a roll of her eyes. "With the exception of Tyler Perry, you're the only man I know who quotes Aretha Franklin lyrics on a regular basis; I don't know how I couldn't tell you were gay before, but I guess hindsight is 20/20."

"LaQuintia, you have to understand just how much your father and I mean to one another," said Bottom Bear as he stepped between father and daughter. "This isn't some Grindr love affair where we just hooked up because we were within 50 feet of one another and needed a quick fix. Your father and I have been quietly committed to one another since you were a child. But there was no way that he and I could be openly together in front of the entire tribe; half of our tribesmen still buy their jeans at K-Mart for Christ's sake! Do you honestly think they'd be open and cultured enough to deal with a gay chief?"

LaQuintia knew that there was a certain validity to Bottom Bear's point but she wasn't trying to hear any of it. "That still doesn't excuse lying to me after all these years! If you two cared as much about me as you say you do than you would have told me. It's not like I can't handle having a gay parent, you know! I watch *Modern Family* just like the rest of the world. I'm not a child anymore, I can handle the truth!"

"You're absolutely right, my daughter" said Chief Wailing Badger as he softly took ahold of his daughter's hand. "I'm very sorry that we lied to you. In our efforts at trying to protect you for so long we misjudged just how much of an adult you've grown up to become. We were wrong and we both apologize to you."

She could see that her father genuinely meant his apology. He wasn't one to admit his wrongdoings often, but she knew that when he did it was most definitely from the heart. But before LaQuintia could tell her father that she accepted his apology there came a loud rustling from the tree branches outside the window.

"What in the world is out there on that branch?" questioned Bottom Bear as he walked toward the window. With all the commotion surrounding the sudden outing of Chief Wailing Badger and Bottom Bear, Princess LaQuintia had completely forgotten the main reason why she was at the tree house in the first place: Rupert.

Bottom Bear reached out the window into the pitch-black night sky and pulled in the teenage boy that had been secretly perched outside on the tree branch the entire time.

"Hey dude, get your hands off of me! This is a Versace shirt you're stretching out," Rupert yelled as Bottom Bear dragged him across the floor of the tree house.

"Who the hell are you and what are you doing in my family's tree house?" Chief Wailing Badger angrily questioned.

"My name is Rupert, sir," Rupert said as he stood up from the ground and looked around the room at all the faces that peered in his direction. "Forgive me for breaking into your tree house. I saw it from a distance and was intrigued so I figured that I would come up and take a look. When I heard you two gentlemen coming up the ladder I quickly made my way out the window and sat on one of the tree branches while you two…well, we all know what you were doing so there's no point in reopening that can of worms again, but it sounded like you were both have a great time if that means anything to you."

LaQuintia was silently trying to signal for Rupert to shut the fuck up with her hands, but the poor boy had already said too much.

"You see Bottom Bear, this is why I said we have to create boundaries between us and these foreign neighbors of ours. A couple days ago that woman walked onto our land asking for help with that chicken and now here we have one of them trespassing inside a royal Sucyamama house. What's next? Before you know it they'll be claiming that they were the first ones to discover this country; this is how these white people tend to operate! We must make an example of this youngster!"

"No father! You cannot do that!" yelled Princess LaQuintia as she darted between her father and Rupert. "It's not Rupert's fault that he's up here, it is mine."

"LaQuintia, what are you talking about?"

"I…I…I know this boy quite well," she softly said.

Chief Wailing Badger and Bottom Bear exchanged worried looks.

"LaQuintia, *how* well do you know this boy?" Bottom Bear asked.

She swallowed hard. "I know him just as well as you two apparently know each other."

"Oh fuck, I was afraid of that," Bottom Bear quickly responded.

"You've got to be joking with me right now," the chief said in a low, monotone voice. Everyone in the tree house could see that his temper was seething and beginning to boil over. "LaQuintia, are you saying that you're in a *relationship* with this young, Tobey Maguire-looking mothafucka? That's why you were coming out to the tree house this evening, wasn't it?"

"Yes father, that's exactly what I'm telling you," LaQuintia said as proudly as her nerves would allow her.

"If I may interrupt for a moment," said Rupert. "I just want you to know that I love your daughter very much sir and I'll do anything to be with her. LaQuintia and I are soulmates and…"

Chief Wailing Badger let out a boisterous laugh, completely cutting off Rupert's plea of love for his daughter. "Love? Soulmates? You've got to be kidding me, boy. That's the same thing Jennifer Lopez said about her relationships with P.Diddy, Chris Judd, Ben Affleck, Marc Anthony, and Casper Smart, and look how well those turned out. This union is bound to end up in flames just like those previously mentioned and I forbid it!"

"But father, love is love! At least give me a chance to explain everything to you. I know once you get the chance to hear our story you'll understand," pleaded LaQuintia.

"I'm sorry LaQuintia, but I refuse. I'm your father and I know what is best for you. You're too young to understand just how wrong this is and that when everything is said and done it will end in heartbreak for both of you kids. You come from two very different worlds and blending those together just won't work."

"I extremely disagree father! Without interracial relationships we wouldn't have amazing entertainers like Mariah Carey, Halle Berry, Derek Jeter, and Tiger Woods," responded LaQuintia. "Okay, maybe that last one isn't the best example since he's kind of a scuzzbucket, but the other three are really good!"

"She's got a point there," Bottom Bear politely interrupted. "I mean could you imagine how boring life would be without Mariah Carey?"

"Shut up Bottom Bear," the chief replied. "I can handle this one on my own, thank you very much! Now I won't hear another word from anyone else in this tree house. Rupert, I'm sure you're a nice boy but it's time for you to pack your belongings because we're taking you home to your family."

"But daddy, please!" yelled LaQuintia.

"LaQuintia, I won't hear another word from you about this matter. It's time for you to bid your final farewells for the young Caucasian is going back to his people tonight."

CHAPTER FOUR

The farewell had been quick and insensitively rushed by Chief Wailing Badger's increased annoyance on the matter. He allowed the children one final goodbye hug before he practically dragged Rupert by his collar through the woods back towards the Higgins household.

"What's with you guys and this constant need to pull on my shirt?" Rupert asked as he trailed behind the chief. "I'm pretty sure I previously mentioned this was Versace after all."

"I don't care if Donatella hand-stitched the damn shirt herself, I'm making sure you're delivered to your family's household myself so that this situation doesn't happen again," said Chief Wailing Badger.

"I'm sure this is a futile attempt sir, but you really have to understand how much I love your daughter. She's honestly the closest friend that I have in this new world. There isn't anything that I wouldn't do for her. We understand how crazy you must think our relationship may be, but like LaQuintia said, love is love. Doesn't that account for anything? I mean, you're banging another dude for God's sake! I'd think you would be a little more open-minded than this."

Chief Wailing Badger came to halt and pulled Rupert in front of him. "Listen here boy, I am Chief Wailing Badger of the Sucyamama tribe! Who I choose to *bang* is of no concern of yours. If I choose to share my bed with Tinkie Winkie, the gay Teletubbie, than that's what the hell I'll do. You think I don't understand what you're saying? Of course I understand, I'm not an emotional simpleton. But I'm also a loving father who doesn't want to see his daughter get hurt in life. So all this talk about love and feelings may work if this were a Nicolas Sparks novel, but you're trippin' if you think it's going to work on me."

Rupert hung his head in disappointment. "I'm sorry sir, I meant no disrespect. I just want you to know how hard I'm willing to fight to be with LaQuintia."

"I suggest you exert your energies into something else because I honestly could give a shit. No daughter of mine, the only Sucyamama princess, shall ever be with one of your kind. Now enough of this nonsense, which direction towards your family's house?"

Rupert lifelessly pointed in the northern direction. "It's just a little bit further that way."

The chief grabbed ahold of his collar once again and continued to drag him in the suggested direction. The two walked in silence for another 10 minutes before they finally came upon the front door of the Higgins household.

"Thank you for walking me home sir, but I can manage from this point," said Rupert as he rustled free of the chief's grasp.

"Oh no, no, no. Your parents and I are going to have a discussion. I want to ensure that this never happens again."

Rupert turned and faced the chief as tears began to well up in his eyes. "No sir, please. I'm begging you. No good will come from that. Please trust me when it comes to this matter."

"Young man, you should know by now that you're begging and pleading won't deter me from doing what I want. Now I suggest you knock on the damn door so I can take my tired ass home and get to sleep. This evening has given me a splitting headache."

Rupert knew that he didn't stand a chance. The chief wanted to speak to his parents and that's exactly what he was going to do. Rupert turned around and proceeded to knock on the door. A few moments later Emily answered the door and quickly embraced her twin.

"Rupert! O-M-G, where the hell have you been? Dad! Rupert's here! He's back! We've been looking all over the place for you, dipshit!" she said as she wrapped her arms around her missing brother. Such a public display of affection towards her brother was typically out of the question for Emily, but with all the insanity going on in the Higgins household lately it felt necessary.

"This brother of yours has been very busy lately," the chief's voice boomed from behind Rupert. "Busy trying to run off with my daughter, that is."

Emily had been so intently focused on Rupert that she hadn't even noticed Chief Wailing Badger standing behind him in the darkness.

"Oh shit," said Emily as she locked eyes with the chief. "I should've known that's where you were, Rupert. What did I tell you about getting involved with that native hussy? Now we have Squanto here knocking on our door and talking reckless."

"My name is Chief Wailing Badger, not *Squanto*, and my daughter is no damn *native hussy*, thank you very much. Such blasphemy will not be tolerated, especially from a little girl who looks like Rosie Perez's stunt double from *White Men Can't Jump*."

"What the hell is going on out here?" said Baxter Higgins as he emerged in the doorway and began to survey the situation at hand. At the first sight of his missing son he immediately took ahold of him and wrapped him in his arms. "Damn you, Rupert Higgins. Don't you know how worried we've been? I thought a bear or wolf had surely gotten to you out there in the wilderness. Now get your ass into the house, I believe this *chief* and I need to have a word."

Baxter pushed his children into the cabin and closed the door behind him. If the situation turned ugly he didn't want the twins to witness any potential bloodshed.

"Would you mind telling me what the hell you're doing with my child?" he politely asked the chief as he placed his hands into his pockets.

"I'm returning your lecherous child after I discovered that he had been taking advantage of my daughter and trespassing onto my tribe's property. You're quite lucky I did the neighborly thing and returned him unharmed. Next time he might not be so lucky," said the chief as he crossed his arms across his massive chest.

"Is that a threat?"

"Take it however you would like, I could really care less, but I don't want to see your son around my daughter again."

"Listen here *chief*, you think I want my son running around with some native chick? We're a civilized people. We come from a country of class and fine breeding. The last thing I want is any child of mine fraternizing with some savage from your kind. You keep your daughter away from him and I'll make sure I do the same."

The chief scoffed. "You see, that's what's wrong with you foreigners. You think you're so much better than us. You think because you pull up with your fancy clothes and your cute little cabins that all of a sudden my people are supposed to bow down to you and your claims of superiority? I hate to break it to you, but my people have been on this land for hundreds of years and will continue to run shit whether you like it or not. Ya'll are rookies in this game, we're the O.G.'s around this place and don't you forget it!"[98]

"Well maybe it's time to be out with the old and in with the new," said Baxter as he stepped closer to Chief Wailing Badger. "You know, I could honestly care less what you and your people do on the other side of those woods. You could be sacrificing goats to Hades for all I care, but stay away from my family. I'd sooner let R.Kelly babysit my kids before I would allow them in your company *ever* again."

Chief Wailing Badger stepped closer so that he and Baxter were

---

98 W.A.S.P. Translation: The members of the Sucyamama tribe were the "Original Gangstas" of the "new world."

nearly nose-to-nose. "That's fine by me. I'd hate for our *savage* tendencies to rub off on your *perfect* children, anyhow."

The chief promptly turned around and began to storm off back towards the woods, but not before Rupert came barging out of the front door, carrying something in his hand, and running towards the chief.

"Wait, Chief Wailing Badger! Please wait!" he yelled.

"Rupert! Have you lost your mind, boy? Get your ass back here!" Baxter yelled after his son.

The chief turned around and came face-to-face with the boy that had already ruined his night. "What do you want now?"

"I'm sorry, I just wanted to give you this in hopes you could give it to LaQuintia," he said as he handed the chief a book. "It's a book of poetry that she and I used to read together in the woods. It has some of my favorite poems written inside. We would spend hours reading from this book and I know how much she would appreciate having it. If you promise to give this to her as a token of the love we shared, I swear I'll never bother her again."

The chief looked down at the lovestruck boy. He could tell in his eyes that Rupert was being as genuine as possible; he was offering up something dear to his own heart in order to make LaQuintia happy. The chief could see that he truly did love his daughter. He quickly snatched the book out of Rupert's hand and turned around and continued his march towards the woods. Refusing to utter a single word in response.

Rupert stood there in the darkness and watched as the chief disappeared into the woods carrying his book of poems; clinging to the hope that the chief would indeed give her the memento of their special time they shared together.

"Rupert Higgins! Rupert Higgins! Bring your ass back into this house!" Baxter yelled from behind. "You've caused enough drama for one week, young man!"

The young boy turned around and slowly meandered back towards the cabin. He knew he was in a world of trouble for running away from home. But he wasn't aware of what the ripple effect of his actions would mean for the future.

Chief Wailing Badger slowly made his way through the woods and back towards his tribe. The night had surely taken it out of him. He was exhausted, to say the least. As he got closer to the Sucyamama village, he looked down at the book he was carrying in his hand. Part of him wanted to throw the book of poems into the shrubs and just be done with it, but another part of him prevented himself from doing such a thing. He wasn't sure what it was, but he couldn't just dispose of it like it meant nothing. He may have been a hard-ass, but he wasn't completely devoid of any romantic notions in life.

Upon entering his teepee, the chief found Bottom Bear and LaQuintia sitting around the fire in what looked like a deep discussion. The young princess refused to make eye contact with her father as she wiped the tears from her cheeks.

"How did it go?" asked Bottom Bear.

"It went fine," the chief answered. "His father was every bit the dickhead that I thought he would be."

"What is that in your hand?"

"It's a book of poetry that the boy wanted me to give to you, LaQuintia," the chief said as he extended his hand and passed the book to his daughter. "He said you would probably like to have it."

The distraught young princess took hold of the book and pressed it against her chest. "He and I would read from this for hours during our times together. I will cherish this forever."

Bottom Bear rubbed her shoulder as a means of comfort. "It was very nice of you to bring that back with you, chief. Don't you think so, LaQuintia?"

The princess shook her head in agreement. He hated to see his daughter so upset, but the chief was only doing his best to prevent her from getting hurt. He was only looking out for her best interests. Wasn't he?

"It's been a long evening, everyone. I think it's time we all went to bed. Tomorrow is a new day," said the chief.

"I think you're right," said Bottom Bear. "I shall return to my teepee and see you both in the morning."

"Why?" asked LaQuintia, in a solemn tone of voice.

"What do you mean?" Bottom Bear responded.

"I mean why are you going back to your teepee? That cat's out of the bag already, why don't you stay here with father? Haven't you two been hiding your love for long enough already?"

Chief Wailing Badger and Bottom Bear looked at one another. In nearly 15 years of dating, they had never spent a full night together out of fear of being discovered. And now, here they were, being given the blessing to do just that, by the chief's own daughter of all people.

"Are you sure you're comfortable with that, LaQuintia?" the chief asked.

"Why would I be uncomfortable with it? Like I said earlier, love is love. I'd be a hypocrite of epic proportions if I tried to turn my back on that claim now, wouldn't I?" she stated as she stood up and made eye contact with her father for the first time since he'd entered the teepee. She casually began to walk toward her bed before she turned to face the two men on the other side of the room. "Regardless of how mad I am at you right now father, and believe me I'm still pretty effin' mad, I'm happy that you two can now love openly and not have to keep it a secret any longer; at least in front of me. Just don't mess around with one another when I'm home cause that would kinda gross me out; not cause you're gay but just because every child should retain the right to view their parent as a non-sexual being."

The chief didn't know what to say. The last thing he expected to experience when he came home this evening was for his relationship with Bottom Bear to be openly accepted by his daughter. He would have expected to see Michael Sam having brunch with Rick Santorum before getting LaQuintia's seal of approval this evening. He found himself truly baffled by the turn of events that the night had taken. Bottom Bear reached out and grabbed ahold of his partner's hand and gave it a squeeze. In all the years he had known the chief he had never seen him so awestruck before. A single tear ran down his cheek.

Princess LaQuintia lay down in her bed, the poetry book still in hand, and pulled her fur blankets over herself. The day had gone in a direction she could have never foreseen. A direction she wasn't sure could ever be reversed.

Many days passed but Princess LaQuintia's heartache refused to subside. She had reverted back to her sullen ways of when she and Rupert had been forced to "consciously uncouple" weeks prior. She sat around the teepee and read from his Rupert's book of poetry and refused to see anyone. Chief Wailing Badger and Bottom Bear tried to pry her with treats and promises of a new suede two-piece ensemble with matching Jimmy Choo pumps, but it was to no avail.

The chief was racked with guilt. He knew he had done the right thing for his daughter, but he hated seeing her in such a state. She had become so depressed he was afraid nothing could pull her out of it.

It wasn't until late one November afternoon did things seem to take a turn for the better. Bottom Bear, Princess LaQuintia, and the chief were sitting in silence inside their teepee when they heard a familiar voice beaconing from outside.

"Hello there! Is anyone home? We come in peace!"

All three of them filed out to find Jane Bigglesworth, along with her husband, Arthur, standing in the exact same position they had encountered her last time. This time she didn't have a chicken in hand, but rather an envelope.

"Hi there, it's great to see you all again," she said. "Do you amigos remember me from last time?"

The chief leaned over and whispered to Bottom Bear, "Seriously, does she honestly think we're Mexican? First we're *muchachos* and now we're *amigos*; someone needs to buy this bitch a map."

He then turned his attention back toward Jane. "Yes we remember you, but not this man you've brought along with you."

"Oh yes, please excuse my manners. This is my husband, Arthur."

"Greetings hombres, it's a pleasure to meet you," said Arthur with a wave.

"Oh Jesus Christ, not him too," the chief whispered again, but this time paired it with a dramatic eye roll.

"How may we help you?" Bottom Bear interjected in an attempt to keep the peace. "Do you need more assistance with another fowl?"

"No, no no! Not this time at least," replied Jane with a laugh. "My husband and I wanted to come by to personally invite you and your family over to our home for a feast we're throwing tomorrow. I know it's short notice but we really wanted to thank you for how kind you've been to us since we arrived. A meal in your honor is the least that we can do."

Jane walked up to the chief and handed him the invitation with a kind smile plastered across her face. Chief Wailing Badger was in shock. Were these foreigners really inviting his family to come share a meal with them? Are they really opening their home to the Sucyamama people? It seemed virtually impossible to the chief. He turned his head and saw Bottom Bear and LaQuintia, both with eager smiles on their faces.

"You're inviting us to come dine with you?" asked the chief, wanting to verify exactly what was being offered to them.

"Why yes, for sure," answered Arthur. "Like my wife said, we apologize for the late notice but we do hope you can come join us. We've invited quite a few people from our colony to come as well so this could be a good way for all of us to get to know you and your family. Maybe you can even bring some of that roast turkey we've heard you guys are so good at cooking? My wife, God bless her, she may have a set of tits like a 22-year old Playboy Playmate, but her roast turkey always seems to come out a little dry."

"Guilty as charged," said Jane with a giggle.

Princess LaQuintia could barely contain her excitement at the prospect of dining with the foreigners. "Can we go, father? Please?" she pleaded as she grabbed ahold of his arm and held it close.

"I don't know, LaQuintia. I'll have to think about it."

"What is there to think about?" she questioned further.

"Right now is not the time to discuss that my daughter. I need some time to think over an invite such as this."

"But why? It's just a nice simple dinner with our neighbors, and it was so gracious of them to extend the invite to us. It can't hurt to share a meal and get to know one another a little bit."

"Your daughter has a point," said Bottom Bear.

Chief Wailing Badger squinted his eyes and gave his partner a scorching look of disapproval. "And you never miss a chance to let me know when the princess makes a valid point, do you?"

"That would be correct, chief," said Bottom Bear with a smirk.

The chief looked down and saw the sheer joy and anticipation that was written all over his daughter's face. It was a look he hadn't seen in a very long time; a looked that he greatly missed; a look that he didn't want to go away anytime soon.

"I suppose a feast between our people *could* be beneficial for all," said the chief, finally agreeing. "It was rather nice of you to think of us at all so I greatly appreciate that."

"Oh wonderful!" exclaimed Jane as she grabbed ahold of Arthur's arm and pulled him close. "I'm so excited now! Well, we hate to rush off but I have to start getting this feast prepared, don't I? Our friend Lucy and I will be up all night cooking and baking if I don't get a move on it soon. Anyway, I would say come by our place around 5:00 tomorrow evening; it's the property over by the great oak tree across the woods. Oh, I'm so excited! And please don't forget those turkeys, I'm dying to have a taste. Adios!"

The Sucyamama tribesmen watched as their foreign neighbors excitedly trotted off back towards the woods.

Chief Wailing Badger turned to face his partner and daughter. "*Adios*? Seriously? I'm surprised she didn't request that we bring tacos and burritos to the feast."

"I'm very proud of you, chief," said Bottom Bear. "I never thought I'd see the day when you'd agree to dine with the foreigners."

"Me too, I'm kind of in shock," said Princess LaQuintia. "But proud nonetheless."

"Well, like I said to them, I do greatly appreciate the fact that they extended the invite to us. That was very nice of them. But I feel as though I need to reiterate something very important to you, LaQuintia; just because I've agreed to dine with some of these foreigners, that doesn't change how I feel about you dating one of them. This changes nothing in regards to that."

LaQuintia looked up and met her father's gaze. "I understand father, I know." As she slowly turned around and walked back towards the teepee she couldn't help but begin to smile from ear-to-ear. Though he may have been sticking to his guns about her relationship with Rupert, LaQuintia couldn't help but feel overjoyed at the subtle progress that she saw her father making. She knew change wouldn't occur overnight, but the fact that he was willing to sit down and dine with some of the foreigners was surely a step in the right direction. Surely he would begin to see that some of them were not nearly as bad as he had imagined them to be.

Maybe all hope for Rupert and I isn't completely lost just yet, she thought to herself as she stepped back inside her home. *But I won't count my chickens before they hatch. We still have to get through dinner first.*

Meanwhile, back outside the teepee, Chief Wailing Badger and Bottom Bear had more to discuss.

"I really am quite proud of you for accepting that invitation," said Bottom Bear as he patted the chief's shoulder. "You know that I've been wanting us to meet with these foreigners for awhile now. I think this is a great step in the right direction."

"I don't know why you're so excited, who do you think is going to be roasting turkey's for the rest of the day to bring to this God-forsaken feast? I suggest you hop to it, mister"

Nearly 24 hours had passed since she had extended the invitation for dinner to Chief Wailing Badger and his family, and Jane Bigglesworth was still running around her kitchen like a wild woman.

"Lucy, please do me a favor and take those biscuits out of the oven for me," she commanded to the young lover she shared with her husband. "And can you also please check with Arthur and make sure he lights all those candles on the outside table. Guests will surely be arriving soon and I want the table setting to look exquisite."

Arthur and Jane had invited nearly 30 people over to their home for this feast and in preparation they had set up a grand table outside with a gorgeous white linen table clothe, fresh flowers, their finest China, and enough bottles of red wine to give Olivia Pope a spontaneous orgasm upon sight.[99] It was to be the grandest affair since they landed in this new world and Jane wanted to make sure it was talked about all season long, for all the right reasons.

"Of course I'll handle all that for you, Jane," said Lucy as she gently slapped Jane's derriere and then proceeded to remove the biscuits from the oven.

"How did the macaroni and cheese come out? Can you taste it for me and let me know? I'm afraid I put in too much cheese," Jane said, worryingly.

"Jane, you can never have too much cheese in macaroni and cheese. Have you learned nothing from Patti LaBelle's cookbook?"[100]

"I know that's right, bitch," Jane said with a giggle. "I want to make sure it's just right."

"I've tasted the macaroni and cheese and it's delicious," Lucy

99   I'm convinced Kerry Washington's popular TV character from *Scandal* is single handedly keeping the red wine business thriving.
100   Patti LaBelle's cookbook should be deemed as the second installment of the Holy Bible.

reassured her. "You should stop stressing out so much. I haven't seen someone freak out so much about a dinner party since the time I brought Ol' Dirty Bastard, God rest his soul, as my guest to Sarah Palin's Christmas party. Though, I suspect she was less concerned with the trimmings and more concerned with hiding her jewelry."

"I know, I know, I just want this evening to be special that's all," insisted Jane. "This is the first time that the colony is going to dine with the natives and I'm so worried that I'm going to fuck it up somehow."

"You needn't worry, everything looks and smells delicious," said Lucy as she grabbed ahold of Jane and embraced her to ease her nerves. "And I can't forget to mention how lovely and sophisticated that table setting looks outside. It looks like we're about to dine at Lisa Vanderpump's house!"

"Thank you so much, Lucy. There's no way I could've pulled this dinner off without your help."

"Don't even mention it, that's what side bitches are for,"[101] Lucy said with a wink.

"Okay, enough fooling around. Can you go make sure that Arthur lights those candles now? The sun is starting to go down and we need to make sure we've set the perfect ambiance when people begin to arrive. And take the macaroni and cheese platter with you, as well."

Everyone inside the Bigglesworth household continued their frantic hustle and bustle right up until the point when the first guests began to arrive. First came Samuel and Lydia Collins, then came Timothy and Ester Smith, followed by Joseph and Theresa Mills, and so on and so forth until nearly the entire village had arrived. All except the Higgins clan, that is.

And while they may have been missing in attendance, they were still the main topic of conversation on everyone's lips.

"Have any of you been to see Mary yet?" asked Ester.

---

101   Usually side bitches are just used for a quick roll in the hay, but Lucy's bond with the Bigglesworth's was a bit more special than that.

"Not yet, have you?" responded Theresa.

"No, I can't bear to go see her like that," said Ester. "Why I hear she's completely lost all her marbles and just sits and stares into space all day as she recites prayers over and over."

"Oh dear, how horrific," said Theresa as she took a sip of her wine.

"Not nearly as horrific as having to scrub that damn Captain Todd's blood off my damn bathroom rug for the past few weeks," Lydia interjected. "That's the last time I host a dinner party at my house, I tell you that fucking much."

As everyone stood around the beautifully decorated table and made small talk with one another about their daily doings, Jane finally caught sight of her guests of honor. Off in the distance, four statuesque bodies, bronzed-skin and draped in calf-skin suede outfits, approached the massive dinner table; each of them carrying a delicious looking turkey in their arms.

"Oh my, chief!" Jane exclaimed as she rushed to greet her guests. "I didn't realize you would bring so much. It looks amazing. Please bring the birds over to the table and I'll introduce you all to everyone."

Ester huddled together with Theresa and Lydia and whispered, "Let me get this straight: she invites the natives to come have dinner at *her* house, but she has *them* prepare the main course? Tacky much? How much you want to bet she's going to have them wash the dishes at the end of the night as well?"

The three gossipmongers laughed amongst themselves as they watched Jane greet the natives. Even in Mary Higgins absence, they still didn't miss a beat.

Jane led her guests towards the table and instructed them where they could place the succulently roasted turkeys.

"Attention everyone!" Jane announced. "I'd like to introduce you all to the members of the royal Suckyourmother family."

"No, it is pronounced *Sucyamama*," the chief interrupted as graciously as possible.

"Oh, I'm so very sorry, it's the royal Sucyamama family! That's my bad!"

"It's no problem at all. I am Chief Wailing Badger, the leader of the Sucyamama tribe. This man to my left is my second-in-command, Bottom Bear. The ravishing young beauty to my right is my daughter, Princess LaQuintia, and next to her is her best friend, Raindrop Twerk."

Ooooooh, Raindrop Twerk huh? thought Lucy Skeezabeth as she intently listened to the chief's introductions. *Judging by that name I'm going to have to get to know her.*

"Thank you so much for that great introduction, chief. We're so honored that you decided to come dine with us this evening. Would you all care to take a seat?" said the hostess of the evening.

"That would be very nice," said the chief. While he had agreed to come to this feast, there was a part of Chief Wailing Badger that was still very apprehensive about the evening. One of the first things he noticed upon their arrival was that Rupert and his family were not among the guests that had shown up to dine this evening; a fact that Princess LaQuintia quickly noticed as well, which had translated into a defeated look on her face. As they all took their seat at the table, the chief casually reached out and took ahold of his daughter's hand and gave it a soft squeeze. The tacit showing of affection between father and daughter was lost on everyone except Bottom Bear, who had caught it out of the corner of his eye and immediately knew what it was in reference to.

After everyone took their seats the real feasting began. The food looked like glimmering treasures strewn across the table. The golden glazed turkeys, the crispy crust on top of the macaroni and cheese, the buttery whipped mashed potatoes, the savory green beans with little bits of bacon lingering throughout the casserole dish, the burnt layer of marshmallow on top of the sweet potatoes. The spread looked so grand that no one even wanted to touch it. But, of course, they eventually began to dig in because these were some hungry bitches.

As the night progressed, and the wine bottles continued to pop, everyone at the table began to open up and share more and more. The settlers began to learn about the rich culture of the Sucyamama tribe. The chief and his family began to learn about the hardships and struggles that the settlers had faced in order to make it to the new land. A true understanding and respect began to form between the two cultures. They began to stop looking at the fact that they dressed differently and started to look at the individuals underneath the clothes. They stopped hearing all the differences in the way each other spoke and focused on the real *meaning* behind the ways they communicated. They may have been different in so many ways, but with a little compassion, and a lot of wine, a new bond of friendship began to form during that first dinner. And with that new bond of friendship, all the little, insignificant matters that they once held against one another began to fall by the wayside.

But, of course, the evening couldn't go off without a little drama.

After the main course had been served, and the burnt orange pumpkin pies were about to be sliced, the dinner party was interrupted by a few *surprise* guests. Arthur Bigglesworth had first spotted the mysterious figures coming down the trail towards his cabin. At first Arthur didn't know what to do so he nonchalantly tapped his wife on the shoulder and directed her to look in the direction his eyes were pointed.

"Oh shit," Jane sighed as she caught a glimpse of who was making their way to crash the party.

Within a few moments, the rest of the dinner party had become aware as well. An audible gasp came over the table once Baxter Higgins fully stepped into the light, his twins Emily and Rupert trailing behind him.

Princess LaQuintia's face lite up with joy when she saw Rupert come into view; a look that he reflected back to her upon seeing her beauty in the subdued candlelight of the table.

"You listen here Baxter Higgins, if you've come to start a rift between us and these fine tribesmen than I suggest you be gone," bellowed

Arthur. "We ain't with that play play shit tonight!"[102]

"Put a sock in it, Bigglesworth. I haven't come here to fight," said Baxter as he slowly made his way towards Chief Wailing Badger's direction. "I've come to speak with the *chief*."

Chief Wailing Badger stood up from his chair and faced Baxter Higgins. The chief was having a splendid evening and really didn't want to rough Baxter up, but he didn't like to be run up on during dinner parties so if it came down to it he was ready to put them paws on him.[103]

"I came to apologize to the chief," said Baxter.

The whole crowd looked on completely stunned. Baxter Higgins had always voiced his displeasure for the native people and now here he was apologizing to them? Everyone was confused. No one more so than the chief.

"You came to apologize to me?" he asked.

"That's right."

"And what are you sorry for?" the chief asked as he placed his hands into his suede pant pockets.

"You returned my son to me. You didn't have to do that. He was trespassing on your land and you still returned him home to his family, safe and sound. I know you could have made an example out of him, but you didn't. For that I'm grateful. I apologize for the way I spoke to you the other night, it was wrong of me."

The chief was flabbergasted. After his first encounter with Baxter this was the last thing he had expected from him. "Well, I suppose I should apologize to you too then. I'm sure I spoke out of line to you as well. I believe at one point I even referred to your daughter as a bootleg Rosie Perez. For that, I am sorry."

"We were both speaking to one another out of a place of fear that evening. After I had a chance to think it over, I came to the realization

<hr/>

102   W.A.S.P. Translation: Don't start no drama, won't be no drama.
103   W.A.S.P. Translation: By stating that he was going to "put them paws on him," he's basically stating that he's ready to throw fisticuffs if necessary. The chief ain't no punk.

that maybe I was judging you and your people unfairly. I've made a lot of bad assumptions in my life lately and trusted a lot of things that have been proven to be false. So I figured this was a good enough time as any to start making some changes."

"I can deeply respect that," said the chief as he stuck out his hand in hopes for a handshake to officially bury the hatchet. Baxter reached out and grabbed ahold of the chief's hand.

"I don't suppose there's any room at this table for my children and I, is there?" asked Baxter as he signaled for Emily and Rupert to come towards him.

"I believe we can find some room," said Jane as she reached out and handed Baxter a plate. "Please help yourself."

"Yes, you all must eat up, but first there's something important that must be done," said the chief as he reached out and grabbed ahold of Rupert's arm and directed him to his chair next to Princess LaQuintia. "I believe this is where you belong, young man."

LaQuintia was touched by her father's expression of acceptance. She leapt up and embraced him with all her might. "Thank you daddy," she whispered in his ear. "Thank you so much."

"Anything for my daughter," he whispered back. "You love hard, just like your mother did. I never want to extinguish that flame within you. This boy loves you and I can see that. I will support whatever makes you happy."

Princess LaQuintia kissed her father on the cheek and took her seat next to Rupert. They knew they had a long way to go to make it work, but it was surely progress for the both of them.

"All right everyone, time for some more wine and dessert!" announced Lucy Skeezabeth as she began to cut into the first of many pumpkin pies that would be consumed that evening. "Does anyone know where the Kool-Whip is? I could've sworn I remember seeing it recently."

"Oh, I know where it is," said Jane as she got up and leaned in close to Lucy's ear. "It's on the nightstand in our bedroom. Remember we were using it on Arthur last night?"

Lucy let out a giggle. "That's right. How could I forget, you naughty little minx."

The first meal between the Sucyamama people and the settlers was a smashing success.

The wine continued to flow. The stories continued to be told. The feelings of thanks and gratitude continued to build. Everyone enjoyed it so much so that they vowed every year, during the last week of November, before the harsh winter months began, they would get together to remember this night of love and acceptance. The night when their differences had melted away and the only thing that remained was the respect and appreciation they had for one another.

And that, ladies and gentlemen, is the real story of how Thanksgiving came to be in America.[104]

---

104   Well, not really, but wouldn't it be cool if that's how it actually happened? ;-)

ACKNOWLEDGEMENTS

I have to start by saying how incredibly grateful I am to have such a wonderful and supportive family. Mom and Dad, thanks for always allowing me to be myself (even when I'm sure it drives you both insane). A guy couldn't have asked for better parents. To my brother Kevin and his beautiful wife Megan, thank you both for being pretty damn cool and bringing the coolest little baby into the world. I love me some D.Q. and I can't wait to meet her little brother very soon!

To Damien Pierre for being the most amazing and supportive best friend in the entire world. Camp Glory and beyond!!! We made it!!! Can't stop, won't stop!!!!

To my amazing Stacy Ann Payne-Gray, your friendship means more to me than you'll ever know. You're my heart and I love ya.

Tamara McKenzie, thanks for staying fly all the damn time and being my soulmate sister. We sippin' Grigio....slow!

To my NYC family: Laura, Vanessa, and Antonio. I can't even tell you how much your frienship and support means to me. You guys have been there for me through some of the toughest experiences in my life and I love you for it. #Chewbacca

Troy Agard, thanks for always being my voice of reason. The positivity and light that you exude out to the world is nothing short of amazing. Never ever change.

To Grandma and Grandpa D, Grandma and Grandpa "By The Lake," and Sylvia Caporale. Thank you all for being the best grandparents a guy could've ever asked for.

To Kristy Polito, thanks for just being yourself. You're a sweetheart.

I love you all :-)

Michael Anthony McLafferty is a proud graduate of Florida A&M University, class of 2008, where he received his bachelor's degree in Journalism and Sociology. He enjoys spending time with family and friends, eating virtually anything deep-fried, and taking selfies whilst wearing Zara jackets. He currently lives in New York where he roams the streets eagerly awaiting the moment when he runs into Mariah Carey.